THE CROYDON ENIGMA

Jacqueline Beard

The Croydon Enigma

The Constance Maxwell Dream Walker Mysteries are published by Dornica Press

The author can be contacted on her website
https://jacquelinebeardwriter.com/

While there, why not sign up for her FREE newsletter.

ISBN:1-83-829554-2

ISBN: 978-1-83-829554-7

First Printing 2021

Dornica Press

Coming Soon

The Constance Maxwell Dreamwalker Mysteries

The Cornish Widow
The Croydon Enigma

Also, by this author:

Lawrence Harpham Murder Mysteries:

The Fressingfield Witch
The Ripper Deception
The Scole Confession
The Felsham Affair
The Moving Stone

Short Stories featuring Lawrence Harpham:

The Montpellier Mystery

Novels:

Vote for Murder

The Croydon Enigma

PROLOGUE

Diary of Constance Emma Maxwell

Wednesday, June 8, 1932

It's not raining, which is the only saving grace about today. Everything else is grey and miserable, with problems heaped on problems and no future pleasure in sight. The only break in the clouds is my planned trip to see Mary in Bosula next month, assuming I last that long.

I'd list my worries, but they would run off the page, and there's only so much writing I can do in a day. But, in no particular order, my problems include love, friendship, nightmares, poor judgement, killers at large and Grace. And though my bad dreams are the most sinister of my concerns, it's love or the lack thereof that troubles me most.

Love is in the air for everyone but me. Stephan St John is pursuing Cora through the Royal Mail, or so she writes in her letters. Cora is not receptive to his advances while she is in London, trying to negotiate a divorce. Elys and Jory

1

announced their engagement to the horror of Mrs Ponsonby, who cannot face the thought of employing another domestic. Even Mr Moggins has been conducting an unsavoury flirtation with the young hotel cat. She is barely more than a kitten, and I have had sharp words with him about it, to no avail. Kit Maltravers and Charlotte Napier will wed next year. I doubt I will make the guest list for the evening reception, much less the wedding, which is as well as I might disgrace myself and cry. But as decent as he is, Kit wouldn't look at me twice, and I have consigned him to my list of unresolvable problems. The only other man I know who is even remotely attractive is Carrington Blake, who lives in Bosula. He bears more than a passing resemblance to Kit, but after sloshing red wine down his shirt last Christmas, I doubt he holds any fond memories of me. I am destined to be a sad, lonely spinster if I live long enough.

These last words sound flippant, but the prospect of something untoward happening seems terrifyingly likely. Since my brush with Annie Hearn, I have resisted dream travel and have only once found myself on the cliff walk. As soon as I realised, I returned to my body. No more running, arms outstretched in joy for me these days. Dream travel has lost its appeal, and I am resigned to living in a shrunken world again. Instead, I am plagued by vivid nightmares, each one longer than the last and coming with increasing regularity. Crossley is always there in one guise or another, most often as himself but on one notable occasion as a rat with Crossley-like features. Had his baleful eyes been less consumed with hatred, the whiskers might have suited him. But Crossley was the ultimate king rat. His slitty, red-rimmed eyes, yellowed fangs and a tangle of tails binding him to his ratty henchmen horrified me. I slept with the lamp on for a week after that dream. Nothing has ever shaken me quite as much, not even meeting Crossley on the astral plane.

Thankfully, the nightmares are not real. I do not separate from my body, nor do I travel as much as an inch. They happen inside my head, and though it feels as if Crossley is probing my mind, he isn't there. I will be safe if I don't go back to the astral realm, and I won't. I promised Peter, and I am determined not to let him down.

Talking of Peter, he is missing in action. I haven't seen him for weeks. Peter has succumbed to the lure of Oliver and Felicity Grenville's drama group and involves himself only in thespian matters. He spends a lot of time with Freddie Parsons, a young actor recently arrived from Cambridge. Mr Whitstable has changed the hotel books for the last few weeks, and Peter is neglecting not only his friends but his library too. So, I am battling problems on all fronts and have no friends to share them with.

My life is lonely and made more complicated by my overactive conscience also contributing to my insomnia. It's Annie Hearn, you see. I don't know what to do about her. I made a mistake, a grave mistake when I blindly believed her story without any evidence. Every instinct screamed her innocence. I knew it, I felt it, but I was wrong. She is a wicked woman, driven by some nameless need for destruction. And I, who knew with certainty that she was alive from the touch of her handkerchief, could not detect her guilt from handling the object. She seemed so naïve and guileless, as if her depraved behaviour was not her doing. But having seen her diary and her sister's too, there is no doubt. The question is what to do about it. I wish I'd never found out. If only I hadn't poked my nose into future events that didn't concern me, I might still exist in blissful ignorance. Instead, I find myself in the unique position of knowing about a crime before it has happened. And about two attempts at poisoning that are years in the future. I have all the time in the world to warn Betsy Poskitt and her husband, but how can I? Why would she believe me? It is only a short time since Annie Hearn moved in with her sister in Long Sandall. They are no doubt settled together and enjoying Annie's newfound freedom. I could write and tell Betsy, but she will think that I'm mad.

I telephoned Oliver Fox in the week when fretting about it got the better of me. He was very kind. He listened without speaking until I had finished all I needed to say, then he advised me not to do anything at all. Fox agreed that nobody would believe me but reasoned that it would be worse if they did. Changing the future might have consequences, and I should settle for knowing the truth. That's easier said than done, but he is right. I've wracked my brain and found no alternative solution to the problem.

Then there's the matter of Grace. I barely noticed it at first, but the name kept cropping up in daily conversation. And before I knew it, I heard it every day, as if something fatalistic was trying to draw my attention. First, it was Mr Moggins' girlfriend, the little hotel tabby cat. I crossed paths with her while returning from a beach walk last week and bent to stroke her as one of the hotel maids was shaking crumbs from the linen tablecloth.

"Is that your cat," she asked, pointing to Mr Moggins, who was rubbing noses with the tabby.

I nodded.

"Well, keep him away from Grace," she said. "We don't want any accidents."

I thought nothing of it until chatting with Dolly the following day, and she happened to reveal that her middle name was Grace. On Wednesday, to my disgust, Mrs Ponsonby kept up a relentless dialogue about Charlotte Napier's grace. Charlotte, it transpires, is part of the ballroom dancing group. Goodness knows why a young woman wants to waste her afternoons gliding around the dance floor with a group of women old enough to be her aunts, but she does. And marginally less irritating than compliments about Charlotte Napier was Ely's constant whistling. For reasons best known to herself, her tuneless rendition of Amazing Grace bothered me repeatedly all weekend. I had almost written the grace thing off as a series of coincidences when I noticed a new picture in the hallway. Cora had purchased it for Mrs

4

Ponsonby during our Christmas break in Bosula. I was beginning to think Mrs P didn't like it as it had lain in its original wrappings since December. But it was the lack of fixings that Jory kindly rectified that caused the delay, and he hung the painting on Saturday morning. On Sunday, I took a closer look at the boat in the foreground and saw its name was Grace. Coincidences are sinister, not passive events swirling by like leaves on a blustery day. They have meaning. This one does. I just don't know what it is yet. But something is in the offing. I can feel it coming.

CHAPTER ONE

Trouble at the Hotel

Thursday, June 9, 1932

The world seemed a happier place when I woke today, probably because I had slept for eight hours for the first time in ages. I was refreshed and ready to go, having enjoyed a cooked breakfast in the dining room with the sun streaming through the window. Now, as I walk across the sand towards the cave as sturdy and straight-backed as I have been for many a week, I can see something is wrong. There are muddles outside the cave indicating a problem, and I wish I'd stayed in bed. As I grow closer, I see that it's a book. It shouldn't be there, and it lies splayed open, spine proud, and liberally coated in sand. I gasp at the sacrilege and crouch down beside the little paper corpse. Though dirty and crumpled, it is salvageable. I brush the sand particles away with my skirt, tuck the book in my bag and enter the cave where chaos reigns. Books, crates, my chair and my lamp are all strewn across the stone floor. Someone, it seems, has tossed the suitcase full of books in the air and hurled the furnishings on top of the pile. It is vandalism of the worst kind, and tears fill my eyes at the thought of my beloved books lying unloved on the ground.

I take the suitcase and open it. The handle has broken, but the structure is intact. I can still store books inside. Fortunately, the cave is dry, and my books, my little darlings, have not suffered water damage. One by one, I lift them into the case, straightening their bent corners and flattening covers. I right the chair, put the lamp on the little table and search the cave for clues.

It is empty, and I can't see anything at first, but as I step towards my chair, something crunches beneath my foot, and I look down to see a dull brass circular shape poking above the shingle. I take the object, walk to the front of the cave and inspect it. The unpolished bangle is plain but etched inside is the shape of a sun with a slash through the centre. The symbol is meaningless, and it doesn't account for the mindless destruction, which I can't help taking personally. Barely anyone uses the cave except the occasional tourist, and they don't have any motive for vandalism. I can only assume that the fisher boys have been running amok again. They are a lively lot, full of fun and generally without malice. This wanton damage is not their way. At least, my cave is largely unscathed, and the books are safe for now. I cast an anxious look around before leaving and try not to think too hard about it as I make my way to the hotel. I can't secure the cave and can only hope for the best. I will keep the bangle because if it was the fisher boys, they might have misappropriated the item, and it will have to be returned to its rightful owner. Elys might recognise it, and if she doesn't, Jory will. I'll take it back to Pebble Cottage as soon as I've been to the hotel. I reach the slope and heave myself onto the first step. I am drained, which is strange after such a good night's sleep.

I lean heavily on my stick, reach for the railing, and as I turn towards the cave for a final time, something catches my eye on the rocky path. I lift my stick and turn it upside down, inspecting the base. As expected, it is sandy, but a substance like blotchy crimson paint coats the bottom two inches. I touch the damp sand and lift my fingers to my nose. It smells metallic. I didn't notice any blood in the cave, but one of the boys might have cut himself. Perhaps the blood pooled in the rocks, and shingle blew in and covered it. I walk towards a patch of grass and wipe it away. It wouldn't do to make a mess in the hotel.

#

The reception desk is empty when I enter, so I head straight for the library, opening the door with trepidation. But I needn't have worried. Peter is inside and busily exchanging books as if he'd never been away. I make my way over, and he greets me with a broad smile.

"It's been too long," he says, beaming.

"I haven't been anywhere," I reply waspishly.

"Sorry, Connie, but I've been rehearsing solidly for weeks."

"I know," I sigh. "But I miss you. When will you have more time?"

Peter opens a book as if the answer might lie inside. "I don't know," he says uncertainly. "We only opened in May. It's a lot of fun, Connie. Come and see us? We're decent for amateur performers."

"It's not that easy," I say. "Mrs Ponsonby won't let me out alone, and if I ask to go, she'll want to join me."

"Then let her," says Peter. "There won't be any talking during the production, so what difference does it make who you go with?"

"Don't you have an intermission?"

"Of course."

"Then that's reason enough not to take her," I say. I am just about to elaborate on the many reasons why Mrs Ponsonby is even deeper in my bad books than usual when Roxy Templeton enters the room clutching a register. She advances towards us.

"Can I have a word?" she asks.

"Of course. Go ahead," says Peter.

She glances sideways at me. "Privately."

"Is that necessary? Connie is a trusted friend."

"This is not a personal matter," says Roxanne Templeton, curling her pretty lips.

"Don't mind me," I say, grabbing the nearest book. I head towards the sofa and sit down, tucking my stick unceremoniously underneath. I watch as the Templeton woman leaves the room with Peter in tow, then examine the book. I've chosen badly. It is a children's book called Swallows and Amazons, and I grew out of childish reading years ago. Still, I am settled, and it's too much trouble to change it, so I open the cover and begin the story. By the time Peter returns, I am engrossed in the tale of the Walker and Blackett children and their adventures in the Lake District. Peter sits heavily beside me, and I look up. His mouth has settled into an uncharacteristic frown.

"What's wrong?" I ask, reluctantly lowering the book.

"That bloody woman," whispers Peter fiercely.

"Who?" I ask, feigning ignorance. Peter knows how I feel about Roxy Templeton but champions her cause every time I point out her shortcomings.

"Roxy bloody Templeton."

I stare at him disapprovingly. I've seldom heard Peter swear during our long friendship, and he must be livid to do it twice. "What's she done?"

"She's trying to stop the local people using the hotel library," he says.

"Oh, no." I feel my eyes widen as I contemplate the prospect of losing one of my few daily treats. "But why?"

"Some of the guests have complained about the lack of books."

"Then I'll only take one at a time in future."

"I don't believe her," says Peter. "There are more than enough books to go around, and they're changed every week. She's using it as an excuse."

"But why would she?"

"I don't know. Perhaps you're right, and she's not a pleasant person."

I lean back and slump into the sofa. "That could be it. Roxy has never liked me, and hardly anyone else uses the library. What a spiteful thing to do."

"It hasn't happened yet," says Peter grimly. It won't affect Peter if they close the library to visitors, but he is a good friend and knows how badly I would feel.

"Is there anything we can do?" I ask.

"No. It's in the lap of the gods. Miss Templeton is in charge of the office now that Dolly is back in reception. She's making a recommendation at this stage but decided to warn me."

"And knows you'll tell me, so I'll be fretting about it. Roxy Templeton is a nasty piece of work."

"She suggested that I ought to encourage non-residents to stay away."

"What on earth for?"

"Because if it happens voluntarily, she won't need to make the recommendation."

"Then I'm damned whether I do or don't." I shake my head as a distraction from the tears pricking in the back of my eyes. My world is already so tiny that it is hardly worth bothering without easy access to my books. "Do you think I should stay away?"

"No," hisses Peter. "I don't. When Mr Booth invited you to use the library, he intended it to be for the long-term. Just because he's managing things from a distance is no reason to think he's forgotten. Let her make her recommendation, and if she does, then I'll write to him. I'll ask him to make a special case for you under the circumstances."

I bite down a surge of anger at Peter's words. I don't want to be a special case. I want to be treated the same as everybody else. But I can't succumb to matters of pride without running the risk of losing access to the library.

"Thank you," I say. "I appreciate your suggestion, but I'll write to Mr Booth. He's a kind man, and I will throw myself on his mercy, but not because of my leg. It shouldn't matter. I'll ask because nobody who stays here will ever love this room as much as I do."

Peter leans over and squeezes my hand. "Good for you, Connie," he says. "Now, tell me why you're looking so tired."

"I'm not sleeping well," I say.

"You're not dream walking again?" The question is curt, accusatory. He has gone from my saviour to a villain in seconds.

"No. I promised I wouldn't, and I have resisted whenever it threatens. I've only been on the cliffs once, and I forced myself back."

"Good," he says. "Good. You mustn't do it. Then why are you suffering from insomnia?"

"I'm having a lot of bad dreams and the occasional nightmare."

"About what?"

"I can't remember," I lie. I don't want to mention Crossley. Peter will worry.

He nods his head. "As long as you are safe," he says. "Anyway, we've got next week to look forward to."

I stare dumbly, then remember. The hotel summer ball is early this year, and it's all Peter has spoken about for months. I am dreading it. Everyone who is anyone will be there, including Dr Kit Maltravers and his perfect fiancée. Frankly, I would rather avoid it, but I promised Peter I would go.

Nevertheless, I wonder if it's worth making an excuse. "Mrs Ponsonby is in full mother hen mode," I say. "I'm not sure she'll let me attend.

Peter purses his lips. "You don't need to worry on that score," he says. "It's already arranged."

"How?" I ask, trying not to show my disappointment.

"Mother sorted it," says Peter putting his finger to his lips. "Ask no questions, tell no lies. Anyway, you'll want to meet Frank, won't you?"

I refrain from saying no. However pleasant Frank may be, he is an actor, and they will probably spend all night talking about the theatre and other things that don't concern me. "I didn't know Frank was going," I say petulantly.

"He wasn't," says Peter. "But he is now. You don't mind, do you?"

"Of course not," I lie, but I do. Still, I owe it to Peter to honour my word and behave well in front of his friend. "I need to go," I say, getting to my feet.

Peter nods. "If I don't see you before, then I'll see you next Friday. Will you need an escort to the hotel?"

"Don't be silly," I say. "I'll meet you in the lobby."

"Don't be late."

"I won't." I flash Peter a smile and leave the room, then make my way to the reception. Things are looking up. Dolly is there and she is working through a large pile of keys in the middle of the desk.

"Rather you than me," I say.

She looks up. "Connie, dear. How are you?"

"All the better for seeing you back where you belong, Dolly."

"I've missed being here," she says. "It was lovely at home with my parents, but a much longer convalescence than I expected."

"But you're well now?"

"Yes, much better," she says, "though the doctors never got to the bottom of it."

Roxy Templeton emerges from the back office and walks past the desk on her way to the dining room.

"Reception looks much better with you in it," I say unnecessarily loudly, and I can almost feel Roxy bristling as she strides along the walkway.

Dolly and I exchange glances, and she giggles. "Really, Connie. You'll get me sacked," she says.

"Don't be silly. You're part of the furniture."

"I mean it. I can't risk upsetting Roxy."

"Why not? You're her senior and have been here far longer."

"She holds a lot of power," says Dolly and her face falls. "We got on well when she started, but that all changed when I returned. I think she resents being back in the office. She's cold and distant, and I know she says things to the other girls."

"What things?"

"I don't know, but they suddenly stop talking when I walk into the kitchen. Nobody knocks on my door for an evening chat like before. Once upon a time, my room was like Piccadilly Junction, always buzzing with visitors. Now, it's a lonely place."

I gaze at Dolly's pale face. Her eyes have lost their sparkle, and she can barely raise a smile. My heart breaks for her. "Is there anything I can do?"

"Not really," she says.

"Dolly, do you read?"

"Not much."

"When I feel lonely, I pick up a book."

"We're not allowed in the library," Dolly replies.

"Well, go to my cave next time you've got a free day. You can read for as long as you like. I know you'll still be alone, but I visit most days, and you'll get such comfort from the books."

Dolly opens her mouth to reply but doesn't get the chance as a shadow looms behind me and I turn to see the unwanted form of Edgar Sutton.

#

"Edgar, how nice." I paste an insincere smile on my face as I meet his eyes. He tips his hat and nods.

"How are you, Connie?" he asks.

"Very well," I say, "And you?"

I shouldn't have bothered. Edgar takes this as a sign of encouragement and relates an interminable story about an abscess under his tooth which took a long time to treat. I couldn't be less interested in his medical problems, and I'm still seething about the remarks he made to Charlotte Napier at the Pottses supper party last year.

"Let it go," Elys had said after I'd complained to her for the tenth time. She thinks I make too much of these things. I made a special effort not to dwell on it and thought I'd finally buried the slight deep in my memory. One look at Edgar's smug face, and I now realise the hurt is as raw as ever.

"So, I said, fix it right now, or I'll sue you," says Edgar, standing with his hands on his hips. This is my cue to reply, but I don't know who he's talking about because I wasn't listening. "You didn't, did you?" I ask, choosing what I hope is a safe option.

"No. I didn't need to. Sugden repaired it there and then. He wasn't going to risk damaging his reputation. It's a nuisance paying Harley Street prices, but at least they take complaints seriously."

"He won't do it again," I say, throwing Edgar a rare opportunity to boast.

He draws himself higher. "No. You've got to know how to handle these people," he says.

"I'm glad you're feeling better now," I continue. It's time to go, and I have better things to do than chat to loathsome Edgar.

"This is for you," says Dolly, passing Edgar a brown envelope.

"Good. That's what I'm here for," he says, smiling. "I say, Connie. Are you going to the summer ball?"

"I'm not sure yet," I reply. I'm still hoping to get out of it, and Edgar is one of the many reasons why.

He opens his mouth to speak, but Roxy Templeton appears. She flashes him a beaming smile as if he was the most important guest in the hotel. His eyes follow her as she struts towards the library, wiggling her behind. Dolly rolls her eyes, and I smile, but Edgar is staring with his mouth wide open.

"I haven't seen her before," he says, without taking his eyes off her retreating form.

"Funny that," I say. "Roxy was on reception while Dolly was poorly."

"I must have been back in London by then," says Edgar. "She's rather lovely. I suppose it would be bad form to ask her to the dance?"

I ignore the rhetorical question, but Dolly does not. "Why?" she asks.

"Fraternising with the staff," Edgar replies with a wink.

"But you're not staying here," says Dolly, and I realise that she's irritated by his crass reply.

"No, but I'm a gentleman, all the same," says Edgar without batting an eyelid, seemingly oblivious to his offensive remarks. Dolly scowls, but neither of us answers.

"I don't suppose you'll have a partner," says Edgar turning to me.

"Sorry?"

"A partner for the ball. Do you have an escort?"

"Weren't you listening? I don't know if I'm going yet."

"Keep your hair on," says Edgar. "Perhaps I haven't made myself clear. I'm offering to take you."

I stare at him in amazement, both surprised and appalled at his suggestion. He mistakes my horror for delight.

"There," he says, slitting open the brown envelope and withdrawing two tickets which he waves under my nose. "One for you and one for me," he says, depositing them on the reception counter.

I don't know how to respond and stare at Dolly, aghast. She grimaces in sympathy. Dolly knows me well enough to detect my discomfort.

"It was clever of you to buy two tickets not knowing if Connie would accept," she says.

"Oh, I didn't buy them for Connie. Lola Hazel was coming, but she's cried off," says Edgar. "Still, it's her loss, and I'd rather do the decent thing and take Connie."

"Would you?" I ask sceptically.

"Of course," he says. "It's a good deed in a naughty world."

"A good deed?" My knuckles turn white as I clench my stick.

"I don't mean it like that," says Edgar. "It's just an expression."

"You don't mind taking someone in my condition?"

"No. It's not as if we'll be dancing."

"What will we do?"

"I'll escort you to the ball and bring you home again. We can dine together. You won't mind if I spend time on the dance floor with other girls?"

"You haven't got anyone else to bring, have you?" I ask. Edgar is a first-class dancer and would never endure someone who can't dance unless he had no other choice or was madly in love with them. Neither case applies to me – we have never got along, and I can only assume that Edgar can't bear the indignity of attending alone.

"Don't be like that," he says.

"Admit it. You're asking me because you don't have a partner."

"Oh, for God's sake, Connie. It's just a dance. Don't come if you don't want to. You could show me a little more appreciation. It's not as if anyone else is going to ask you."

Dolly jerks her head back in shock at his words, and I let them settle on me like a swarm of hornets. A red mist descends. I feel my hackles rising, and it's all I can do not to scream.

Edgar snatches the envelope from the counter, turns on his heel and takes a stride. But I am furious, and for once, I am quicker. As he turns to go, I drop my stick. It rattles in front of him just as he descends the stair that has so often dogged me in the past. And, just as I intended, he stumbles over my stick and trips down the step, falling face-first onto the tiled hallway.

"My God," he screams, pushing himself off the floor into an untidily seated heap. He clutches his bloodied mouth and spits into his hand. Two white objects appear through the crimson mess. "They're my front teeth. Look what you've done." He holds his hand out and shakes his head as if he can't believe his eyes.

Roxy Templeton scurries into the hallway together with Roberto, the waiter. They help Edgar to his feet and sit him in the foyer. His swollen lip is bloody, and the tip of his nose is red raw. "Get a jug of water," hisses Roxy and Dolly rushes to the dining room, shooting me a sympathetic glance. I am still standing, one hand on the reception counter and staring at my stick, wondering if I have the nerve to pick it up. Roberto sees me, jumps to his feet and hands it over.

"She tripped me up," snarls Edgar.

"It was an accident," I say.

"No, it wasn't. You did it deliberately, you bitter little cripple." Edgar's bloodied face is twisted and angry. His newly grown moustache doesn't disguise his sneering disgust. "And to think I was trying to help you."

Roxy pats his shoulder. "I'm sure Connie was her normal clumsy self."

"No. She attacked me," says Edgar. "You shouldn't let her in here. This place is going to the dogs."

I can almost see a light bulb going off in Roxy's head. "If that's what you think, then rest assured that we will look into the matter."

"You'd better," says Edgar, wiping his face with a napkin.

"It was an accident," says Dolly, passing the jug to Roxy

Templeton. "I saw it. Connie dropped her stick, and it rolled down the step. The timing was unfortunate, but that's all."

"Why, you little liar. You would say that."

Dolly's face pales, and her hands shake slightly, but she persists. "It was an accident."

Mr Brookbank, the hotel manager, appears in the hallway. Roberto is with him; he must have slipped off to find him while Edgar was complaining.

"What's going on?" he asks.

Edgar and Roxy fall over themselves to condemn me as an aggressive danger to the hotel, but when Dolly gives her opinion, Mr Brookbank seems satisfied.

"I'm sorry this happened," he says to Edgar. "Please accept my apologies and come and dine here next week on us." He scribbles a note onto a business card and hands it to Edgar.

"What about my teeth?"

"I can't help you with that," says Mr Brookbank.

"But it happened on your premises."

"Even so. There are limits to our culpability."

Edgar stands in front of the doorway, glaring at me through narrowed eyes. Then he thrusts his teeth in his trouser pocket, spins round and stalks from the hotel. Mr Brookbank, Roberto and Roxy retreat to the rear while Dolly chews her lip nervously.

"I can't believe you did that," she says.

"He deserved it."

"Connie, you shouldn't have. This won't be the last you hear of it."

I watch as Dolly finishes sorting the keys and know that she is right. I leave the hotel, already regretting my impulsive act and hope that it won't come back to bite me.

CHAPTER TWO

A Disturbed Night

Wednesday, June 15, 1932

I wake to feel a tugging at the back of my head, the same pull that usually brings me safely back to my body. I clutch my temple and sit up, glancing bleary-eyed at the clock. It is only two o'clock, and I've already woken once. I sigh, knowing another broken night is ahead.

My headaches have become a regular occurrence. They began not long after I stopped dream walking. And the more I resist, the more frequently they happen. I don't know why, and I am sorely tempted to telephone Oliver Fox and ask him. It is almost as if my mind cannot settle without a regular release from my body. I feel trapped, restless and heartbroken about my standing in this little local community. Although Edgar is staying with the Potts family, Tregurrian is too close for comfort. And there's a chance that he will be at the Summer Ball on Friday unless his damaged mouth leaves him too embarrassed to go. Chance would be a fine thing.

I yawn, longing for sleep, but now that my mind is on Edgar, reminding me of my stupid, rash actions, I know it won't happen. My insomnia was bad enough before, but every night since Edgar fell down the step, sleep seems further away, and I inwardly cringe at the thought of my behaviour. I was lucky he didn't break his neck, or worse. I have never thought of myself as impulsive, and though I'm quick to rise to temper, I have always been able to contain it. I don't know what got into me. Pride, I suppose, though what I have got to be proud about escapes me now.

I sigh, plump my pillows and reach for a book. Perhaps if I read, I might fall asleep before dawn. But the back of my head tingles again, and a throbbing pain at the base of my skull soon follows. It is almost as if something is tugging me into the astral plane. I rub my head and turn a page, but the pain increases, and I lose concentration. My eyes drift towards the window. It is dark, but I can just see the pale outline of the moon in the sky. And a moth. A giant moth. I gasp. Excessively large insects are scarce in Cornwall. I must be heading for a false awakening.

I plunge my hand into the mattress to test, but it stops dead. I am still in my body, yet the winged shape at my window flutters persistently. I adjust my position and take a closer look, trying to ignore the palpitations in my chest as the pulse in my neck throbs to the beat of its wings. And as I stare at the creature, I realise it isn't a moth at all. It's a perfectly normal-sized bat. I sigh with relief, although its presence at my window still commands my attention. It hovers persistently as if it is trying to get in, though I know it's safely outside. I look away and resume reading my book, managing to get to the end of the page, though I can't remember a word I have seen. But I feel the bat's presence and look up again. It is still there, but it has multiplied exponentially. A swarm of bats hang menacingly outside, wings beating while emitting high-pitched screeches that rip through my mind. My ears are on fire, and my brain burns amid the torturous sound. I think of escape. I could leave now if I allowed myself to dream walk, finding protection on the cliff tops by Beacon Cove. But would I truly be safe? My fingers vibrate, and the pain in the back of my head is tingling again. I resist. The pain grows until it cascades through my skull like a volcanic eruption. There's no choice now. I'll have to dream travel to escape this torture for fear that it will kill me. But just as I start to relax and accept the inevitable, I hear a sound on the landing. The staircase squeaks, and I realise that someone is awake and going downstairs.

The noise is enough to stop me in my tracks, and instead of succumbing to an unwanted astral experience, my head clears. The pain evaporates, and when I look at the window, the bats have vanished – each creature gone as if it never existed at all. I clutch my chest. My heart is still beating, fit to burst. Have I just had another nightmare? I can't have. I was wide awake through the whole experience, almost feeling as if under attack. I recheck the clock. Barely ten minutes have passed, yet it feels like a lifetime. There is no chance of sleeping again tonight, and my thoughts turn to the household and who might be awake.

Elys is back in her room now that Coralie Pennington has gone, and when she returns in a few short weeks, Elys will go back to her mother's house and come in daily again. So, the footsteps either belong to Elys or Mrs P. They have piqued my curiosity, and I decide to find out who is on nocturnal manoeuvres. I grab my stick with trembling hands, make my way downstairs, and walk to the front of the house. The parlour and dining room doors are ajar, and there is no sign of movement or light in either place. I retreat to the kitchen and open the door. Elys sits at the wooden table, nursing a glass of water and sobbing as if her heart would break.

"Oh, you poor thing. What's wrong?" I ask, forgetting my fear of the bats at the sight of her stricken face.

"Go away," she says. Her cheeks are blotchy red, and dark shadows lurk beneath her eyes.

"Not until you tell me what's wrong."

"I don't want to. Leave me alone."

I stand by the table, not knowing what to do. I yearn to reach out and hug her, but she is spiky and hostile. Elys never behaves like this. Sensible, trustworthy Elys is wise beyond her years. Watching this alternative version is like seeing a fishing boat on a calm, windless day, suddenly capsized by violent, unexpected waves.

"I'm not going anywhere," I say, lowering myself to the chair beside her. I take her hand, and she snatches it away. "Tell me what's wrong, Elys," I say, determined to get to the bottom of her strange behaviour.

"No."

I stand and reach for the heavy skillet on the worktop. "Tell me, or I'll drop this, and Mrs Ponsonby will hear."

"You wouldn't."

"Try me." I feel awful at putting Elys under pressure, but I can't walk away when she's so unhappy.

"It's a private matter," she says.

"Oh." I am taken aback. Elys has no obligation to tell me anything personal, and I've just approached the problem like a bull in a china shop. Is there no end to my lack of judgement? "I'm sorry," I say. "I only want to help, but of course, you don't have to tell me if you don't want to."

Elys sighs and puts her head in her hands, looking as if all the fight has left her. "I know you do," she says. "It's just so hard to talk about."

"Then don't, but let me get you a hot drink. Warmed up milk and honey will make you feel sleepy. Perhaps things will feel better in the morning."

Elys doesn't argue, and I quietly set the pan to boil, get two cups and spoon a dollop of honey in each. I stand in silence as the milk heats. Elys says nothing. She is staring at the same place on the kitchen table as if she has discovered a fascinating detail in the knotted blemish. I pass her a cup, and she puts her hands around it but doesn't drink. I take a sip from mine and wince as the hot liquid burns my mouth, then I leave it to cool.

Elys looks up. "It's Jory," she says unexpectedly.

"Is he ill?"

"No. He's an idiot."

"Oh, I see."

"No, you don't," she says waspishly, and I fear I will lose her again.

"Sorry, Elys." It's not much of an apology, but it's all I have. I glance at her hand as I wait for her reply and notice a glaring absence. She follows my gaze.

"I gave it back."

"Your lovely ring?"

Elys nods. "I threw it at him on Sunday."

"Why?"

"Because Jory Clark is a selfish, unfeeling, disloyal piece of work, and I don't love him anymore." Her voice breaks, and tears course down her cheeks.

"I'm a rotten judge of people, but even I know that's not true," I say, stroking her hair. Elys squirms away, and I remove my hand. "Tell me what he's done?"

"He accused me of going with Isaac Langley."

"Going where?"

"For goodness' sake, Connie. You're not that naïve."

My face reddens as I realise what she means. "Why did Jory think that?"

"Because that's what Isaac told him."

I want to ask if there's any truth in it, but Elys is so upset and angry that it's not worth the risk. I settle for silence, and the tactic works.

"There's no truth in it, in case you're wondering," she says.

"Then why did he say it?"

"I don't know. If I did, I could have convinced Jory that it wasn't true."

"You must have denied it?"

"Over and over again. Jory was alright at first, but as time went on, he couldn't get it out of his head, and he kept asking why Isaac would say such a thing if it didn't happen. He tried to believe me, but trust wasn't there in the end. We had a big fight on Sunday, and that was that."

"Is there no chance of a reconciliation?"

"I don't see how," says Elys, sipping from her milk. "They're all teasing him about it."

"Who?"

"The other fishermen. Everyone except Bertie that is. He's a little older and more mature. Perhaps I should take up with him."

Her bottom lip trembles as she speaks, and it's clear that her heart is still with Jory.

"What are you going to do?" I ask.

"Nothing. If Jory doesn't trust me, then what's the point?"

"Why don't you ask Isaac about it? Surely he wouldn't lie to your face?"

"How would that look?" asks Elys. "Talk about adding fuel to the fire. If I'm seen within a mile of Isaac's cottage, tongues will wag. Everyone knows each other's business around here. You should know that."

"What if I ask him?"

"How will you get there?"

"Where does he live?"

"A good two miles away, next door to Mrs Rose."

I grimace. I could walk a mile at an absolute push, but a two-mile round trip is beyond my ability.

"Don't worry. There are plenty more fish in the sea." Elys thinly smiles as she finishes her drink, then walks to the door, head bowed.

"I'm going back up now," she says. "I won't sleep, but I've got things to do tomorrow, and I ought to try. You should do the same."

I watch her depart and want to tell her how much I long for a good night's sleep, but Elys is distracted and now is not the time. She has given wise counsel in the past, but she must look after herself. A flash of inspiration hits me at the same time as a yawn. The doctor gave Mrs Ponsonby sleeping pills when she broke her arm a few years ago, and I don't think she took them all. I quietly rummage through the kitchen drawers, hoping against hope that I might find them. But if there are any left, they are not here. Mrs Ponsonby must keep them in her room. Sighing, I collect both cups and rinse them in the sink. There's no point in leaving evidence for Mrs Ponsonby's eagle eyes. Then I ascend the stairs, filled with trepidation, knowing I will either be awake all night or immersed in another nightmare.

CHAPTER THREE

Sorrow at the Summer Ball

Friday, June 17, 1932

The dreaded day has finally arrived, and I'm dressed to the nines in another outfit made by Elys, wearing the least offensive shoes I can find. I don't look bad if I say so myself. Mrs Ponsonby is in the parlour, pacing up and down as if sending her chick off to catch worms for the first time.

"Ah, there you are," she says, smiling as she catches sight of me in full evening dress for the first time. "You look very nice, Connie," she continues.

"Thank you," I say, opening my evening bag and examining the contents. I've stashed a lipstick, a couple of spare kirby grips, and some loose change inside the tiny space.

"Ah, that reminds me," says Mrs Ponsonby. She reaches towards the handbag she keeps by her chair and extracts her purse. "Here you are," she says, passing me half a crown. I gasp in surprise. It is more money than I have had in a long time and since she's paid for my ticket already, I probably won't need it.

"Thank you," I mutter, almost lost for words.

"Have you got a clean handkerchief?" I can't believe my ears. I am not seven years old, and she doesn't need to ask, but equally, I don't need to look inside my bag to know that I haven't.

"Connie," she gently chides. "I'll ask Elys to fetch one." Mrs Ponsonby strides to the bottom of the stairs and shouts for Elys. Silence. Tutting, she reaches for the bell on the hall table and jangles it loudly. "Where is that girl?" she complains. "I don't know what's got into her lately."

Seconds later, Elys rushes through. Her pale face suggests that she didn't get back to sleep on Wednesday night and probably hasn't since. "Get Connie a hanky," says Mrs Ponsonby, "quickly now."

Elys sighs and ascends the stairs two at a time. Mrs Ponsonby regards her disapprovingly. "I thought he'd be here by now," she says.

"Who?"

"Peter, of course."

"I'm meeting him at the hotel."

"You're going without an escort?"

"It's only a few yards away," I say.

Mrs Ponsonby shakes her head. "How very modern of you."

"You wouldn't have wanted an escort though?" I say perceptively. Mrs Ponsonby is nothing if not independent and, in her youth, was probably indefatigable.

My words hit the mark. "You're right," she says. "I would have gone alone. But it's different for you."

"Why? Because I can't walk?"

"No, dear. Not that, but I worry. But you're right in this case, and I've no objection to you going alone if you promise me that Peter will walk you back."

I nod. It's a small price to pay for a bit of freedom. "He will," I say.

Elys returns, clutching the monogrammed handkerchief she gave me for Christmas. She never said, but the neatly embroidered initials look like her work. I tuck it into my bag and pull a black cape over my shoulders.

"Have a lovely time," says Mrs P as I leave.

I walk towards the hotel feeling liberated, but when I glance back, the curtains twitch, and I see Mrs Ponsonby standing by the window. Her eyes bore into my back as I make my way to the front of the hotel. She doesn't trust me an inch, even supervising a two-minute walk. But I shrug it off, determined to make the most of the evening now there's no backing out of it.

I enter the foyer feeling nervous. I hadn't considered what I might do if Peter didn't arrive. But he has, and a dark-haired young man, sharply suited with pale green eyes and a slightly receding chin, accompanies him. Though not overweight, his companion's moon-shaped face and rosy cheeks give the young man a hamster-like, though not unattractive, appearance. He is clean-shaven, and I can't estimate his age, but he must be closer in years to Peter than to me.

"Frank, this is the lovely Connie. Connie, meet Frank Parsons."

Frank extends his hand, and I shake it. His grip is firmer than I expected.

"Pleased to meet you," I say.

"Likewise. Peter has told me a lot about you."

Frank's grip may be firm, but his voice is shrill and carries a faint accent. It does not strike me as the versatile voice of an actor, and I suspect it limits his range.

Roberto approaches us, weighed down with a tray of

drinks. "Would Madam like a glass of wine?" he asks, proffering the salver. The polished glasses stand in rows with red wine on one side, sparkling white on the other and something that looks like orange juice in the middle. My hand hovers over the centre of the tray, but Peter beats me to it.

"We'll have none of that," he says, taking two glasses of white wine and handing one to me and one to Frank. "We're here to enjoy ourselves." Peter selects a glass of red for himself.

"Oh, I say, look at that," says Peter pointing to a large board at the entrance to the reception area. "Consommé to start and filet mignon," he says, "washed down with vanilla eclairs."

"That's too rich for me," I say. "I'm having the salmon mousseline with roast duckling." My stomach growls at the thought, and I wish I'd eaten something before I left.

"I'll have what you're having," says Frank, looking towards Peter.

Roberto flits past again this time carrying a tray of hors d'oeuvres laid out in neat rows. There must be half a dozen different choices. Peter takes a devilled egg; Frank takes a devilled egg. Roberto leaves and returns ten minutes later. Peter takes a red onion tartlet, and Frank follows suit. By the time Roberto makes his fourth pass, it is clear that Frank is a sheep, following Peter's lead to the letter. He is starting to irritate me, and I am surprised that Peter hasn't noticed it himself. Perhaps he approves of this evident hero worship.

Roxy Templeton appears, dressed in a formal version of her usual uniform with ankle-length skirts and a sparkling brooch pinned to her chest. She bangs the dinner gong, and we make our way into the dining room. Pristine table clothes cover the round tables, two dozen of which are laid out in the capacious dining area. One by one, we approach another board at the entrance to the dining room. I glance at Peter in panic when I realise that it is a seating plan.

"Don't worry," he whispers. "Mother made the booking for

one party."

Peter is right. The planners have seated us together on a table by the window. It is still light, and I gaze at the sunlight dappling the sea. The sparkling wine is working its magic, and I feel excited for the evening and unusually sociable. The table, laid for eight, is almost empty. We are the only ones there, probably because we were at the front of the queue. I watch as the remaining guests file in, chatting as they search for their tables.

"Look at the name tags," says Peter. He is sitting in the middle and can't check for himself. I reach to my side. "Philip Protheroe," I say, staring at the name blankly.

"Never heard of him," says Peter.

"Charlotte Napier," says Frank, grabbing another. My heart sinks. What fresh hell is this? The only thing worse than being on a table with perfect Charlotte would be if Edgar Sutton arrived. I rise and scrabble frantically to read the other name cards. Kit Maltravers will be sitting next to Charlotte, and Mrs Protheroe and Miss Angelica Protheroe are in the other seats. I exhale with relief.

"What's wrong, Connie?" asks Peter. I chew my lip. I haven't seen him for a week and as far as I know, he hasn't heard about Edgar, but now I come to think of it, he was in the library when it happened and might be aware.

"Nothing. I'm glad Edgar Sutton isn't on this table."

"I doubt he'll be here," says Peter. "The silly ass tripped downstairs and split his lip open."

"Who told you?" I ask.

"Dolly," says Peter.

I offer silent thanks to Dolly for her loyalty, relieved that I don't need to explain myself to Peter.

The Protheroes take their seats and introduce themselves. Philip Protheroe is a land agent operating out of Newquay. He comes from a long line of land agents, and two of his brothers conduct their business in other Cornish towns. He is an agreeable man with a ready wit, educated but not full of self-importance. His wife is timid but pleasant and his daughter, thank the Lord, is the same age as me. We fall naturally into conversation and when he sees how well we are getting on, Philip Protheroe swaps seats with Angelica.

Peter pours me a glass of water and another glass of wine. The waiters appear, take orders for our choice of starters and place a basket of rolls on the table. I am settled and happy with just the right amount of alcohol to have lost my social inhibitions without losing control.

"They're late," says Peter, during a lull in the conversation. He nods to the two empty seats to Frank's right. I cross my fingers under the table and hope they won't arrive at all. I don't like the idea of eating in front of Kit Maltravers, who sets my heart fluttering with a single glance. And the thought of enduring Charlotte's benign sympathy for the duration of the meal makes my stomach churn.

"They might have changed their plans," I say.

Peter's face falls, but Frank looks relieved. "That's a shame," he says.

It is anything but, and I nearly say it. But Charlotte, for some inexplicable reason, is a friend of Peters. I often forget this and don't want him to think the worst of me for being unkind. It doesn't matter anyway, for just as the waiters bring the first plates of salmon, Charlotte and Kit come through the door and fuss around the seating plan. The door opens again, and Edgar Sutton walks inside. My stomach churns as the trio make their way towards our table.

"No, I'm afraid it's full," says Charlotte, turning to Edgar, who is sporting a giant scab on his lip.

Edgar tuts loudly and searches the room, noticing the table at the furthest end with six instead of eight occupants.

"Looks like you're over there," says Kit.

"I don't know anybody on that table," lisps Edgar, regarding the empty seats with a thunderous expression on his face. His partial denture is ill-fitting, and his speech has suffered accordingly. No doubt, the false teeth are temporary.

"I say, fancy moving over there?" he asks Peter. "I'll give you a crown for your trouble."

Peter glances towards me, and Edgar notices my presence for the first time.

"You," he scowls. "The least you can do is give me your seat."

Peter's eyes narrow, and I know he is wondering what Edgar means.

"We're together," says Peter.

"And are you together?" asks Edgar, turning to the Protheroes.

"I'm afraid so, old son," says Philip.

Mr Brookbank, the manager, is hovering surreptitiously in the background. Seeing the commotion, he advances to the table.

"Can I help," he asks.

"I'm not satisfied with the seating plan," says Edgar. "I demand to sit with my friends."

"Did sir book as a party?" asks Mr Brookbank.

"No, sir did not. But neither was sir told that there would be a seating plan."

"Then I can't help," says Mr Brookbank. "Unless one of the other guests is willing to move."

"Peter, be a darling," says Charlotte. "Please."

Peter looks at Edgar, and I can see he is considering offering his seat. But one glance at my panic-stricken face, and the words stay firmly inside.

"That won't be necessary," says Kit Maltravers. "I'll sit over there. It's no trouble."

Charlotte's face falls. "No, Kit. I want you here."

"I don't mind," says Kit.

"It's good of you, old man," says Edgar. "Though I'm willing to sit over there with Charlotte if you'd rather stay here. In fact, I'd prefer it." Edgar looks pointedly at me, then nods towards the other table.

"Very well," says Kit, sitting next to Frank. Edgar takes

Charlotte's hand and guides her towards the other table.

"There's a better class of customer over there," he mutters as he passes, looking sideways at me. Charlotte lags behind, holding onto his hand, the picture of abject misery.

Kit unfurls his napkin and places it on his lap. A waiter scurries over to take his order, but like a perfect gentleman, he apologises for being late and tells him to bring whatever is easiest. Then he breaks open a bread roll, butters it and introduces himself to Frank. Kit already knows the Protheroes, and before long, our table is buzzing with interesting conversation and genuine laughter. Frank is naturally shy, but Kit has sensed this and is drawing him out of himself with a series of observations about theatre. The wine flows, the entrée arrives, and silence falls as we devour beef, duckling, or in Sarah Protheroe's case, nut roast. By the time dessert arrives, we are in full flow again, and everyone is slightly tipsy. Despite my earlier reservations, I am thoroughly enjoying myself – so much so that I don't mind being left to my own devices when they clear the tables, and everyone takes to the dance floor.

Edgar and Charlotte lose their sullen looks as they foxtrot to the sound of the Beer Barrell Polka. Kit stands good-naturedly, watching them spin elegantly around the room. Peter is dancing with Angelica Protheroe while Frank stands uncomfortably chewing his nails. I get to my feet and join him. I know a fish out of water when I see one and think about the many times I have been in his position as I offer a friendly word. But it's too much like hard work. Frank's answers are monosyllabic, and he asks me nothing in return. He was so different chatting to Kit Maltravers, and I am frustrated at my lack of social skills. Eventually, I use my leg as an excuse and return to my seat on the edge of the dance floor, where I observe proceedings through increasingly blurry eyes. I am unused to drinking and have had more wine than on any other occasion. And that's having declined Peter's last two attempts to fill my glass.

I'm not drunk, but I'm so pleasantly relaxed from the alcohol that I might get a good night's sleep for once. There's not much to keep me here now that the dancing has begun. I've had a lovely time and a delicious meal, but it's a good time to leave. I decide to stay for one more round of dancing and watch Charlotte and Kit, together with Peter and a new, unknown partner, joyfully swinging around the floor. The music ends, and Georgio, the assistant manager, plays a gramophone record while the band decamps for a break. Peter joins Frank, and I wave towards him as I make my way to the bathroom. It is time to freshen up and go home.

I see Charlotte Napier as soon as I open the door. She is talking to Peter's dance partner, a young dark-haired girl and is holding out her hand. Charlotte hasn't seen me, which suits me very well, and I lift my stick off the floor and make my way to the nearest cubicle, happy to be out of her sight.

"It's beautiful," says the unknown girl.

"It should be," says Charlotte. "It's a real diamond."

"Can I try it on?" Charlotte must be hesitating and says nothing for a moment.

"I don't see why not," she says, eventually.

I flush the toilet and emerge to see the other girl passing the ring back.

"Oh, it's got soap in it," says Charlotte, rinsing the ring under the tap. She glances at me but doesn't speak.

I am advancing to the sink when I hear a thud on the wall outside. Something falls heavily against the door, which swings open to the sound of a metallic clatter like raining pots and pans. The three of us exchange glances, then Charlotte and the girl head for the door while I trail in their wake.

Outside, a grey-haired man sits surrounded by silverware. A hostess trolley lies on its side, wheels still spinning – teapots, milk jugs and cutlery spilt across the carpet as far as the eye can see. The man groans and shifts onto his elbow, staring groggily towards us. Mr Brookbank arrives, soon followed by Georgio and Roxy. Mr Brookbank rolls his eyes and takes one arm while Georgio puts his head under the other. They carry the man, legs trailing behind him, into the nearest room and shut the door firmly behind. Roxy emerges a few moments later.

"Don't worry. He's fine," she says brightly.

"Some people don't know when to stop," says Charlotte before disappearing down the corridor. The girl follows in her wake, and I limp slowly back to the dance floor. I haven't moved much, but the long evening and lack of sleep have taken it out of me.

Peter and Frank are sitting at the table when I return. Peter is on the wrong side of tipsy, and Frank looks far happier than he has done all night. I chat with them for a while, but they are talking theatre, and I feel excluded.

"I think I'll go," I say.

"I'll walk you back," says Peter watching the band return. They are barely seated before the musicians start again, launching into fast-paced jive music. Peter taps his feet excitedly.

Frank taps him on the shoulder and points to a picture of Rudolph Valentino gracing a wall a few yards away, but Peter misinterprets his actions. Angelica Protheroe is standing beneath the portrait, swaying to the music and clearly in need of a partner.

"Do you mind?" he asks. I shake my head. Peter is full of life tonight, and I can't deny him this small moment of pleasure. I smile as he takes Angelica by the hand and leads her to the dance floor. Within seconds, they are throwing themselves into the moment as if their lives depended on it. I cast a glance at Frank, who is watching sombrely and wonder why he hasn't been on the dance floor himself – shyness, I suppose. Then, out of the corner of my eye, I see a very animated Charlotte Napier gesturing dramatically at Mr Brookbank. I watch as he summons Roxy Templeton and Georgio, who shake their heads vigorously in response. The music draws to an end, and couples hover on the outskirts of the dance floor, waiting to hear if the next piece of music is to their liking. But before the band strikes up again, Mr Brookbank takes to the stage and gestures for quiet. Most people stop talking, but a few young men in their cups ignore him. He nods at the drummer, who lowers the hi-hat cymbal with an almighty crash: everything stops, and silence reigns.

"Ladies and gentlemen," says Mr Brookbank. "Sorry to interrupt your evening, but a diamond engagement ring has gone missing in the last hour. I hope this has come about by accident and not design, but please check your possessions in case. The item in question is precious, both sentimentally and monetarily. I will have no choice but to call the constabulary if we can't find it.

I chew my lip. I know exactly who the ring belongs to and when it happened, and I rack my brains trying to remember in what order we left the ladies' room. Around me, people are patting their pockets and examining their bags in a very English way knowing full well that they didn't take it but going through the motions, nevertheless. Don't be silly, Sarah," says Philip Protheroe, watching his wife turn out the contents of her handbag.

Cooperation slowly turns to irritation. One of the men steps forward and confronts Mr Brookbank.

"This is a fine way to treat your guests," he says.

Mr Brookbank apologises and gestures towards the back. The music quickly resumes, and the guests slowly return to the dance floor.

"I wonder what that was about," asks Peter. We chat for a while, and I can see from Peter's demeanour that he is dying to dance again, but Frank won't stop talking. Every time there is a natural lull in the conversation, Frank fills it. Peter checks his watch. Time is slipping away, and it won't be long before the dance is over. I don't know why I'm still here when I'm tired to the bone, and I am relieved when Peter asks if I want to go back. I am about to reply when Georgio approaches and whispers in my ear.

"Please follow me to the office," he says.

Puzzled, I agree and remove my stick from under my chair.

"What's going on?" asks Peter.

I shake my head and trail behind Georgio as he leaves the room. He opens the office door and waves me inside, where I see Roxy Templeton sitting behind one desk and Mr Brookbank behind the other. Georgio pulls out a chair, and when I am seated, Mr Brookbank clears his throat.

"I have received a report of a most concerning nature," he says.

"Have you?" I reply. I don't know what else to say.

"I'm afraid I have," he continues. "Were you in the ladies' room when Miss Napier showed off her ring?"

My heart flips. I can see where this is going. "Yes," I say, seeing no point in denying it.

"Did you see her take the ring off?"

"Yes. A dark-haired girl tried it on. Have you spoken to her?"

"Miss Roberts? Yes, we have."

"It doesn't matter. She returned the ring to Charlotte. I saw her."

"That's correct, and they both agree."

"Me too. Charlotte had the ring, and then she washed it under the tap, and that's the last I saw of it."

Mr Brookbank ignores me. "In what order did you leave the room?"

"Charlotte went first, I think, then Miss Roberts and me. Oh, I see what you're suggesting. I didn't take the ring, and I didn't see it left there. Charlotte had it, as far as I know."

"No. The commotion outside was a terrible distraction, and Miss Napier left her ring in the sink."

"Are you sure?"

"Quite sure."

"She might have made a mistake and put it in her handbag."

"Miss Napier is distraught. She has searched everywhere

she can think of and has no reason to lie. I have offered to conduct a thorough investigation of the hotel, but she wants the police called in. So, if you know where that ring is, you must tell me, for your own good."

"Are you accusing me of taking it?"

"No. I'm advising you of the consequences of concealing a crime. This is the second time this month that you've..." Mr Brookbank looks at the ceiling and searches for the right words. "...that you've drawn attention to yourself," he continues. "Both Miss Roberts and Miss Napier say that you were the last person in proximity of the ring. The hotel's reputation is at stake, and I've no choice but to act."

I shake my head, aghast at his words. I wish I could remember if the ring was there or not when I left the room, but I wasn't paying attention. Whatever happened, I had no hand in it, and the unfairness of his words pierce my heart.

"Have you anything to add?" he asks.

"No, except that I didn't take it," I say. My voice wobbles, and I am on the verge of tears.

"You must stay away from this hotel until we resolve matters," says Mr Brookbank. "No more visits to the library, no more hanging around disturbing Dolly. I am very sorry, Miss Maxwell, but my position is untenable if I let things carry on as they are. Georgio will escort you out."

My hands clench tightly around my stick as I stand, feeling swamped by shock and desperation. How has it come to this? Georgio takes my arm and gently manoeuvres me towards the door, but I wrench it away.

"Don't worry. Things have a habit of working themselves out," he says in his lilting continental accent. I know he is trying to be nice, but I am beside myself and cannot even return to Peter.

"Goodbye, Miss Maxwell," says Georgio, and before I know it, I am outside the hotel. It is dark, but not so dark that I can't see a trio of people standing by the garden wall: Kit, Charlotte and Edgar Sutton. Edgar smirks, but Kit steps towards me before Charlotte pulls his arm.

"Leave her," she says.

I stumble away, faster than is good for me, desperate to leave before my sobs become audible. I feel their eyes boring into me as I walk the last humiliating yards to Pebble Cottage.

CHAPTER FOUR

Crossley Returns

I stumble through the door of Pebble Cottage, slamming it behind me and hurling my stick to the floor. It clatters across the hallway, landing at the foot of the stairs. Mrs Ponsonby emerges from the parlour.

"What on earth has happened?" she asks, staring in puzzlement at my streaming eyes.

"Go away," I rage.

"What is it? Has someone hurt you?" She reaches for my hands. I try to tear them away, but she grips me firmly.

"Let me go," I say. Hurt has turned to anger, and I can't contain my fury.

"Calm down, Connie."

"I said, let me go."

I wrench my hands away, and she nearly falls over as I push past.

"Where is Peter?" Mrs Ponsonby barks.

I ignore her and make for the stairs, but she is quicker and gets there first.

"How should I know?"

"You were under strict instructions not to walk back alone."

"I'm always under strict instructions. Why can't I live a normal life?"

Mrs Ponsonby doesn't respond for a moment, and when she does, it isn't an answer.

"It's not good enough," she says.

"What isn't?"

"Your behaviour."

"My behaviour?" I snap, knowing I am angry with the wrong person but unable to control myself all the same. "What about your behaviour?"

Mrs Ponsonby wears a puzzled frown. "I don't know what you mean."

"You're just a bloody liar," I say. A combination of the awfulness of the evening together with the wine has given me a bravery that wouldn't exist under usual circumstances. Mrs Ponsonby recoils as if I had slapped her.

"How dare you!" She stands in front of me, shaking with rage as Elys comes downstairs in her nightdress, rubbing her eyes.

"What's going on?" she asks.

"Go back to bed," says Mrs Ponsonby.

"Don't," I say, still consumed with unspent fury. "You can hear this, Elys. Mrs Ponsonby is a bloody liar. She isn't a Mrs at all. She hasn't got a husband and never had one. Mrs Ponsonby has lied for years. So," I say, turning to face Mrs P, who by now is pale and trembling herself, "don't tell me about my behaviour when yours is even worse."

I lunge for my stick and push past her, but I am forced to stop when Elys grasps both banisters and blocks my path.

"Apologise," she says, and I reel at her words. If I expected any reaction from Elys, it would be benign sympathy. Instead, she is seething with silent condemnation.

"I beg your pardon?"

"Apologise to Mrs Ponsonby," she repeats icily, emphasising the Mrs.

"I will not."

"Go to bed, Elys," says Mrs Ponsonby in a softer voice. Elys catches her eye, turns and walks away.

"I will write to Coralie and Mary Newson tomorrow," says Mrs Ponsonby. "Your visit to Bosula will not take place. I cannot have you conducting yourself like this. I must be able to trust you, and you have violated my rules in every possible way."

"No, not Bosula," I say. "I'm sorry. You don't know what's happened tonight. If you did, you would understand."

"I'm sure I would," says Mrs Ponsonby. Her voice is gentle, almost kindly, but her next words pierce like spears. "You must behave properly, Connie. This outburst, however justified from your perspective, is unforgivable from mine. You cannot go anywhere without me until you learn some self-control. Your safety is paramount. The Bosula visit is cancelled. Please don't mention it again as I will not change my mind. Use your time to reflect on your actions tonight, and we will talk again tomorrow."

She walks into the parlour, and I consider following her. But I know I've overstepped the mark and it's pointless arguing. I have lost everything in the space of a few hours – my library access, my trip to Bosula and my reputation, all in one fell swoop. I fall sobbing on my bed, utterly broken, weary and hopeless. And I'm not at all surprised when I wake to find myself on the astral plane.

#

Shimmering particles of light surround me as I hurtle through time towards an unknown destination. I feel weak, only partially formed, my hands translucent and hazy. There is nothing controlled about this journey. I am not in charge; it is happening to me, and I hold no influence upon it. I make a half-hearted attempt to will myself home but I don't care enough. My safety has taken a low priority, and I have nothing to look forward to. I passively watch as the light fades and dark shadows loom around me. I don't know what they hold, and it isn't important. Let fate take me where it will. But the darkness clears to indigo blue, and eventually, I find myself outside the front door of a townhouse that I recognise. I'm in Berlin. I have been here before, and I know what, and more importantly, who is waiting inside.

Despair drives me forwards. No good will come of meeting Crossley, but I am here and can only assume that it's because he wants me. Throwing caution aside, I climb two sets of stairs and pass through the door into the attic room. As I expected, Felix Crossley is inside, but he is not alone. I stand at the rear where I watched him conduct a ceremony last year. I thought he would know as soon as I entered, but he is so engrossed in what he is doing that it's blunted his senses to my presence. I lurk in the background and watch as he stands in front of a woman kneeling naked before him. Her flaxen hair is greasy, and she has lowered her eyes in subjugation. The woman looks utterly broken.

"Look at me, Renate," he commands. She doesn't move.

"I said, look at me." His voice rises as he tips her chin. She looks into his eyes, and I move nearer for a better view. When I am close enough to see her expression, I expect to see fear. Instead, she gazes at him with adoration.

"You disobeyed me," he says.

"I'm sorry."

"Sorry isn't good enough."

"What can I do to make it up to you?"

Crossley sighs. Hair sprouts from his once balding head,

and I realise that he shaves it.

"Let me think about that," he says, producing a jewelled silver knife from his robes. He strokes the blade, then runs it gently over her throat.

"Do you love me?" he asks.

"More than life itself."

"Good answer. I so badly wanted you as my scarlet woman."

"I am. I am."

"No. I have taken another."

Her face crumples. "But why?"

"Because you disobeyed me."

"I couldn't do it," she says. "She's my friend."

"And that's the problem," says Crossley. "You should have loved me enough to do it anyway."

The woman is sobbing now, her voice a strangled whine. Snot streams down her nose, and she wipes it away with the back of her hand.

"You'll have to leave, of course," says Crossley.

"But I've nowhere to go and no money."

"That's your problem."

"Don't you love me anymore?"

"No. Not at all."

"Then there's no point." The woman prostrates herself in front of him. "Please don't make me go," she cries. "I love you."

"Renate von Gluck, consider yourself banished," says Crossley, pulling his foot from her grasp in disgust. "Go."

"I'll kill myself," she wails.

Crossley hands her the knife. "Be my guest."

The woman kneels and stares at Crossley, searching for the slightest hint of compassion. But Crossley stares disinterestedly, examining his nails.

Renate von Gluck raises the knife in the air, holding it tightly with both hands. I cannot stand by and let it happen, though Crossley undoubtedly would. Despite the danger, and though I cannot touch or influence the outcome, I shoot towards her in a desperate attempt to save her life. It works. She doesn't see me, but Crossley does, and he raises his arm.

"Stop," he booms.

She stays her hand two inches from her bosom, then stares at Crossley like a saviour. He watches me, hypnotic eyes boring into mine as if they are trying to pin me down, then he orders her to leave.

"I don't know where to go," she says.

"Go anywhere, or you'll face the wrath of Baphomet."

The woman turns pale and scurries away, breasts heaving. She hasn't seen me and does not attempt to cover her shame. Under other circumstances, I would feel embarrassed, but I am both intrigued and fearful, yet full of cavalier bravery born of despair.

"Well, well," says Crossley, his voice low and triumphant. "This is most unexpected. I have tried to catch your attention for many months. Your resistance is a source of great irritation."

"What do you want with me," I reply, not knowing whether he will hear, but he does.

"Come closer," he says. I don't want to, but I can't help moving towards him. He looks me up and down, then reaches towards me, suddenly thrusting his hand into my midriff. I recoil, my reactions the same as if I was inhabiting my body, but I feel nothing.

Crossley gloats. "I had to be sure," he says. "You can't always believe the evidence of your own eyes."

"What do you want," I repeat, feeling as if I must be dreaming. What would a man like Crossley want with a slip of a girl who has never left Cornwall?

"Where do you come from?" he probes as if reading my mind. But I know he can't, or he wouldn't need to ask.

"Guess," I say.

The smug expression falls from his face. "Tell me," he commands.

"No."

"Do you know what would happen if I plunged this knife into you?" he asks.

"Nothing," I say. "It can't hurt me."

"Correct," says Crossley. "I can't harm you while I am in my physical body, and you are in your astral one. But what do you think would happen if you faced me in the flesh?"

"I think it's obvious," I say condescendingly. Crossley is a large man, and though quick-witted, I am small and encumbered.

"And if we were both in our astral forms?" he continues.

I consider the question. Truthfully, I don't know.

"I'll tell you," says Crossley.

"I have dedicated twenty years to the study of astral travel. I am strong in ways you cannot imagine. If our paths cross on the astral plane, there can only be one winner. So, I suggest you answer my question if you don't want me to demonstrate.

I haven't taken my eyes off Crossley's face. He stares like a serpent, a spitting cobra, with deep, black impenetrable eyes. They hold me in a vice-like grip, and I am sinking deeper into a reverie.

"Tell me your name," he whispers. I can feel my lips moving, but no sound emerges.

"Try harder," he commands. His syrupy voice is compelling, and his words infiltrate my better judgement. I could make him happy by telling him what he wants to know, and I want to please him.

"Good girl," he whispers. "That's it. Keep going."

I whisper my name in a voice so low that he can't hear me.

"One more time," he says, and I detect a note of irritation in his voice. It is enough to set a small part of my mind free, and I idly wonder why he is still in his physical body where he wields less power. It must be because his transformation is not instantaneous. In this situation, I already hold the balance of power. Summoning all my resolve, I break free of his gaze. It splinters the trance, and I feel a tugging in the back of my head. I want to return. Even Pebble Cottage with an angry Mrs Ponsonby is safer than this, but I know Crossley will follow. Even now, he is muttering under his breath, trying to open his pineal door. I banish thoughts of Cornwall from my mind, and the first thing I think of is Oliver Fox. Where does he live? I visualise his card. I can't see the house number, but the street name is clear. Worple Road, Wimbledon.

The scene changes. I am flying backwards, dappled sky surrounding me as I land heavily by a street sign marking my desired destination. I have made it, but with a high-risk strategy. Crossley is more dangerous on equal terms. If he follows me, it will be in his astral body. He will have the whip hand with powers I can only imagine. I cannot stay here, putting Oliver Fox at risk. Ignoring the pull on my scalp, I run in a southerly direction for mile after mile before floating half a foot above the pavement when I can't feel him anymore. My concentration lapses and I look around to find myself in the centre of Croydon, where I take stock of my surroundings. My desperate run has left me in the middle of a long straight road. I turn to face the large Victorian villa to my front, and a feeling flashes through me akin to the moment I touched Annie Hearn's handkerchief and knew she was alive. And as I regard the angular attic window, I know without a doubt that I will visit 29 Birdhurst Rise again.

CHAPTER FIVE

The Final Straw

Saturday, June 18, 1932

I am not speaking to Mrs Ponsonby. Fear of Felix Crossley
may have left me eager for Pebble Cottage, but that does not
extend to seeing Vera Ponsonby, who has denied me the only
thing left that has any meaning. I've been looking forward to
the Bosula visit for months, not only to see Mary but Coralie
too. I miss her so much, and since Coralie left, the house is
quieter and stricter. Mrs Ponsonby is incapable of having fun
and wouldn't know a good time if it bit her in the ankle. She
should have been a prison warden and would have felt deep
satisfaction locking doors and sneering at inmates from the

corridor. I've never liked her, but the depth of my loathing has plumbed new lows.

The weather is foul today, as befits my current mood. It has been raining off and on all morning. After breakfast, I started for the cave having nothing better to do, but by the time I reached the sand, it was too wet to continue. I'm not allowed in the library and can't walk any great distance. My life is over and all because that witch wouldn't forgive my outburst, just once. If she'd endured one second of the humiliation I suffered last night, she wouldn't have reacted the way she did. Without the hotel, there is no Dolly, no Peter and no books. I don't know what I will do with the rest of my life, trapped inside this tiny cottage with a broken-hearted housemaid and a woman who doesn't have a heart at all. I mooch into the kitchen, looking for Elys. She is rolling pastry at the kitchen table with an expression no less miserable than mine.

"Have you apologised yet?" she asks as I enter.

"What?" I was aghast at the suggestion last night, and time has not improved its attraction.

"Have you said sorry to Mrs Ponsonby," she repeats, regarding me like a naughty child.

"No, I haven't," I say. "Why should I?"

"Do you remember what you said?" She puts down the rolling pin and stands with her hands on her hips, making dusty white patches on her housecoat.

"Not really." I didn't consider my words in the heat of the moment. They flew straight from my mouth with no regard for the consequences.

"Well, you swore at her twice," says Elys.

I screw my eyes closed. I hadn't remembered that when I replayed last night's events in my mind this morning. "She deserved it," I say.

"She was worried about you. I was listening upstairs and heard every word you said. Mrs Ponsonby was trying to help, and you rewarded her by blurting out a secret you have no business knowing."

Elys is angry, and her eyes flash dangerously.

"Did you know?"

Elys doesn't answer.

"For goodness' sake, does everyone know but me?"

"It's none of your business what Mrs Ponsonby calls herself," says Elys. "She's always looked after you."

"You've only been with us for a couple of years," I reply.

"But I've lived in Porth Tregoryan all my life," Elys retorts. "Mrs Ponsonby isn't perfect. There are days when I could cheerfully wring her neck but has she ever caused you a moment's worry other than not letting you out of her sight?"

"No," I concede. "But I might as well be a prisoner."

"Don't start that again. I'm sorry your life isn't what you want it to be, but that's no reason to be quite so unpleasant to your guardian."

I take a deep breath and consider her words. "I had an awful night, Elys. Hear me out, and you'll understand." I sit at the table and relate every sordid detail as she rolls the pastry and crowns a beautifully constructed meat pie. And when I finish, she slams it in the cooker and sits beside me.

"That must have been dreadful," she says. "Really dreadful. But don't you think things would have felt better if you'd let us help?"

I think of her reluctance to tell me about her. For a moment, I consider dropping the matter, but I can't bear her hypocrisy.

"I didn't want to talk, like you didn't want to talk about Jory," I say. "If she'd let me go to bed and sleep it off, I wouldn't have been so angry."

Elys nods. "I take your point," she says.

"And now, I can't do anything. If only I could go to Bosula."

"Mrs Ponsonby won't change her mind," says Elys. "She's already written the letters. They're on the sideboard for posting.

"I should burn them," I say.

"It won't help. She'll write others." Her words sting, but Elys is right. I've brought this on myself, though Mrs Ponsonby is partially to blame. But for once, I had a genuine reason for wanting to be left alone and not talk about the awful events at the ball.

"Why don't you do some drawing later?" asks Elys. "Mrs Ponsonby is going out, and you'll have the parlour to yourself.

"I haven't got the energy," I say, "or the enthusiasm."

"Read a book then."

"I've only got one I haven't read, and there's precious little chance of replacing it."

"I'll go to the reading rooms next time I'm in town," says Elys. "We'll work something out with Peter."

I think of Peter and wonder whether he's heard anything yet. He didn't come to look for me. For all I know, his feet are firmly in Charlotte Napier's camp, and he has disowned me and thinks I'm a thief. I stare miserably at Elys.

"I know it wasn't entirely your fault, but try saying sorry to Mrs Ponsonby," she advises. "An apology goes a long way. You won't get to Bosula in July, but perhaps it will be enough to set things right for later in the year."

I leave Elys in the kitchen and take a turn around the garden as I consider my options. Elys is right once again. Mrs Ponsonby is my captor, and there is no point in this unpleasant standoff. It's not a war I can win, and I decide I will apologise, but not straight away. It will sound more sincere if I give it a couple of days.

I am in the bedroom when Mrs Ponsonby departs. I hear her shouting to Elys as she leaves the cottage, reminding her to pay Jory for this week's fish. I am surprised that Jory is still delivering under the circumstances and quietly pleased that Elys hasn't confided in Mrs Ponsonby, who doesn't know they've fallen out. I empty the contents of my wardrobe as I haven't had a clear out for a month or two. With a long afternoon looming, I might as well do something useful. Ten minutes later, I'm already bored and feeling peckish too. I decide to visit the kitchen for a snack, but on leaving my room, I see something that suggests Mrs Ponsonby is equally distracted. Her bedroom door is standing ajar. Not only is it not locked, but she hasn't even pulled it shut. Although I am in as much trouble as I have ever been, the open door is irresistible. I have been trying to get inside her room for years. I know what it looks like as she tolerates me being there as long as she's present, not that I do it very often as I have no desire to be close to Mrs Ponsonby in any room, much less her lair.

I push the door fully open and enter, making a beeline for her closet. I expect it to be closed as it always has been on the few occasions I've passed the bedroom door before, but it's open too. Suddenly the day has meaning, and I push past the door with alacrity, eager to lay my eyes on her secrets. The cupboard is underwhelming. Small, sparse and dusty, it contains two large trunks and a writing case. And that is it. Nothing more. I try to lift the lid of the first trunk but regret it immediately. The lock won't budge, and now there are fingerprints over the surface. I blow into the dust, hoping it will naturally re-spread, and to a degree, it works. It is not clear whether Mrs Ponsonby has locked the second trunk, so I risk another go, but it is also closed.

I am seething with frustration when I reach the writing case, but it looks like a better bet. There is no evidence of a lock, so I flip it open and pull out a pile of large brown envelopes. My fingers tremble with excitement as I withdraw the contents of the first. Inside is a document written in flowing italics. And on closer inspection, I find myself holding the deeds to a house called Netherwood in Bury St Edmunds. I haven't heard of this house or its location, but it doesn't sound like Cornwall. I am trying to decipher the owner's name when I hear a click, and Mrs Ponsonby walks in clutching an umbrella. She stares at me in stunned silence, and, not knowing what else to do, I hand her the deeds.

"You've done it now, Connie," she says, voice trembling with emotion. "I can't keep you safe here. I'm selling the cottage, and we're moving away."

CHAPTER SIX

A Change of Scenery

Sunday, June 19, 1932

I woke yesterday feeling terrible, yet sure that things couldn't possibly get any worse. But that was before Mrs Ponsonby caught me rifling through her papers. Today, she is holed up in the parlour with the door shut, and when I peeped through the keyhole, she was tallying accounts. It looks like she meant what she said about moving and is calculating our finances. I want to confide in Elys, but I can't because if Mrs Ponsonby sells the house, Elys will need to look for another situation. And it's all my fault. I feel awful, and I don't want to leave Porth Tregoryan. It is the only home I have ever known. I can't imagine what I'll do without Peter and Dolly. And although things are difficult now, they won't be forever. I didn't take Charlotte Napier's rotten ring and sooner or later, someone will find it. Then she will have to eat a lot of humble pie. But at the moment, my situation is too humiliating for words.

I can't face Elys today and having nothing else to do, I head towards my cave. It is a beautiful day outside. Seagulls swoop low in a cobalt sky, and the tide sloshes gently against the sun-kissed shore. I remove my shoes and pad across the beach, my limp more pronounced without the built-up shoe, but finding small pleasure in feeling the sand under my feet.

I reach the cave with slight trepidation, remembering my broken books, but it is exactly how I left it. And after a cursory look, I drag the chair outside the front and sit watching the shimmering sea. The sun beats down on my uncovered skin, but I don't mind. Everything has gone wrong, yet I find myself searching for a glimmer of hope. Any small ray of positivity will do because if I can't find one, then not only has my world collapsed, my haven disappearing before my eyes, but I'm not safe anywhere. Crossley is pursuing me across the astral plane. I don't know why he wants me, but I'm in no doubt that he does. Sighing, I pick up a book and try to enjoy reading in the sun's warmth, but I can't concentrate. Shutting out my problems isn't feasible. There are too many to ignore. I will have to confront them one by one and see what I can do to make them go away. I shut the book and return to the cave. I left a jotter and a pencil inside the suitcase, and I need to write to think. I locate the notebook immediately, but the pencil is missing, and I don't recall picking it up among the damaged books. I inspect the stony floor, swishing sand away with my stick for a better view.

I find nothing on the rocky floor where the books once lay, but when I move my search to the edges of the cave, I see a disconcerting pool of congealed blood beneath the sand, the same blood that stained my stick a few days ago. I can't tell if it's human or animal or how it came to be there. There isn't enough blood for serious injury, but more than you'd expect from a cut. All in all, its presence is unsettling, but not enough to keep me away from the cave when I've nothing else to do in the world. A few more swishes with the cane, and I uncover the pencil. I wipe it clean of sand and settle back in my chair. Then I compile a brief list of my problems and think about potential resolutions. My conclusions are disheartening. I can't change what I did to Edgar. I don't know where Charlotte's ring is, but I could write to Mr Booth and ask him to reinstate my library rights. But what's the point if we're moving home? As for Crossley, he's another unresolvable problem. So far, I have evaded him, but I know from the other night's events that I am vulnerable in a weakened state of mind, and I need to know how to protect myself from him. That solution, at least, is obvious. I must contact Oliver Fox. But how?

Ordinarily, it would be easy. I would ask Dolly. But I am barred from the hotel, and I don't know how far they will go to stop me from entering. But if Dolly's on reception, there's a reasonable chance she's alone. Guests are unlikely to recognise me, so I only need to worry about the staff. I glance at the black underbelly of a stray cloud on the horizon, and it reminds me of Crossley's bottomless eyes. I can't spend another sleepless night worrying about him. The risk of being caught is nothing compared to his sinister meddling in my life.

I tear the page from the notebook, replace it in the case, and make my way along the shore. I have walked too quickly, and my hip aches by the time I reach the steps. But I push on. I'm going to try and see Dolly, and I'm not procrastinating. If I don't do it now, I'll talk myself out of going at all. I cling to the rail for a moment, then taking a deep breath, I walk through hotel door, trying to look confident and emerge into the reception hall, before ducking back again. Dolly is there, but so is Georgio. They are chatting at the desk. It would be so much easier if I were dream walking, and for a moment, I contemplate trying, but it's too dangerous. Instead,

I cower in the doorway, hoping that nobody comes in from outside. After a moment or two, I hear Dolly laughing, then silence, and I crane my head around and snatch a peep. Georgio is walking in the direction of the library, and Dolly is still there. I grab the opportunity and make for her desk as quietly as possible. She sees me approach, and her face falls.

"What are you doing here?" she hisses.

"I need to use the phone," I say.

"I can't let you. I'll be in terrible trouble."

"Please. I'm desperate."

"Not now," says Dolly.

"When?"

Dolly looks anxiously at her watch. "There's a staff meeting in the dining room at three o'clock," she says. "Everyone will be there except for me. I'll let you in the back door at five minutes past the hour. But that's it, Connie. I need my job, and I can't afford to upset Mr Brookbank."

"I won't ask you again. I'm very grateful, more than I can say."

"Please go," says Dolly, glancing up the corridor.

I leave immediately, knowing I can't afford to upset Dolly and risk her cooperation. But I don't want to go home in case Mrs Ponsonby sees me, and I am already worrying about how to get to the rear of the hotel, which is easily visible from the cottage. I decide to take a route across the front of the hotel garden and along the terrace instead. It means a steep climb for a few yards at the end, but it will take me to the back door with little risk of being seen by the occupants of Pebble Cottage. I've got half an hour to get there, which is more than enough time even with an arduous climb, but I can't hang around the rear door in case one of the hotel staff shoos me away. I settle for perching on the bottom step near the seafront for fifteen minutes and wish I had Mr Fox's card on my person. But I think I remember his number and I know he lives in Wimbledon. The operator should be able to connect me at a push. I don't wear a watch and must rely on estimating the time, and when I think fifteen minutes have passed, I tackle the route to the rear. I stumble once and tear my tights as I scrape my knee on the rocks, but even so, the climb is easier than anticipated, and I wedge myself into a gap between the hotel and the garden fence watching the back door for signs of Dolly. It doesn't take long before the door clicks open and Dolly peers outside. I reveal myself, and she beckons me over and ushers me through.

We tiptoe down the corridor. Dolly is ashen and clearly uncomfortable with her decision.

"Use the one in the office," she says. "I can shut the door on you. Be as quick as you can."

I make straight for the telephone and lift it from the cradle before sitting at what is probably Roxy Templeton's desk. The operator answers. "Wimbledon 251," I say, and she connects me. The telephone rings, and I wait with bated breath. It rings four times, and it occurs to me that I hadn't considered the prospect of Oliver Fox being out, but on the fifth ring, he answers.

"Oliver Fox," he announces formally.

"It's Connie," I say. "Connie from Porth Tregoryan. I'm in trouble, and I need your help."

#

"Is it Crossley?" asks Oliver Fox.

"Yes, how did you know?"

"By the urgency in your voice," he replies. "You sound frightened."

"I am. Crossley is trying to control me, which I've resisted up to now. But I succumbed on Friday night, and he saw me."

"Where did it happen?"

"In a townhouse, in Berlin. He's converted the attic and conducts ceremonies with his followers. He's cruel, Mr Fox. And he wants to know where I live."

"Good," says Fox. I stare at the telephone handset in disbelief.

"What's good about it?"

"It means he doesn't know already, and he can't easily get to you."

"It hasn't stopped him trying to pull me into the astral plane."

"Yes. You are in danger, but we can do something about that. I can help you defend yourself."

"Oh, thank you. I hoped you would say that. What should I do?"

"There's no quick fix to this, Miss Maxwell. It requires study and concentration. If I had more time, I would return to Cornwall and see what progress we could make in a few weeks. But as it is, I am under pressure to complete a series of articles for The Occult Review, and I need to employ an assistant."

"What for?" I ask.

"Transcribing my written notes into a readable form. Didn't I mention that I'm writing a book on astral projection? Over the years, I've collected several dozen journals of research notes. But they're all over the place, and I need someone to type them out and collate them. I've got a desk and a Remington typewriter. Now all I need is a willing assistant."

"I'll do it," I say, the words bursting from my lips without any consideration of the consequences.

"Can you type?" he asks.

"Yes. My last governess taught me. And I learned shorthand too if I can remember it."

"We have a spare room," says Fox. "I can't pay you much, but you could live in, and I would be in a far better position to protect you. When can you start?"

"Monday week," I say.

"That will do nicely. Shall I collect you from the station?"

"I'll let you know."

"As you wish. We're on the corner of Langham Road. Goodbye, Miss Maxwell, safe journey and take great care."

I place the handset on the cradle with shaking hands,

amazed at the decision I have just made. I don't have the means to get to Wimbledon, but it is the right thing to do. I will be safe there with Mr Fox, and if Mrs Ponsonby is determined to drag me away from Porth Tregoryan, then I might as well leave under my own steam. I sit back in the chair, contemplating my next move. I have little money, which won't be a problem when I'm there, as I can work for my keep. But getting to Wimbledon is a different matter. I screw my eyes tight as I try to remember Mr Fox's address. It is on Worple Road, but I don't know the house number. He said it was on the corner of Langham Road and I mustn't forget. I open the desk drawer and scrabble for a pen and paper to write it down. The drawer is spotlessly tidy, and I locate a newly sharpened pencil with ease. There are no scraps of paper, but a smart day book nestles beneath a desk tidy. I open it to find a series of neatly written notes relating to various aspects of housekeeping, then turn to the back and carefully tear out the last page. I've left a ragged edge, but by the time they notice, I will be long gone. I replace the pencil beside a lipstick and nail file and conclude that the desk must belong to the Templeton girl. But as I shove the daybook in its place beneath the desk tidy, I dislodge something taped to the top of the drawer, and it falls with a clunk. I don't need to pick it up to see that it is a diamond ring, and my hands fly to my mouth as I realise who it belongs to. Roxy Templeton has concealed Charlotte Napier's engagement ring in her desk. Why? Surely, she cannot dislike me enough to take it with the sole purpose of incriminating me? Yet this selfish act has ruined my life. I stare at the jewellery, wondering what to do with it. Telling Dolly would be a sensible option, but how would she know I hadn't brought it with me? She might think my request for the telephone an excuse to return the purloined object to the scene of the crime. I immediately change my mind. I may need Dolly's help again, and I don't want to give her any cause to doubt my integrity. I could take the ring with me, but what would I do with it? And it would make everything a great deal worse if someone found me with the thing in my possession. But I won't leave it where I found it. Goodness knows what further mischief the sly Miss Templeton would put it to if left to her own devices. I think for a moment, and then an idea comes to me. I reapply the tape to the top of the drawer and take the ring. Then I place it in the back of the drawer of the opposite desk, which must belong to Georgio or Mr Brookbank. With a bit of luck, one of them will find it before Roxy notices that it's missing from hers. Then, in the fullness of time, my name will be cleared, even though I won't care because I will be long gone. How though? How will I get to Wimbledon when I can't even walk? I do so wish I could drive.

I return to Roxy's desk knowing that I must leave shortly, or Dolly will worry herself into an early grave and, worse still, I might get caught. But thinking about driving has inspired me. Mary Newson can drive. I had planned to see her in a few weeks anyway, and once she hears that Mrs Ponsonby has cancelled the visit, she might feel minded to help me escape. Nothing ventured, nothing gained, and I feel full of confidence that my life will be more fulfilling, not to mention safer, if I can only get to Wimbledon. I pick up the handset again and ask for the operator. Ten minutes later, my plan is in place. Mary was sympathetic and cooperative. A free spirit herself, she already disapproves of the confines of my life, and when I was in Bosula last year, she took great pains to encourage me not to let my injury limit my choices. It's something I've always known, and even a few years ago, I still pushed myself as far and hard as I physically could. Now, I resent my crippled leg and often give in to feelings of inferiority. An occupation and a new start are exactly the right ways to change my fortunes. I will miss Peter, Dolly and Elys very much, but with Mrs Ponsonby on the warpath and determined to move us, I will miss them anyway. I am still musing about this when the door opens to reveal Dolly.

"You've got to go," she whispers, glancing anxiously

behind. "I can hear them moving."

"On my way," I say, scrabbling for my stick, but it has rolled under the desk, and I drop to my knees to retrieve it. The door slams shut, and I hear Dolly speaking. "Have you finished, Mr Brookbank?"

"No need to shout, Miss Grey," he says, and the door opens.

I gasp. I am too late. Thankfully, I am under Miss Templeton's desk, and the modesty board almost reaches the ground; almost, but not quite. If I move a muscle, he might see me, and I can only hope that Dolly can distract him before he comes through the door. She doesn't get a chance. I hear Roxy Templeton barking orders in the distance. Then, there is the sound of footsteps outside as the rest of the staff walk through the reception area. But external steps are the least of my worries. Mr Brookbank is now in the office and whistling as he makes for his desk. I hear him rearranging paperwork, then he stands and scrapes his chair back before walking towards the desk I am currently squatting beneath.

I can't see anything of him except his feet, but I hear a click as he takes the telephone handset and starts dialling. He is not sitting at Roxy's desk, thank goodness. But the furniture groans, and I realise he has either plonked himself on the desk or is leaning against it as he makes the call. I am still on my hands and knees, my back sore and stiff. I hope he won't take long and wonder who he is calling on a Sunday, but sadly, it's not a business call. I suffer the excruciating embarrassment of listening to Mr Brookbank telephoning a lady friend; a lady friend who is not his wife. I am not the only one risking an illicit call from the office today, and he must be desperate to risk telephoning from a shared office. I soon find out why. He has planned to meet the lady this evening and cannot make the appointment. He quickly rearranges it to the following night and returns to his desk no doubt to give the impression of a hard-working hotel manager. It is a pity that I'm going away. I could possibly use this newfound piece of information to get my library rights returned. Mr Brookbank starts singing to himself, and I take the opportunity to adjust my position to a more comfortable seated one in the realisation that I may be there for some time. But then the door opens again, and someone else enters.

"Ah, Miss Templeton. I thought you were busy?"

"I am," says Roxy. "I'm just fetching something."

My spirits sink and my heart thuds. If Roxy tries to sit at the desk, she will see me, and my humiliation will be complete.

"Hurry up then," says Mr Brookbank irritably.

I hear an audible sigh, and Roxy yanks the top drawer open. I close my eyes, waiting for the worst, but she grabs something and slams it again. Then the office door clicks shut, and she is gone.

I finally trudge through the doors of Pebble Cottage a little after six o'clock. Mr Brookbank had spent three long hours at his desk before resuming duties elsewhere. As soon as he left, I escaped through the hotel front door without seeing Dolly or anyone else. But I encountered Elys and Mrs Ponsonby after entering Pebble Cottage, who both regarded me with stony silence. Too tired for tea, I went to my room, and I am now in bed, eyes heavy with sleep. Something tells me it will come quickly tonight.

CHAPTER SEVEN

Experiments at Worple Road

Monday, June 27, 1932

I have escaped my old life, and I am currently sitting in the back bedroom of Oliver Fox's home in Worple Road, still shocked that I've completed my audacious plan. It is now six o'clock and almost time for supper in my new location, and I am full of excitement to see what the evening brings. The ruse went like clockwork. I woke this morning and packed a suitcase which I'd moved from the outhouse last week. It was risky. Elys wanted to change my bed on Friday, but if I'd let her, she would have seen my luggage. So, I spent a frustrating day in bed pretending to be ill and slept late on Saturday. The subterfuge worked. On the rare occasions that Elys works on Sundays, it is only for a few hours, so she didn't go near the bed. And I rose at dawn this morning to complete my packing and slid it back underneath while I waited.

Mary planned to arrive at eight thirty with strict instructions to watch for my signal. Mrs Ponsonby was due to travel into Newquay, and I knew that Elys would do the laundry on Monday and would be in the kitchen for most of the morning. As long as those two events happened simultaneously, I would be home and dry. And sure enough, Mrs Ponsonby sailed out of the door at quarter past eight, and I watched from my room to make sure she went in the right direction. She disappeared out of sight, and as soon as I was confident that Elys was busily engaged in the kitchen, I dragged my case downstairs and stashed it by the side of the cottage behind the dustbin. As planned, my red scarf was already billowing outside my bedroom window when Mary arrived ten minutes later. She pulled the car up outside Pebble Cottage and helped me stow my luggage before pulling off at speed once I was safely inside. Nobody saw a thing, and we set off towards Bodmin light-hearted and triumphant.

I'd only asked Mary to take me as far as the railway station. I couldn't manage the onward trip by myself but thought I'd take a chance and throw myself on the mercy of the rail staff for help. But Mary was one step ahead. She often exhibited in London and had several friends there. After making a few phone calls of her own, she took me all the way to Croydon, then drove herself to Piccadilly to catch up with a fellow artist and make a weekend of it. It was just as well.

When we arrived in Wimbledon, we quickly found Worple Road, but there were several houses at the junction of Langham Road, and my confidence plummeted when I realised that I didn't know which one belonged to Mr Fox. But Mary parked the car, strode straight to the first property, and knocked on the door. A minute later, the housekeeper directed us to the opposite house.

"Shall I wait?" asked Mary as I stood nervously on the corner.

"No. You've done so much for me. It's time I took charge of my future."

I waved as she drove off then, taking my bag in one hand and my stick in the other, I made for the door of the red brick gabled building in front of me and loudly knocked.

That was four hours ago. Since then, I have unpacked and made myself at home as requested by Mrs Bertha Callaway, wife of Oliver, or Hugh as she keeps calling him, and the only occupant of the house when I arrived. Writing and astral travel are not his only interests, and the reason my host needs an assistant so badly is that he works as a civil servant during the day. But he has taken pains to tell his wife all about me without being indiscreet about my unusual ability. She knows I will assist him with his paperwork, and so far, she has been friendly and open. Bertha has already said that she spends too much time alone, and it will be good for her to have another woman in the house. She's not been well of late and will soon take a short trip with a friend to stay in a guesthouse on the south coast. I must have inadvertently reacted because she reached for my hand and told me not to worry about the domestic situation. She had already intended to employ a live-in domestic servant to cater and clean while she is away. And I am glad she's been so thoughtful, for, in my naivety, I trusted everything that Fox told me. And for all I bothered checking, he could have lived alone and spent his days like an ageing lothario preying on silly young women. Fortunately, he is not that way inclined. And judging by the reading material in his bookcase, dominated by books on the occult and other unusual topics, Oliver Fox is everything he claimed. In fact, while I waited for my supper, I spent an interesting half an hour reading through one of The Occult Review magazines he'd left in my bedroom, and to which he had indeed submitted an article. So, I am confident of his provenance and keen to see him again.

"Miss Maxwell?" A voice calls uncertainly from the stairs. I take my stick and walk towards the door, stifling a yawn. The journey, though enjoyable, has taken it out of me. I am hungry and tired, excited, yet a bag of nerves.

"Yes?" I ask.

"It's almost time to eat."

"I'll come straight down."

As I descend the stairs, the door opens, and Oliver Fox steps inside. "Miss Maxwell." He smiles, removing his hat, which he places on the hatstand in the hallway.

I return the smile with one of my own as he places a battered attaché case on the floor and slides it under a chair.

"Did you have a pleasant journey?" he asks.

I am about to reply when Bertha Callaway arrives and plants a kiss on his cheek. I look away, discomfited at this display of affection.

"Come on," she says. "It's your favourite."

I follow them through to a small dining room, only large enough to fit a table and six chairs. But as small as it is, the room overlooks a pleasant garden and the outlook more than makes up for the lack of space.

"Sit down," says Bertha, pointing to a setting at the end of the table. Fox takes his position at the head and Bertha sits beside him once she has deposited a platter containing a large suet pudding surrounded by carrots and onions. It is not my usual fare, but I am starving and my mouth waters.

Bertha serves her husband first, then carves a large portion for me and piles vegetables by the side. I am somewhat taken aback at the size of the helping and surprised that Bertha didn't offer me the opportunity to serve myself. But these thoughts evaporate as soon as I taste the rich steak and kidney filling. The suet pudding is light and fluffy, and the filling rich and luscious. I eat every morsel and scrape my plate clean. If I were alone, I would have mopped up the gravy with a slice of bread and butter, but I remember my manners and refrain. Bertha asks her husband about his day, and he goes through the motions, though I can tell that he is anxious to talk about our project. But he waits until Bertha takes the dishes into the kitchen before mentioning it at all.

"Now," he says. "As you will have gathered, I work during the day – not every day, but most, and devote the evenings to writing, poetry and research. So, you can come and go as you please when I'm not around, but I'll need you at the weekends and between the hours of seven and ten each night."

I nod my agreement. The proposed hours seem entirely reasonable. I am about to ask him where I will be working when Bertha returns with a tray of dishes. She places them in front of us, and I find room for the tinned fruit she offers.

"Was there any mail, my dear?" asks Fox.

Bertha nods. "Yes. It's in your office."

"From my publisher?"

"I don't know. You'll have to open it."

"Are you a regular writer for The Occult Review?" I ask, searching for something sensible to say. Fox and his wife are talking easily together, and I feel like an intruder in their domestic world.

"Yes," he says, "but this particular piece is not for that magazine. It's a piece of poetry, and I've published it in my real name. Talking of which," he continues exchanging glances with his wife, "we need to establish some rules."

I raise an eyebrow. I have just escaped one regimented life and have no wish to rush headlong into another. I needn't have worried.

"I keep two distinct identities," Fox says. "My real name is Hugh Callaway, and in that guise, I am an actor, author, poet and civil servant."

"I see," I reply, not entirely sure where this is leading. "It's confusing, though," I say. "I've never called you that."

"And I'd prefer it if you didn't," says Fox. "You'd be surprised how cynical people are about esoteric matters. The subject was more acceptable a few years ago, but my superiors in the civil service would look down on me if they knew the extent of my involvement."

"I understand," I say, nodding my head.

"Good. Then you won't mind referring to me as Mr Fox?"

"Not at all. I'll find it much easier."

Oliver Fox smiles and slurps the last mouthful of fruit juice from the spoon. "Very nice, dear," he says to his wife, then turns to me. "You're not too tired to join me in my office?" he asks.

I shake my head. "Not at all. I'm eager to begin."

I thank Bertha Callaway, and we leave the room and cross the hallway. Fox ushers me into his study, and I immediately see why the dining room is so tiny. It would act as the study in a typical household, but Oliver Fox has commandeered the largest reception room to accommodate two desks and an extensive array of bookcases. The smaller desk is under a bay fronted window looking out over the road, upon which a battered Remington typewriter rests. A notebook, pencil, eraser and ruler sit tidily to one side below an inkpot and fountain pen.

"This is your desk," he says unnecessarily. "Do take a seat."

I perch on the chair and turn it to face him. He sits on the corner of the other desk, reaches back and picks up a notebook from a pile on his desk which he passes to me. I take it and stifle a grimace. The cover is yellowing with age, and a nasty water stain runs along the bottom right-hand corner. It has seen better days, and I open the front sheet with trepidation. Mr Fox writes in a spidery cursive hand with no regularity to the formation of letters. I wince at the sight of the scrawled page, knowing that it will take me time to gain sufficient familiarity for quick typing. But it doesn't matter, I suppose, as time is not pressing. Fox notes my response.

"It's awful, isn't it?" he says. "And some journals are even worse. But some are better." He takes another more recent notebook and hands it to me. I look inside. It appears his writing has improved over time.

"Do you want me to start tonight?" I ask.

"No. Begin tomorrow. You'll need me around until you get used to my ways. My writing is bad enough, but I've used my own brand of shorthand in there too. You're bound to get stuck at first. And I'd like us to devote an hour every night to astral travel. I will do everything I can to help you and keep you safe, but we'll need to experiment first so I can learn more about your abilities."

"It hasn't happened since we last spoke," I say.

"Dream walking or feeling as if you're being summoned?"

"Neither. The last time was shortly before we spoke. I'd resisted it up until then and haven't felt anything strange since."

"I'm surprised," says Fox. "I can't see Crossley giving up that easily. But I know you've mostly resisted his advances. Why do you think he broke through?"

"I don't know," I say disingenuously. I know full well. My defences were down because I was too miserable to care. But I can't bring myself to tell Fox why I was feeling broken and low that night.

"Are you sure?"

"I was more tired than usual," I say, settling for a half-truth.

He nods. "Are you too tired now?"

"For what?"

"To try a spot of dream walking here in this room. You mustn't go beyond these four walls, though."

"I'll need a candle," I say doubtfully. I have only tried dream walking publicly once, and that was in front of Peter. The thought of doing it in front of Fox makes me feel hugely self-conscious.

"Over here," he says, gesturing towards a day bed in the corner. I need my stick more than ever as I make my way across the room. My leg feels as if it's dragging behind. I know it isn't, but tiredness has this effect.

"Shall I light the flame?"

I nod. Fox lights the candle, and I stare at it, but his presence is limiting. I know he is there, and I cannot find it in me to drift. After five minutes of tortuous effort, I tell him. He smiles understandingly.

"We'll try tomorrow," he says. "You should retire for the night."

I don't need to be told twice and quickly return upstairs. When I next wake, it is Tuesday and well past breakfast time.

#

Tuesday, June 28, 1932

I complete my ablutions and go downstairs to find Bertha Callaway slumped across the dining room table. I stand in the doorway for a few seconds, reeling at the shock, then walk towards her intending to check her pulse. But as I draw close, she hears me, raises her head and weakly smiles. Then, mustering unseen reserves of strength, she pushes herself to a seated position.

"What must you think of me?" she says, gesturing for me to take a seat.

I shake my head. "No, let me fetch you a glass of water? Are you unwell?"

Bertha sighs. "I feel feeble this morning," she says. "Tired, weak and out of sorts."

"You should see a doctor," I say.

"I saw one last week," she replies, "and a few weeks before that too. They don't know what's wrong and have suggested I take a short break with plenty of sea bathing."

"That sounds just the ticket."

"It is, and I'm looking forward to it," says Bertha. "It's a shame Hugh can't join me, but that's what happens when you're married to a busy man. Now, what would you like for breakfast?"

"I'll get it." Bertha looks done in, and I don't expect her to wait on me.

"No, no. You're our guest," she says, glancing at my stick. She evidently feels sorry for me, and I won't have it.

"I can manage," I say, "and anyway, I'm here to work, and I expect to pull my weight."

"If you're sure?"

"I'm certain," I say, and she tells me where I can find everything I need for a decent breakfast. Ten minutes later, I return, bearing a tray with two cups of tea and a plate of buttered toast. I've sloshed tea into the saucers while carrying the tray. I badly wanted to prove my capability to Bertha. She's sick, and for once in my life, I am stronger. But as I hooked my stick over my arm, my balance wobbled. Bertha pretends not to notice the messy presentation.

"Thank you. That's just what I needed," Bertha says, taking her cup and raising it to her lips. We chat for a while, and I watch the colour return to her face. Then once I have eaten the last piece of toast, I return the empty tray to the kitchen and head for the study.

I sit at the desk examining the notebooks, feeling like an adult for the first time in my life. I count fourteen jotters and start arranging them into piles from the oldest to the newest. Then, I insert a piece of paper in the Remington and begin to type. It is a slow job and horribly inaccurate. I leave spaces wherever I can't read Fox's writing and soon realise that I must type everything twice to finish the job if I want to produce a tidy page. After an hour of typing, my head aches and I find myself gazing ahead at my new surroundings.

Worple Road is not pretty. It is a wide thoroughfare with several hundred houses on each side. The view from the study looks out towards the other side of the road, and although the properties are not unattractive, they cannot compare to the beauty of the Cornish coast. I feel a pang as I think of my bedroom in Pebble Cottage and my eyes fill with tears as I contemplate my cave. During a typical day, I would have risen, crossed the beach and be reading by now. The air would be full of shrieking seagulls, and I would inhale the salty sea air with a blanket over my lap and a mug of hot cocoa. I shake my head, and the thoughts tumble away. I won't let them back. It is too painful. This is my new life, and I will make the best of it.

My eyes grow weary, and the page starts to swim. If I continue, I will fall asleep or be too tired to assist Mr Fox tonight. So, I take my stick, don my coat and set off to explore my new surroundings. I leave the house knowing I must exercise restraint. I can't walk far and must learn to navigate a suitably short route. I turn down Langham Road and immediately notice a left turning a little way down. It is only a short distance, and I turn into Stanton Road, hoping for a quick ten-minute turn around the block. I have vastly underestimated the distance, and by the time I trudge to the end of the road, I am nearly exhausted and worried that I won't make it back. I stop and look behind. I can't face returning the same way, and after a short rest, I head towards Worple Road and take another left. By the time I see the Fox residence, my legs are trembling with exertion, and I feel light-headed.

"Are you alright?" I jerk my head around to see a young man leaning over the fence. He is watching me with obvious concern.

"Yes, quite alright," I say, flushing red with embarrassment.

He isn't fooled. "Sit down," he says, pointing to a chair on the front lawn with a newspaper beside it.

"No, really."

"I insist." He guides me towards the chair, quickly pulling the paper out of my way.

"There," he says. "I expect it's the sun."

"I expect so too," I agree, quite happy to accept his explanation which doesn't imply bodily weakness.

"I'm Jim, by the way," he continues, extending a hand. I shake it, noting his firm grip.

"Connie," I say.

"Where are you going to, Connie?"

"Over there," I say, pointing to Mr Fox's house and feeling foolish that it's only three doors away.

"Ah," says Jim, and his face lights up. "Such a nice couple, Mr and Mrs Callaway. My mother is going away with Bertha for a few days. Has she mentioned it?"

"I know Bertha is going sea bathing," I say, "but she hasn't mentioned your mother."

"They go to church together," says Jim, as if I ought to know. He pauses for breath.

"I'm sorry I interrupted you," I say. I am starting to feel awkward about sitting with a stranger. And now that I've taken the weight off my feet, I am feeling more energised.

"Don't be," says Jim. "I was only reading the paper and catching a bit of sun. It's nicer out the front at this time of day."

"Well, I'll leave you to it."

"I'll walk you back."

"There's no need."

"No, but I'll feel better if I do," he says.

There is no point in arguing, so I don't.

"Are you staying long?" he asks.

"Yes. I am Mr Fox, I mean Mr Callaway's clerical assistant," I say proudly. Jim looks impressed.

"Good. Then I expect our paths will cross again if I'm not at work."

"Where do you work?"

"Z division," he says, puffing out his chest.

"I'm sorry?"

"Metropolitan Police, Z division," he repeats. "I'm a police constable."

"Oh, how interesting. And where is Z division?"

"Croydon," says Jim. "I've got time off for good behaviour, hence the sunbathing."

Jim is good-humoured, and his smile reaches his eyes. It is my first full day in Wimbledon, and I already feel as if I've found a friend. "Well, enjoy it," I say. "You'll be back at work soon enough."

"Look after yourself," says Jim and saunters back to his chair.

I don't mention the encounter to Bertha when I go inside. She is reclining on the sofa, skin pallid, and her temples flecked with moisture.

"I should call a doctor," I say as soon as I see her.

"No, don't. I'll be fine after a little rest." I take her at her word and return to the study, where I put in a few uninterrupted hours of work until a tap at the door herald's Bertha's arrival. She is carrying a tray of sandwiches.

"You shouldn't have," I say.

"I need to keep going," says Bertha. "And I've got dinner to cook."

I open my mouth to speak, but she has already turned away. The afternoon flies by as I work, feeling more confident as my familiarity with Fox's handwriting improves. And before long, I hear the front door open, followed by the murmur of voices as Bertha greets her husband. I remain in the study, giving them a chance to talk about their day, but it doesn't take long before Fox calls me for dinner. Fox eats quickly, and I sense his impatience. It is all very well for him, but he does not have to perform like a dancing bear. His dream walking experiments might be necessary, but I can't pretend to be looking forward to them. Nerves make me lose my appetite, and I spend dinner aimlessly pushing a pork chop around the plate, taking tiny mouthfuls and going through the motions. I am glad when Bertha takes it away without asking if I've finished. I'm in no better mood for the blancmange that follows, but it is easier to get down. Then the dreaded moment arrives, and I follow Oliver Fox through to the study for the first of our attempts at dream walking.

CHAPTER EIGHT

The Croydon Mystery

"Over there," says Oliver Fox, gesturing to the day bed at the end of the room. He takes the chair from the desk and drags it behind him, then sits a few feet away.

"I don't think I can do this," I say.

"Are you frightened?"

"Yes. But it's not just that. I can't perform to order."

"On the contrary. You have a remarkable success rate that I can't hope to emulate."

"It's not a competition."

"I know, Connie. But I don't know anyone as naturally gifted as you."

"I don't want to," I say. Working as an adult and helping

Bertha Callaway filled me with confidence this afternoon, but the thought of returning to the astral plane, leaves me feeling like a child again, and to my horror, I find myself on the brink of tears.

"We could leave it," says Fox, and a rush of relief courses through me. "But what will you do if Crossley comes again?"

"You said you would show me how to protect myself," I reply.

"Theory is all very well, but practise is necessary, which means leaving your body."

I slump forward and put my head in my hands, massaging my temples with my thumbs. Work and walking have sapped my energy, and I am in no mood for an argument, which is likely to happen if Fox pushes me any further.

"Let's try something else then," says Fox. "Lie down and put your feet up."

I hesitate, but Fox nods. "Go on. It's perfectly safe."

I do as he asks and stare upwards, watching the remains of a spider's web dangle from the light fitting.

"When did you last see Crossley?",

"Over a week ago," I reply. "It hasn't happened since we spoke on the telephone."

"Have you travelled at all?"

"No, and I don't want to."

I see Fox nodding his head from the corner of my eye, but the web still holds my gaze. It is both relaxing and annoying. I will have to clear it away tomorrow when I'm alone in the room.

"Have you felt him, Connie?"

A shudder travels through my body.

"I don't think so," I say.

"How were you feeling last time you met?"

"Terrified. Crossley is wicked, and I don't know why he wants me."

"That's not what I mean. How were you feeling in yourself? Tired? Energetic?"

I see what he's driving at. "Miserable," I say, blurting the word out without thought. I squirm uncomfortably, hoping he doesn't ask why.

"Interesting," says Fox. "I wonder if your mood affects your resistance?"

"Probably," I reply. "I have considered that myself."

"Are you comfortable?"

"Yes."

"You seem preoccupied."

I tear my gaze from the light fitting and turn to Fox. "It's nothing."

"Can you bring yourself to recall your encounter with Crossley?"

The hairs stand up on the back of my arms, but I knew this was coming, and I will cooperate. "Yes. What do you want to know?"

"Everything you remember."

I close my eyes and recall the events of that night, then faithfully relate them to Fox.

"Did Crossley follow you?"

"I don't think so. I couldn't feel him."

"Are you sure?"

I recall my final glimpse of Crossley, eyes slitted in concentration. "He was still talking to me," I say. "But his mind was elsewhere. I think he was trying to separate from his body."

"Which means he can't do it instantaneously and gets distracted," says Fox.

I nod. "Yes. It's true."

"How did you get away?"

"I thought of you," I say, embarrassed at the possible implication, but Fox understands.

"You came here?"

"Yes, but I didn't want to endanger you, so I ran."

"Oh, dear. Such a risky prospect, and one I hadn't considered. You are absolutely certain that you haven't felt

Crossley's presence here?"

"Positive," I say. My heart flips as I comprehend his fears. I haven't brought danger to his door, but I could easily have done so.

"I realised my mistake as soon as I saw the road sign, and I ran for miles, just in case," I explain. "But I promise you that I couldn't feel him, and I don't believe he followed me."

Fox nods. "How did you return to your body?"

I chew my lip as I try to remember. "The usual pull at the back of my head," I say. "It was easy. I didn't get stuck at all, thank goodness, although..." My words trail away as I remember the gabled house with the liver-coloured brick.

"Although what?"

"I found myself outside a property in a curiously named street, and it felt important. I knew without question that I would go there again."

Fox stares quizzically towards me. "Where were you?"

I close my eyes and try to visualise the building. "In a quiet, residential street in Croydon. Birdhurst Rise," I say, reaching deep inside my memory.

Fox turns pale. "Are you sure?"

I nod. "Quite certain. But returning to my body was straightforward enough."

"Wait there." Fox jumps up and starts rummaging through his desk drawer. I push myself onto my elbows and watch him. "Perhaps it's just a coincidence," he mutters to himself. He pulls another drawer out and slams it back again, and I watch the tower of notebooks wobble. "Did you see the house number?" he asks sharply.

I nod. "Yes, I've got a good memory for numbers," I say.

"What was it?"

"Twenty-nine. Why?"

Fox proceeds to his bookcase, then runs a finger along a set of cream covered booklets, identical except for the date. He withdraws one and opens the page. "Yes, I thought so," he says, placing it face down on the desk. "Well, well. I wonder if they are relevant?"

"What?" I ask.

"The murders."

#

"Murders?" I echo. Fox snatches the booklet and returns to his chair, then scoots it forward until he is sitting near enough to show me. I trace the numbers down the page and stop at 29 Birdhurst Rise.

"Mrs and Miss Sidney," I say. "No, sorry. I'm still none the wiser."

"Don't you read the newspapers?

I scowl. The subject of Mrs Ponsonby's aversion to news is a never-ending source of irritation to me.

"No, as it happens, I don't."

Fox stares as if I had just sprouted a second head. "Really?"

"Really. I don't know what you're talking about."

"Three years ago, someone poisoned Miss Vera Sidney and her mother to death. It was quite the local cause célèbre."

"Arsenic, I daresay."

"Oh, so you know about it?"

"No. I don't. But we've not long had a case of our own."

"Oh yes. I remember your involvement in the Annie Hearn case."

"It was more than a passing interest. I attended the inquest and saw her acquitted."

"Poor woman," says Fox.

"That's what I thought."

He raises an eyebrow. "You don't believe her?"

"She dies," I say.

"Everybody dies."

"Not from poison."

"Someone poisoned Annie Hearn? I haven't heard the news."

"And you won't hear it for another thirty years."

Oliver Fox crosses his legs. "How do you know?"

"I saw it," I say, relieved that he is one of the very few people who might believe me. Fox doesn't let me down and accepts my word.

"So, you've travelled into the future," he says.

"Yes. But don't ask me how, because I don't know. I kept trying until I reached the right point in time. I went to save Annie, but instead, I saw her die at her sister's hand."

"That's quite incredible," says Fox, his eyes gleaming with excitement. "You took a controlled dream walk into the future to fulfil a purpose. It is new and fascinating ground."

I am slightly disappointed in Fox's attitude. He isn't interested in Annie, only the method I used to find her.

"And you did it more than once?"

"Yes. But I'm not doing it again. I don't want to know about the future."

"I wish I had your ability."

"It's inexact," I say. "I tried numerous times to get to Annie before it worked. I can't turn dream walking on at will, no matter how easy it sounds."

"Of course not. But don't you think it's odd that you have come across two poisonings in such a brief space of time?"

I shrug. "This is the first I've heard about the second murder, and I'm disinclined to find out more after Annie."

"And there's no reason why you should though I ought to mention that young Jim Douglass played a part."

"Bertha's friend's son?"

"Yes. That's Jim. He's about your age." Fox glances towards the grandfather clock on the far wall. "Oh dear, this Birdhurst Rise business has been very distracting. Look at the time."

"It's much too late to do anything else now," I say.

"Hmmm. Why don't you retire to your room and try to leave your body from there? I'll stay up for a while and wait."

"Will you see me if you're awake and I'm in my astral form?"

"Probably not," he admits. "But don't worry. Will you try

81

anyway?"

"I suppose so," I say, then collect my stick and leave him to it.

#

I lie on my bed watching the candle without enthusiasm or interest. I don't want to dream walk and fear what will happen if I do. But I cannot hope to make any progress without taking chances. I stare, conflicted, still not sure whether to succumb to Fox's wishes. And what is worse, thoughts of Crowley are spinning around my mind. He's not trying to get in – that generates a sinister, insidious feeling. The fearful thoughts are my own, uncontrolled and tumbling through my mind because I can't switch them off. But if I don't, I might end up anywhere. And I have come to understand that what I think about before my body separates influences my destination. I cast my mind back to the last time I entered the dream state in front of Peter, who softly chanted a pre-prepared phrase. It worked like a charm, and I need to discipline my mind to do the same. I close my eyes and see bubbles of light dancing through my head. My mind is never clear, never dark. Thoughts and ideas arrive in different hues and textures. I imagine wiping them away with my hand and concentrate hard. "Oliver Fox, Worple Road," I whisper aloud. And I keep whispering until the words form a distinct pattern in my head. They are white and zip vertically through my thoughts, bottom to top. When I have fully established the pattern, I stop talking and intently watch the candle.

Five minutes later, I am still watching. The lack of recent activity has made the transition slow to come. But I have gone from being half-hearted to determined, and I persevere. The vibration is so slight when it arrives that it takes me a few moments to notice. It presents itself as an itch on the sole of my foot but soon travels up my leg, and by the time it reaches my upper arms, the feeling is as intense as a knock to the funny bone. I am tingling from head to foot, and as I raise my hand and observe its ghostly form, I feel a sense of relief that I can still enter the dream state to order.

I rise and walk towards the clock. I am still in my room, still in Worple Road, and it's a little after ten thirty. My possessions are as they were when I left, so I'm in the right place at the right time and in perfect control. I pass through the door and go downstairs before entering the study. Oliver Fox is lying on the day bed as if he is fast asleep, and it doesn't take much thought to guess what he is doing. The only way Fox can be sure of seeing me is to enter the dream state himself. But he is not in the room with me. I stand over his body, reach out and touch his head. My hand passes through his skull as I expected it would, but somehow, I know that his soul is not there. He is out of his body, but I don't know where he has gone. I wait for a moment, and drift through the hallway, before flitting from one room to another like a ghost bound to its place of death. But Fox doesn't reappear. It is perfectly possible to be bored in this condition, and I grow irritated. I am tempted to return to my body, but my mind is lively, and the fear has gone. Now that I'm in control, I decide to visit my new friend and race through the front gardens until I arrive at the property where I rested earlier that day.

Full of confidence, I breeze into Jim's house and stop short when I see light coming from the living room. I coyly enter and sidle along the wall. Though I know he won't see me, I can't bring myself to stride into the room as if invited. Jim sits in one of a pair of armchairs, between which is a small table containing two empty mugs. A ginger dog of the spaniel variety lies at his feet. Jim is reading with his legs stretched out, resting on a pouffe in front. I hear a noise, a flush, I think, and a plump woman with a shock of white hair bustles into the room and reaches for the mugs.

"I'm going up now, dear," she says

"Goodnight, Mother. I'll see you in the morning."

She walks towards him and kisses the top of his head, then turns and leaves, and I hear the clatter of china as she puts the cups on the draining board. Jim turns back to his book, flips a page and shrugs deeper into his chair. He is reading with a half-smile playing over his face, and I kneel, cock my head and peer at the front cover. Jim is reading an Agatha Christie book, The Murder of Roger Ackroyd, and I find this endearing. He is like me. I watch him for a long time from my kneeling position, too long. I am physically close in a way that's socially impossible under normal conditions. I see things that others never get close enough to view, like Jim's long eyelashes, surprisingly black against his freckled skin and sandy hair. They should be dark blond, like his eyebrows, but they are intensely, deeply black, more like a woman's eyelashes than a man's. Jim's nose is straight, his mouth generous, naturally curling upwards. Not like mine, which rests in a frown. Jim is an attractive man, and I could watch him all day. But when he turns another page and places his book in his lap, staring ahead as if distracted, I think about what I'm doing. If I were in my body, shame would wash over me at the intrusiveness of my presence in his house. Jim owes me nothing, but after his earlier kindness, the least I owe him is his privacy.

The revelation comes with a physical pull at the back of my head. I do not yield because I will miss Fox that way. Instead, I rise to my feet and dart back to the Fox residence and into the study. Oliver Fox is still absent. I glance at the grandfather clock. It feels like I have been out of my body for a long time, but it is not yet eleven. I will give him another five minutes, and the moment the hour strikes, I will go. But less than a minute later, Fox arrives looking dazed and uncomfortable. He sees me and drifts towards me, but his eyes are glazed, and his head lolls to the side.

"Are you alright?" I ask, perplexed at his condition. He starts as if he is surprised to hear me.

"I am now."

"Where have you been?"

"I don't know. I can't recall." Fox shakes his head and tries to free his memories. He fails.

"Don't you remember anything?" I ask, but Fox jerks back, and his image fades away. Moments later, I hear a groan from the day bed and watch as he sits up and clutches his head. Fox is deathly pale, his skin mottled, sickly and green. He rises and staggers towards his desk, then opens the drawer and scrabbles inside. Fox withdraws a brown envelope with a white label on the front. He opens it and shakes some of the powder into a glass. Then he empties the remainder of his water jug and gulps the concoction. Sighing, Oliver Fox reclines in his chair, legs splayed, then undoes the top button of his shirt. Once comfortable, he looks up and speaks. "Connie, are you still here?"

"Yes. I am."

"Connie, speak to me if you can."

"I'm here. Can't you hear me at all?"

Fox sighs, shuts the door and gets to his feet. He has given up.

I lunge towards him and thrust my hand deep into his heart. He flinches but does not react though he must feel something yet can't reconcile it to my presence. Now it is my turn to finish the experiment. Still ignoring the pull of my nearby body, I claim control. I am strong today, and I will return my way. I go back upstairs, touch my sleeping form and become as one. When I wake the next day, I am supremely confident.

CHAPTER NINE

Meeting Mrs Douglass

Wednesday, June 29, 1932

Fox has left by the time I go down for breakfast, but Bertha is arranging a vase of flowers in the hallway and looking a little better than yesterday. I greet her and make my way straight to the kitchen, determined to be as helpful as possible. Bertha must have expected it and has left all the makings of a good breakfast on the side. I fill a pan with water and, before long, return to the dining room with a cup of tea and a boiled egg with soldiers. Bertha pops her head through the door.

"Do you mind if I join you?"

"Of course not," I say.

"Maud dropped by earlier," says Bertha.

"Who?"

"Maud Douglass. I hear you met her son yesterday."

I try to disguise a wry smile. I expected anonymity here, but it turns out that the gossip in suburban Croydon is no different from that in my sleepy little fishing hamlet.

"He was very kind to me," I say. "I walked too far, and I must have looked frightful by the time I reached his house. He seemed very concerned."

"Jim is a nice young man. And he's a policeman," says Bertha.

"So, I hear."

"Have you got much to do today?"

"Plenty, if I set my mind to it. But I will make a point of taking breaks, or I'll be hard at it all day and of no use to Mr Fox this evening."

Bertha's eyes sparkle. "Good. Maud and I are leaving for Seaford tomorrow, but we're catching up today to finalise our plans. She called in earlier to confirm the time and let me know that she's made a cake. We wondered if you would like to join us?"

My heart flutters with momentary panic. I can hardly sit and chat with Jim Douglass after my close and intrusive encounter the previous night. I won't know how to behave. But Bertha radiates kindness and is keen to include me. It would be rude to decline her invitation.

"Yes, that will be lovely," I say.

She beams. "We'll leave just before eleven o'clock."

I make my way to the study and start transcribing Fox's records. His writing is fascinating and pleasingly relevant. He knows much about astral projection yet seems less able to put it into practice. And I need to ask him what happened last night. Contrary to my controlled ascent into the dream state, Fox spiralled into confusion after his travels. He said he would teach me tips and techniques, but I worry that he isn't capable. I snap from my reverie to see time is slipping away.

It's half past ten, and I ought to be presentable by now. I hasten upstairs, where I splash my face, reapply my make-up and arrive back downstairs in time to meet Bertha in the hallway. She is carrying a basket laden with vegetables from her garden. "There's far too much for us," she says by way of explanation. I'm not really listening. Thoughts of Jim and his mother occupy my mind.

We walk the short distance, Bertha taking exaggeratedly small steps in her efforts to accommodate my limp. It is unnecessary, but she wants to please, and I fall into her unnecessarily slow pace. Presently, we arrive at the Douglass' house. Bertha knocks confidently on the door, and Maud Douglass, who I recognise from last night, greets us with a smile.

"This is Connie," says Bertha.

Maud takes my hand. "Very pleased to meet you," she says, pumping it enthusiastically. She shows us into the living room, where Jim sits in precisely the same place that he was last night. He jumps to his feet.

"Hello again," he says. "Have a biscuit."

"Let the poor girl rest her feet first," says Maud. "Sit here, dear," she continues, gesturing to a cream-coloured sofa under the window. Bertha joins me, and Maud pours tea and passes us the brimming cups.

"Are you packed?" she asks.

"Almost," says Bertha. "Hugh will help me finish when he gets home."

For a moment, I wonder who she means. I still can't get used to Fox's real identity.

"Where are you staying?" I ask.

"At Merryweather's boarding house in Seaford," says Maud, taking a card from the mantlepiece and laying it face up on the table. The proprietor has named her establishment well. I wouldn't mind betting that weather is seldom merry, but it conjures up images of balmy sunlit beaches. "We're going on Rhona Dalgleish's recommendation," Maud continues. "She stayed there last year. Cheap but cheerful, Rhona said, which is exactly what we need, isn't it dear?"

Bertha Callaway nods, making me mindful of her financial position. She carries herself with the air of a middle-class lady, a bit like Peter's mum. But Isla Tremayne is financially independent and would frown on the idea of a boarding house. Oliver Fox works for a living. Their house is presentable, and I had assumed that they were reasonably well off. But the maid only works once a week, and Bertha carries out most of the domestic chores. Now, it appears, she has arranged her seaside break with economy in mind.

"What time shall we leave?" asks Bertha.

"I'll drive you to the station at eight o'clock," says Jim. "That way, you can make the most of the day."

"That sounds lovely, dear. How exciting."

Bertha raises a wan smile. She still looks tired and I hope she can cope with the ebullient Mrs Douglass when she ought to be resting during her break.

"Now, we'll take lunch with us," says Maud, "and we can eat it on the train. Would you prefer egg or cheese sandwiches?"

Bertha is about to reply when Jim interrupts. "Do you fancy a walk?" he asks.

I glance at Bertha, uncertain how to reply.

"Do go, Connie, if you are up to it," she says. "Maud and I may be some time."

#

"I hope you don't me asking you to join me," says Jim. "But your eyes were glazing over, and I thought you needed rescuing."

"Oh, dear. Was it obvious?"

"Not to anyone else, and I won't keep you away for long. Mother wants to meet you as you're going to be around for a while. But they're about to plan their catering arrangements for the week, and dull doesn't begin to describe it."

I laugh. Jim's refreshing candour is endearing. I have spent less than an hour in his presence, including my silent voyeurism last night, yet it feels as if I've known him much longer.

"Do you mind the idea of a stroll after yesterday?"

"I like walking," I say. "I am accustomed to it and go outside most days when I'm at home. Yesterday's difficulties only happened because I got lost and overdid it."

"Where's home?" he asks.

I hesitate. Having run away like an overgrown school child, I wonder whether there is any risk in telling him, especially given his occupation. I settle for providing a general location just in case. "Cornwall," I say.

"Oh, how lovely. We holidayed in Bude when I was small and had a wonderful time. Dad was alive then," he continues wistfully.

I am about to empathise and tell him that both my parents are dead, but I don't know if they are or not. I assume they must be as they have played no part in my upbringing, but they could live in Newquay, for all I know. And I still haven't ruled out the possibility that Coralie Pennington might be my mother, though this is more likely wishful thinking. While my parentage flashes through my mind, another part goes off at a tangent. Jim's talk of Bude reminds me of Annie Hearn, which brings to mind Oliver Fox's comments about Birdhurst Rise.

"Can you tell me about the Croydon murders?" I ask. Jim's eyes widen, before darting back towards the living room door, which is standing ajar. He puts his finger to his lips. "We'll take Teddy, I think," he says and whistles. The ginger spaniel that I saw last night comes bounding in from the kitchen. "Good boy, Teddington," he says, stroking the dog's head. He takes the lead from the coat hooks nailed crookedly to the wall and fastens it to the collar.

"Teddington?"

"Master Edward Douglass, otherwise known as Teddington, Ted, Teddy, or that damned dog depending on

90

my mood," says Jim.

"He looks far too nice to misbehave," I say, still feeling nonplussed by Jim's efforts to silence me. But once we have left the house, all becomes clear.

"Sorry about the subterfuge," he says. "I didn't want to talk about the murders in front of mother. She's very involved in the church and knows Reverend Deane quite well. I doubt his name means anything to you, but he is the Vicar of St Peter's in Croydon. We used to live there until we moved about ten years ago, but I digress. Mother still sees him at church gatherings, and he found himself embroiled in the Sidney saga. He loathed Grace, feared Vera and was very attached to Tom. But it all got too much, and he can't bear to talk about them now. Naturally, mother sympathises with him. She didn't know the Sidney family herself and wouldn't recognise them if she fell over them, but it doesn't stop her from having strong feelings about the matter."

Jim stops and studies my face. "You haven't got a clue what I'm talking about, have you?"

I shake my head. "No. But I'd like to know more."

"It's a long story."

"I've got plenty of time."

"Yes, but we need to be careful how far we walk."

I turn around. The house is already out of sight.

"There's a bench around the corner," says Jim. "We'll sit and chat there."

"What about Teddy?"

"Don't worry. He won't say anything."

I am still smiling when Jim directs me to the bench and, with great aplomb, removes a handkerchief and wipes the seat before I sit. Then, he loops Teddy's lead around the arm of the bench and joins me. Teddy takes advantage of the long lead and explores his surroundings.

"Right," Jim says when we have settled. "Why did you ask me about the poisonings?"

"Mr Fox, I mean Mr Callaway suggested it."

"I see. Well, I worked on the case in a very junior capacity. Hedges and Morrish ran the show. They're both detective inspectors, and I'm a lowly constable, so I didn't get too involved, but enough to know what's what. Hugh must know about it. Everybody around here does. I'm surprised you didn't hear the news in Cornwall."

He looks at me as if he is expecting a reply, but I won't embarrass myself by discussing Mrs Ponsonby and her ridiculous aversion to newspapers.

"Anyway," he continues. "Three years ago, a chap called Edmund Duff died suddenly at his home in South Park Hill Road."

"Croydon, I assume?"

"Yes. All the murders happened in Croydon. Duff had just returned from visiting a friend, felt unwell and his wife, Grace, called the doctor out. His illness got progressively worse, and despite their best efforts, he died. They notched it up to food poisoning but informed the coroner to be on the safe side. Nothing came of it, and life went on. Fast forward to February of the following year that is 1929. Grace's sister Vera became unwell over several days, and it went the same way. The doctor arrived, ministered to her as best he could, but she deteriorated and passed away. This time, the doctor didn't hesitate and wrote out a death certificate stating she died of natural causes."

"But someone poisoned her?"

"Patience, dear girl," says Jim. "I'm getting there. Less than a month after Vera died, Violet Sidney met her end."

"Who was she?"

"Violet Sidney, formerly Lendy, was the mother of Grace Duff and Vera and Thomas Sidney. She lived in Birdhurst Rise, not far from Grace, who happened to be visiting soon after her mother took a dose of her daily tonic – Metatone if I remember rightly. Well, the old lady immediately knew that something was wrong. The medicine tasted foul, and as soon as she saw her daughter, she said she'd been poisoned. And sure enough, she became violently ill. Grace high-tailed it to the doctor's surgery at the bottom of the road, where she hoped to find the family physician. He wasn't there, but Dr Binning was, and he returned with Grace immediately to treat Mrs Sidney. It was the same story all over again. They did their best, but Violet Sidney died, and this time there was no doubt. Something was going on which they couldn't overlook, and there was no question of writing a death certificate. They ordered an autopsy and discovered large quantities of arsenic in her body."

"It's like Lewannick all over again," I say.

"I've heard that name before," says Jim. "But I can't remember where."

"Annie Hearn," I say.

He clicks his fingers. "Yes, of course. It's been a bad few years for arsenic poisoning. Lewannick is your neck of the woods. Is that why you wanted to know about our murders?"

I nod. It's not the reason, but it will do nicely. "Do go on," I say. It was just getting interesting."

"It certainly did hot up after that," agrees Jim. "As soon as they discovered arsenic in Violet Sidney, they had little choice but to consider the possibility that Vera and Edmund might have died the same way, and they applied to have the bodies exhumed."

"Were they disinterred?"

"Oh yes. And the autopsy showed that the bodies were stuffed to the gills with arsenic. No question about it."

"It's lucky they weren't buried in Cornwall," I say, still aggrieved at the knowledge that Annie had got away with at least one murder and possibly many more.

Jim takes my point. "I know. It must have been a bitter blow for my Cornish colleagues," he says. "But our exhumation confirmed what we already knew. Someone had poisoned three members of a small family. And there weren't many suspects to choose from. We expected it to be easy, but it wasn't. There was plenty of circumstantial evidence, but not a scrap of anything we could actually use. Hedges was in a frightful mood for weeks afterwards. He still is, for all I know, but he retired earlier this year, and I've got a new boss now, who isn't mired in regrets."

"Who did Inspector Hedges suspect?"

"Grace Duff, of course. And he's not the only one."

"Then why wasn't she convicted?"

"She's far too clever and a consummate actress. The judge and jury believed every word she said. But everyone who knew her saw the mask slip at one time or another. Rumour has it that her barrister thought she was guilty."

"Did you?" I ask.

Jim reaches down and strokes Teddy's head. The dog looks up and licks his master's hand while Jim sits in silent contemplation. "The truth is that I don't know," he says eventually. "I've just repeated to you what I heard every day in the station, and I've heard it so often that I've assumed it's true. But you know, there wasn't any evidence, and there was a lot of doubt."

I sigh. Somehow, I knew Jim would say that. There is a reason why I found myself outside Birdhurst Rise. I'm not sure what I'm supposed to do, but it's connected to this murder. I don't feel inclined to help Grace, as I did with Annie, but I'm already burning with curiosity. "Where is she now?" I ask.

"Grace?"

"Yes."

"She moved away very soon after the trial. She used to spend money like water and soon ran out of it, despite the legacies she received from her mother's and sister's deaths. The police kept an eye on her for a while, and she took a cleaning job, I think. It was a pretty desperate occupation for someone of her class. But then she moved, and we lost track of her. Hedges heard on good authority that she'd gone to Australia."

I feel a pang of disappointment. Despite my initial

disinterest, I would have liked to talk to Grace, but I don't tell Jim.

"Come on," he says. "We've been out for half an hour, and they'll wonder where we've got to."

"I wouldn't mind seeing Birdhurst Rise," I say as we walk back down Worple Road.

"I'll take you," says Jim. "I'm on holiday for a week, and I've nothing better to do. Are you free tomorrow?"

"Yes, during the day."

"Be ready for ten o'clock. I'll pick you up when I'm back from the railway station."

CHAPTER TEN

Birdhurst Rise

Thursday, June 30, 1932

Jim arrives a few minutes after ten the next day, and I greet him with relief. Though only a little late, I was already worrying that he wouldn't call at all. My day had started early, and I'd watched a weary Bertha finish her breakfast and say goodbye to her husband, feeling saddened to see her go. I've only known Bertha for a few days, but we get along in the same easy way that I do with Dolly. Bertha is easy to talk to and very caring. She is only going away for ten days, but it will feel like a long time. Oliver Fox is behaving strangely. He is still quiet and introspective. I was going to spend a few hours transcribing notebooks last night, but Fox insisted on devoting the whole of the evening to the theory of astral travel, dwelling in particular on control. But it was all theoretical, and my eyelids grew heavier the longer he talked. I remember little of what he said, except his urgent delivery of the words. When I asked him what happened the previous night, he changed the subject. I persevered, but he did not answer. When he returns from work tonight, he wants to resume our practical experiments and insists that I must enter the dream state in his presence on the day bed in the study. Fox is clearly worried about something and not inclined to share.

And then there's the question of the new domestic servant who arrived this morning. Bertha was expecting a girl called Lily Rowntree, who has worked here before. Instead, a redoubtable woman loomed outside the door, rang, and announced herself as Hilda Grady. She is huge. Not overweight or of notably muscular build, but tall and Amazonian. Her appearance puzzled Bertha, who greeted her with an incoherent torrent of words spoken at speed as she grew redder with every sentence. Fox stepped in and explained Hilda's duties for the week, which she acknowledged with an amiable nod. Bertha recovered herself and invited Hilda to sit down, then offered her a cup of tea. As they talked, Bertha relaxed at the emergence of Hilda's pleasant personality, despite her fearsome appearance. And ten minutes later, Bertha was fully reconciled to the new, untested home help.

Bertha might be settled, but I am not so sure. Hilda does not strike me as someone who would befriend a person as low down the pecking order as me. And I couldn't help but notice her eyes flickering over my stick where they unwaveringly settled once I stood up. So, I was glad when Bertha showed her to the kitchen where she's still corralled.

My mind is still on Hilda as Jim drives slowly towards Croydon while giving a running commentary on the area. He diverts to the police station and motors proudly past it before heading to Birdhurst Rise. We crawl up Birdhurst Road, and Jim points to a nearby house.

"That's the doctor's surgery," he says.

"The doctors who treated the Sidney's?" I ask.

Jim nods. "The very same. They're still practising, as far as I know."

We travel past, and Jim pulls the car up outside a substantial villa. He doesn't need to tell me that it's number 29. I recognise it immediately.

"I wonder if it's empty?" I ask.

We look towards the house, and my spirits drop as I see a curtain twitch on the first floor.

"Sadly not," says Jim. "But at least you've seen it."

"Can we look around the area?" I ask. I don't know why because without going inside, I'm unlikely to learn more. But something has drawn me to this house, and I still don't know what it is or why.

"Of course, if you feel up to it."

I try to rein in my impatience. Jim is too solicitous about my walking difficulties. I struggled once, and I don't need him to spoil our friendship by clucking around me like an old hen. It's bad enough when Mrs Ponsonby does it. A tremor of regret flits through me as I think of her. She must be beside herself with worry by now, and she won't have the first idea where I am. Nobody knows except Mary. Not even Peter. I wonder if I should write to Mrs Ponsonby and tell her I'm safe. She won't be able to find me without a return address, so I'm not in any danger from dropping her a note. I make a mental note to do it later as I reach for the car door. Jim is beside me in a flash, opens the door from the outside and holds my hand as he helps me out. His touch is electrifying, and I feel weak at the knees as I stand. He grins at me.

"Where shall we walk?"

I can't speak for a moment for fear that my voice will tremble, betraying my emotions, but Jim spares me the trouble.

"There's a little road to the side. Let's take a turn down there," Jim says. But as I walk past the low brick wall at the front of number 29, my body feels drawn towards the house. The sensation is so intense that I must stop to avoid losing my balance. Jim watches me, perplexed, but says nothing. I plant my stick firmly and try again, but it is no good. The pull sends me reeling, and I fall in a crumpled heap through the pavement, swirling backwards in time until I find myself high above my body, looking down. Jim is kneeling beside my unconscious form, insubstantial and ghost-like, both of us echoes of the future. He is calling my name, and I ought to return, but I'm still under the influence of whatever is drawing me into number 29, and I'm curious. It's not Crossley, so I am unafraid. I yield to the pressure and find myself in the drawing room.

#

The first thing I see is a copy of the Croydon Advertiser lying beneath a brown corked bottle of medicine in the middle of a dining room table. I know before I look that it won't bear today's date, and it does not. Bold italics declare that it's March 5, 1929. I glance around the empty room furnished with a dark wooden sideboard, a table and a storage cupboard. Unusually, there is a gas ring to one side, with a clean pan and a wooden spoon within easy reach. Next to the medicine bottle are the remains of an unfinished lunch. A bowl of rolled oats has barely been touched, but a couple of stripped chicken bones indicate someone enjoyed at least part of the meal.

I hear a noise and retreat as a woman clutching a spoon, and a wine glass emerges from the hallway. She sits in front of the dirty dishes and carefully places the glass on the table. I watch as she pushes the plates into the centre with clawlike, arthritic hands. The woman is tall with high cheekbones and a mannish face. Her thin lips top a prominent, square chin, and her heavy eyebrows lie incongruously beneath a mop of white hair. Clad in a black floor-length dress with a high lace collar, the woman before me looks like a Victorian lady. Her movements are graceful, but her dress belongs in a different era. I can see that she's old, but she wears her years well and uncorks the medicine bottle with a strength that her frail-looking hands belie. I watch with a sense of dread as she pours the dark brown substance into her wine glass. The gloopy, unctuous mixture does not look right, even to my untrained eye. I turn away as she raises the glass to her mouth. I can't stop this happening, and I won't try, but I don't want to witness the exact moment that death takes hold.

Whatever is in the bottle does not work instantaneously. When I turn around, the woman is pulling faces. Her tongue darts in and out of her mouth as she wipes her lips with the back of her hand. She swallows, retches a little and swallows again, then takes the bottle and pours the dregs into the glass before scooping a little out with the spoon. She inspects it, and her eyes grow round.

"Mrs Noakes," she calls. Silence. "Mrs Noakes. Come here at once." Moments later, a plain-looking woman enters the room and gazes at her mistress, eyes heavy with concern.

"Whatever is wrong, ma'am?" she asks.

"It's my medicine. It tasted so awful, nasty and gritty," the woman says.

"Did you shake it before you drank it?"

"I think so, but perhaps not."

"That will be it then," says Mrs Noakes. "I shouldn't worry, Mrs Sidney."

Satisfied, she clears the dishes and leaves. Then the woman sits quietly for a while, presumably finding comfort in her words. She reaches for an apple from the fruit bowl, takes a bite and chews. But when she takes a second bite, she retches again and clutches her stomach. She leans forward, her face pale and her mouth open in shock. Beads of perspiration collect on her temples. I hate what I see, but nothing is pulling me back to my body, and I fear I will witness her end.

Pushing her chair back, Violet Sidney staggers to the

sideboard, picks up a bell and rings it feebly, then sinks back onto the chair. Mrs Noakes returns, wiping her hands on her apron.

"Are you still feeling poorly?" she asks.

Mrs Sidney nods. "I feel so sick, but I don't think I can vomit."

"Have you eaten that apple too quickly?" asks Mrs Noakes, pointing to the remains.

"No. Fetch me a bowl. I feel dreadful."

Kathleen Noakes scurries away and returns moments later with a brown china bread bowl. Mrs Sidney places it in her lap and hunches over it, retching in obvious pain.

I hear a knock at the door, which takes my attention away from the pitiful sight before me.

"That will be Grace," says Mrs Noakes.

"Don't leave me."

"I'll only be a moment."

I watch over Mrs Sidney in the short time her servant is away, and seconds later, Mrs Noakes returns with a handsome dark-haired woman in tow.

"Mother," she cries, "what on earth is wrong?"

"I have taken some poison," says Violet Sidney.

"Nonsense. Where from?"

"My medicine. The sediment tastes foul. I wish I'd shaken it."

Grace flashes a concerned glance towards Mrs Noakes, uncorks the stopper, and smells the bottle. She wrinkles her nose. "It doesn't smell very nice, Kate, but I can't see how poison can have got inside. Can you make up a glass of saltwater just in case?"

Kate leaves the room at once and I am torn between following her and staying where I am. I opt for the latter and watch as Grace Duff kneels in front of her mother and pats her hand. "Don't worry. Everything will be fine, I promise."

Mrs Sidney holds her stomach and groans. I can't bear to watch her knowing how this will end, yet I am unwilling to go outside to re-join my body, assuming time is behaving normally in front of the house.

Kate Noakes returns and thrusts a glass of water towards Mrs Sidney.

"Drink it down," says Grace.

Mrs Sidney tries and heaves again, but Grace encourages her, and within moments of finishing, she vomits into the bowl.

"Any better?" asks Grace.

"A little," whispers her mother before sinking back into the chair. Her hands tremble, and her skin has turned an unhealthy grey.

"I'm phoning Dr Elwell," says Grace, getting to her feet.

"No. I don't want a doctor."

"Well, you're having one. Kate, look after her while I use the telephone."

I follow Grace Duff into the hallway and watch as she dials the operator who connects the line to the surgery. She asks for the doctor and listens for a moment, then replaces the handset without replying. "Damn," she says under her breath before returning to the dining room while I take a shortcut through the wall.

"He's not there," says Grace. "I shall have to fetch Dr Binning." Then she strides towards the front door and leaves. I do not follow in case it provokes a return to my body and I'm not quite ready to go.

Kate Noakes is solicitous and kindly while Grace is out, but she is not alone with Mrs Sidney for long. Barely any time passes before the front door slams open, and a clean-shaven man in his forties strides purposefully into the dining room.

"How are you, Mrs Sidney?" he asks in a broad Scottish accent before snapping open his bag and removing a stethoscope.

"Dreadful. My medicine had such a peculiar taste, and I haven't felt right since I drank it."

"Have you eaten anything?"

"Some chicken and a few spoonful's of pudding," says Violet Sidney. "But I felt so poorly that I couldn't finish it."

Binning places the stethoscope over her chest and listens. But before he has time to draw any conclusions, she retches again and loses the little colour left in her face. He regards her with a frown.

"She thinks something was in the medicine," says Grace.

"She may be right," he replies. "Get her to bed at once."

"I'll fetch a hot water bottle," says Kate Noakes while Grace helps her mother to her feet. I watch as they begin the slow journey upstairs, Violet still grimacing in pain. As soon as the room is empty, Dr Binning takes the medicine bottle and sniffs the dregs. He shakes his head, places it down and examines the wine glass beside it. As Binning holds the glass towards the window, I see it is heavy with sediment. But before he gets any further, Kate Noakes answers the door and admits a pleasant-looking man.

"Binning. What are you doing here?" he asks, offering his hand.

The doctor clasps it. "I'm sorry to say that I'm here to tend to your mother, Tom. She's not at all well, and I've sent her to bed."

"I'll go and see her at once."

I am about to follow him when I feel a blinding pain in my temple. I close my eyes, and when I open them again, Jim is standing over me.

CHAPTER ELEVEN

Medical Matters

"Thank goodness," he says. "I didn't think you'd ever come around."

I stare groggily towards him, blinking as my head swims. I place my hand on the ground and try to push myself up, but Jim stops me.

"Oh no, you don't," he says. "Wait until the doctor arrives."

"Why? What happened?"

"You collapsed," says Jim. "And you hit your head on the way down, so we're taking no chances."

I wonder what he means by we but all becomes clear when I turn my head to the side. A young woman is crouching beside me and has peeled the arm of my sleeve up, revealing a large and bloody graze.

"Don't move it," she whispers. "You don't want to stain your pretty dress. Henry's gone to fetch the doctor. He'll be back in no time."

I smile, but it doesn't reach my eyes. Embarrassment washes over me in waves as I lie there watching Jim exchange anxious glances with the woman. I've only known him a few short days, and I've come a cropper twice. He'll be off like a startled whippet at this rate. I'm nothing but a liability, and I feel like crying, but I don't. I won't.

"Here he is," says the woman as a slight, tanned man kneels beside me. He opens his medical bag, withdraws a flashlight, and shines it in my eyes. I blink and look away.

"I'm Dr Elwell," he says. "How are you feeling?"

"I'm fine," I say. "There's no need to fuss."

"Does anything hurt?"

"Only my pride," I reply, trying to make light of things as best I can.

"She's hurt her arm," says the woman.

Dr Elwell examines my wound. "That needs dressing," he says. "Do you think you can walk to the surgery? It's not far."

I open my mouth to reply, but Jim answers first. "No, she can't," he says firmly, brandishing my stick, which he must have retrieved from the path. "But I can drive her there."

"Good. Let me check for broken bones."

And he does. Dr Elwell is quick and thorough and helps me to my feet, then Jim manoeuvres me into the car.

"Don't worry if you get there before I do. My partner is around somewhere," the doctor says before making his way back down the street.

"Will she be alright?" asks the woman as Jim winds up the window.

"I'll be fine," I say, "and thank you for your help."

"You put the fear of God into me," says Jim as he drives slowly up the road. "I honestly thought you wouldn't wake up."

"How long was I out?"

"A couple of minutes, at least."

I cast my mind back to the moment Violet Sidney opened the medicine bottle. It felt as if I was there for at least an hour. I am wracked with confusion about the complexities of dream walking, and I must speak with Oliver Fox as soon as possible. There are no rules. How can I learn how to protect myself when I don't know where, when or how long I will be in my strange out-of-body existence? But I won't panic in front of Jim as I cannot explain myself. I take a deep breath and thank him for his help.

"It's nothing," says Jim. "I'm glad I could."

"You've gone to a lot of trouble," I say. "And we didn't even get a walk out of it."

Jim laughs. "As long as you're alright," he replies. "I think this must be it." Jim parks the car outside number 1 Birdhurst Rise by a notice bearing a caduceus symbol. He takes my hand, and I tentatively step from the vehicle. But my legs work as well as they ever did, and the pain in my head has receded. If not for the wound in my arm, I could have gone straight home. But fate has given me a reason to speak to the very doctor that Grace Duff was trying to contact, and now I am here, I might as well take advantage of it.

Jim escorts me inside, and we find ourselves in a waiting room with two other people. A tired-looking young lady is poring over a box of cards and looks up as we approach her desk.

"How can I help?" she asks.

"Dr Elwell sent us," says Jim. "My friend has hurt her arm."

"Sit down. He'll be back in a moment," she says, returning to her task. We haven't reached our seats when Dr Elwell comes breezing through the door, puffing slightly. "I'll be with you in a moment," he says, nodding in our direction. But as he speaks, the telephone rings. The girl listens and chews her lip nervously. "I think you'd better take this," she says, passing the handset to Elwell.

The conversation is quick. "I'm sorry. I'll have to leave you in the capable hands of my partner. It's an emergency." He turns tail and disappears through the door.

"Oh, dear. You must have better things to do on your day off," I say to Jim. He smiles and doesn't reply.

A woman and her son, sporting a bandage over his ear, emerge from a door to the side of the waiting room. The young woman at reception seizes her chance and goes inside. She quickly returns and approaches us. "There are two other patients ahead of you, and the doctor can't change the order. I hope you don't mind waiting."

"Not at all," says Jim, looking at his watch.

"Why don't you get something to eat," I ask, realising how long it's been since breakfast. Jim must be starving, but he's too polite to mention it.

"Are you sure?" he asks.

"Certain."

"I'll get you something you can eat in the car."

I smile as he walks away, feeling relieved that he has something better to do on such a nice day. The doctor calls one of the waiting patients, who makes his way stiffly towards the door.

"Back pain, I'll bet," says the middle-aged woman sitting to my left. Since we arrived, she has been quiet, but I've noticed her watching the room like a hawk, and nothing escapes her notice.

"It looks like it," I agree.

"You're not from around here," she says.

"No. But I work in Wimbledon," I say, flushing with pride as I utter the words referring to my new occupation. I never expected to earn a living, and it feels good.

"We've got Dr Binning today," she says. "But I prefer Dr Elwell."

"Dr Binning," I exclaim loudly. I am shocked at the thought of being treated by the man I saw back in time only moments ago.

"He's a funny one," she says. "He doesn't like Elwell, you know."

Really? Why not?"

"Jealousy, I suppose. At least that's what Dorcas thinks. They all want Elwell, don't they? And some of them want him a little too much, but then he's a handsome beggar."

"Is he?"

"Well, Dorcas thinks so. And of course, you know who."

I stare blankly, wondering if she's suffering from some sort of delusion. She's not making any sense.

"Grace Duff, of course."

"Oh. Did they…?"

She nods. "Oh yes. Dorcas was her next-door neighbour in South Park Hill Road. She saw it all the time."

"I'm sorry?"

The woman turns her head left to right, then lowers her voice. "He parked his car outside her house at all times of the day and night."

"Whose car?"

"Dr Elwell's, of course."

"While her husband was alive?"

The woman nods and places her bag in her lap with a sense of satisfaction. "And that's not all," she continues.

"Isn't it?"

"No. Dr Elwell makes friends with the older ones."

"I'm sorry?"

"The elderly ladies, the rich ones."

I try to process what she is saying. "Do you mean?" She doesn't let me finish and nods her head.

"Oh yes. Dr Elwell pays particular attention to his wealthier patients. Dorcas says he has them eating out of his hand. Like that Miss Kelvey."

She's lost me again, and it must show on my face because she stops for a moment and tuts loudly.

"You must have heard of Anna Kelvey."

I shake my head.

"Oh, but you're an outsider. Well, she lodged with Grace Duff for a while and died in questionable circumstances, though they didn't dig her up. But guess who benefited from the will?"

"Grace Duff?" I offer.

"No. The Duff children and Dr Elwell. What do you think of that?"

I don't know how to reply but I'm fortunately saved by the bell. The telephone rings just as the man leaves Dr Binning's office, clutching the small of his back. He walks towards the receptionist, but she is in full flow, and he shakes his head and leaves. She looks up at his retreating form, then gestures towards my loose-lipped companion and beckons her in.

"My turn now," says the woman, getting gingerly to her feet. "Nice to have met you." She shuffles into Binning's office and shuts the door. I stare at her, wondering how she has the nerve to gossip so brazenly to a stranger. But the information she has given is helpful. If the rumours about Dr Elwell having an affair with Grace Duff are true, it would explain at least one the deaths. Yet if Grace has started a new life in Australia and Elwell is still practising in Croydon, then the relationship was short-lived and hardly worth the bother. It makes no sense, nor does it explain what happened to her sister and mother. And when I saw Grace during this morning's unexpected foray through time, she seemed solicitous and eager to help Violet. There was no sign of a guilty conscience.

The door opens, and the woman emerges and walks straight up to the receptionist, who is still on the phone. "Excuse me," she says. The receptionist mouths, "Wait a moment."

"I will not wait a moment," says the woman, slamming her hand on the desk." Three and a half minutes," she says, pointing to her watch. "That's all the time he gave me, and if you think I'm waiting around for you to finish gossiping, then you're wrong."

"Excuse me, please," says the receptionist, speaking into the telephone. Then she addresses the impatient woman. "What is it?" she asks curtly.

"Don't take that tone with me."

I don't discover what has made her so angry as Dr Binning has heard the commotion and gestures from his office. I take my stick and walk towards him, relieved to be away from the embarrassing scene.

"Take a seat," says Binning in a soft Glaswegian accent. I oblige. "How can I help?"

I show him my damaged arm, and he examines it. "We'll clean that up," he says, "but I don't think it needs stitches." He removes the worst of the blood, then takes a pair of tweezers from his drawer. "I'm afraid there's a piece of grit under the skin," he says. "Did you take a tumble?"

"I did, I'm afraid," I say. Then, remembering how brazenly his last patient gossiped, I take a chance. "I fell outside number twenty-nine," I say, watching his face. It doesn't change, and he shows not a flicker of interest.

"This might hurt," he says as he works on my arm. I try again.

"I'm not from around here," I say, "but I believe it's the house where Violet Sidney died."

He looks up. "You're quite correct," he says.

"Did you know her?"

Binning nods. "Elwell was her doctor, but I knew the family."

"How do you think they died?" Binning purses his lips. "I don't want to talk about it," he says gruffly and I know I've gone too far. He digs around my arm for a few more moments before removing the offending object and dropping it in a bowl. Then he bandages my arm and sends me on my way. He doesn't mention the poisonings again.

I make my way outside to find Jim standing in front of a highly polished car parked a few yards away from his. "Are you alright?" he asks.

"As good as new," I say, showing him my bandaged arm. He glances at it but barely takes his eyes off the vehicle. "You seem very interested," I say.

"It's a Rolls Royce," says Jim admiringly. "A Phantom II, if I'm not mistaken."

"Who does it belong to?"

"Dr Elwell," says Jim, pointing to the leather seat. I peer inside to see a printed card stamped Royal Automobile Club inscribed with Dr Elwell's name. "He must be doing well," says Jim enviously.

"I prefer your car," I reply. I've disliked expensive cars since Edgar Sutton spent the Pottses supper party boasting about his Morris Major.

Jim looks doubtful but smiles anyway. "Let's get you home," he says, tearing himself away from the Phantom. I get into Jim's car and almost sit on a brown bag containing a bread roll.

"Lunch," says Jim. "The baker filled it. I hope you like cheese and pickle."

I munch it down, and when I'm finished, I tell Jim about the gossip I heard in the doctor's surgery. "You're quite the detective," he says when I mention Anna Kelvey.

"Not really. I didn't ask the woman anything. She just talked at me."

"I'm afraid I can't embellish any further. I wasn't sufficiently involved in the case to know about Miss Kelvey."

"I understand. I don't expect you to. But it's fascinating. I do hate unresolved mysteries."

"Me too," says Jim. "Unsolved crimes are the bane of our lives. Look, if you're genuinely interested, I'll take you to see Hedges."

"I thought you said Inspector Hedges retired?"

"He did," says Jim. "But he lives in Thornton Heath. It's only the other side of Croydon, and he asked us to drop in on him from time to time. I haven't yet, and it's been a while, but

I doubt his obsession with the case has changed. I'm sure he'll be happy to talk about it."

CHAPTER TWELVE

The Vicarage Tea Party

Friday, July 1, 1932

Jim telephoned Inspector Hedges as soon as we arrived home yesterday, and Hedges has invited us over tomorrow. I don't know what to ask him or how much he will tell me. And I still don't know what I am supposed to do about any of it. Truth to tell, I care little about the victims. I might feel more compassion if I purposefully stepped back in time and spent longer with them, but Oliver Fox has forbidden it. He returned from work last night, and we sat down to a dinner prepared by Hilda, who seems familiar with cooking in bulk. She slopped large portions of mutton casserole into our dishes, and my

113

heart fell at the quantity. But the food was as hearty as Hilda and not in the least unpleasant. I left some, but not for want of trying. As tasty as it was, my stomach is too small to consume that amount of food. Fox made a valiant effort, but he failed too, and the conversation between us was stilted and awkward and so different to the way he was in Cornwall.

He didn't waste a second before heading to his study and instructing me to lie down and attempt to attain the astral state. I did this time, and he observed me and seemed satisfied with what he saw, as little as it was. He had instructed me to leave my body, carry out a circuit of the room, and return. I did as he asked, feeling a satisfying sense of self-control, and returned to my body immediately, wondering how he would know if the experiment had worked if he couldn't see me. But he took me at my word and told me to practise getting in and out of the dream state without ever leaving the house. Then, he taught me how to use shutters in my mind against potential intruders, and I told him I had done this once before while staying at Bosula last year. He seemed relieved and has given me a book to look at so I can improve my technique. I am reading it now as I sit in his study, having taken a break from typing out notes.

Fox is an odd chap. Something is bothering him, and I think it involves our astral travel experience, but he won't talk about it, and I don't know why. He hasn't gone to work today and left before breakfast this morning to take the train to London. I can only assume that it's got something to do with his article for The Occult Review as he took his briefcase. So, I am currently alone with Hilda Grady, who has removed the dining room rug, slung it over the washing line and is now beating it for dear life.

I look up from the book which has failed to grip me and find myself thinking of Jim. I wish I could see him today, but he didn't ask me, and I can't just turn up and invite myself in. I am lonely and missing Peter, and I wonder if I will ever see him again. Guilty thoughts of Mrs Ponsonby are preying on my conscience, and I push the book away, find a piece of paper, and scribble a quick note.

Dear Mrs Ponsonby,

I am safe and well. Please don't try to find me.

Yours truly,

Constance

It sounds a bit curt, I know, but what else is there to say? I search through Fox's drawers until I find a suitable envelope, borrow a stamp and decide to set out for the postbox that I passed yesterday, which is only a short distance away.

"Going somewhere?" asks Hilda Grady as I prepare to leave. She is carrying the rug over her shoulders in a workmanlike manner.

"Only to post this letter," I say, wondering if Fox has asked her to keep an eye on me. I hope not. I have only just escaped the confines of Pebble Cottage and this position should be my chance for freedom. But Hilda carries on with her tasks and I leave as planned.

It's sunny outside, and my heart is light as I exit the house and stroll up the road. I hook my stick over my arm and manage a respectable distance before leaning on it again. I've been practising without my stick for almost a year, and it's paying dividends. Although I will always need something to lean on, I am getting stronger. I reach the mailbox and am posting the letter when I hear footsteps behind me. I turn to find the spaniel Teddy sniffing my ankles with his lead trailing behind him. He has evaded Jim, who is trying to catch him up, so I bend and grab his collar, ruffling his fur as I stand.

"Well done," pants Jim as he reaches us. "That little brute ran off as soon as he saw you."

I smile and tickle Teddy's ears, feeling pleased that he likes me enough to give his master the slip.

"How are you after yesterday?" asks Jim.

"Feeling no ill effects," I say. "It's as if it never happened."

"Good," says Jim. "I was coming to find you, but your housemaid said you were out. I asked her where you were, and she wouldn't tell me."

"You've met Hilda then?" I say.

"Yes," he replies. "She's somewhat domineering."

"I wouldn't pick a fight with her."

"Nor would I. Luckily Teddy spotted you, or I might have turned the wrong way."

"What did you want?"

"I come bearing some timely news, and you'll never guess what?"

I smile and shake my head. Jim sounds just like Peter when he gets enthusiastic.

"You're right. I'll never guess, so you might as well tell me."

"Our local vicar called round to see mother. He forgot she was going away, so I asked him in for a cup of tea. He's a very nice chap, you know. Anyway, it turns out that he was coming to see mother because the Reverend Deane is going to the vicarage garden party this afternoon, and she knows him."

"How kind," I say, wondering where the conversation is leading.

"He's bringing a guest," says Jim. "Someone he knows very well. Someone who has been living in the United States for the last two years."

I shrug, still none the wiser.

"It's Tom Sidney," says Jim. "Grace's brother."

"Oh, my goodness," I say and narrowly avoid mentioning that I saw him briefly during yesterday's dream walk. "What's he doing over here?"

"He's back on business as he does from time to time," says Jim. "And with your recent interest in the poisonings, I wondered if you like to meet him?"

"Is it possible?"

Jim nods. "Yes. I've got us an invitation for this afternoon if you'd care to join me."

I beam. The day had been looking rather dull, and now I'm invited to a garden party.

"I'll need to be back for five o'clock," I say. "I must work for Mr Callaway during the evening."

"I know," says Jim. "I'll take the car. Can you be ready for two o'clock?"

"Of course," I say. Jim takes Teddy one way, and I return to the house and let myself into the study where Hilda Grady is hovering over Fox's desk with a duster in her hand.

"Will you want lunch, miss?" she asks.

"Just a little."

"I'll warm some soup." She does, and once more, I am presented with a large, unappealing bowl of oxtail soup that is surprisingly tasty. I eat alone in the dining room and find myself missing not just Bertha Callaway but Elys and Mrs Ponsonby too. The emotion takes me unawares, and to my horror, an unexpected tear splashes onto the table as I think about our meals at Pebble Cottage. I wipe my eyes and turn my thoughts to Jim. But for him, I would be truly lonely, and I worry about how my life will be next week when he is back at work. I busy myself in the study for an hour before freshening up and changing. Jim arrives promptly at two, and we set off for St Mary's Church, a short drive away.

#

I am dressed in one of the frocks that Elys made last year with my best shoes and a matching hat, and I must say I look pretty good. Jim whistles when he sees me. "You scrub up well," he says, with a cheeky wink and I don't quite know how to react. The journey is quick, and moments later, we arrive at the rectory. "Ladies first," says Jim, guiding me towards an arrow pointing to the side gate. We go inside, and Jim approaches the vicar, standing with a small group of people.

"Where is everyone?" I whisper.

"We should have waited," says Jim. "It's only just started. We're some of the first to arrive."

"Ah. Young James," says the vicar, offering his hand.

Jim winces, and a blush settles over his cheek. "Good to see you again, Vicar. This is my friend Connie."

"Delighted to meet you. Now, James. Reverend Deane will arrive shortly. Why don't you help yourself to tea and cakes in the meantime?" He points to a trellis table in the middle of the lawn containing an urn, trays of cakes and dainty sandwiches.

"I wouldn't have eaten if I'd known how much food would be here," I say.

"I'm sure you'll find room for some of that delicious-looking Victoria sponge," says Jim. "And if you don't, I will."

We help ourselves to two teas and sit down under an apple tree. Jim asks about my life in Cornwall, and without giving too much away, I tell him about the cottage, the hens and the beach.

"It sounds idyllic," says Jim. "I would love to visit one day."

"You must," I say, knowing it can never happen. But it feels good to pretend. Jim and I are gossiping like a pair of old maids when a shadow looms beside us and a man in a dog collar appears.

"Reverend Deane," says Jim, getting to his feet. "How are you?"

"Very well," says the reverend. "How is your dear mother?"

"On her travels. She's gone off to Seaford for a break."

"How delightful."

"This is Connie," says Jim, gesturing towards me. I make a move to stand, but the reverend spots my stick and holds his hand up. "Please don't get up on my account," he says.

"Is that Tom Sidney?" asks Jim, seizing the initiative.

"No. That's Mr Sidney," says the reverend, pointing to a different man with a tanned face and gleaming white teeth.

"I'm surprised you don't recognise him."

"I had little to do with the case," says Jim.

"No. Indeed."

"I'd like to meet him."

"Why?"

"To make his acquaintance. The poor fellow has been through the mill these last years. It's only right to be friendly."

The reverend, who seemed offside, is suddenly back on it. "I'll introduce you," he says, walking towards Tom Sidney. "Wait here."

I beam at Jim, and he returns my smile with a twinkle in his eye. "That worked like a dream," I say admiringly.

"Didn't it?" says Jim. "Though what we'll talk about, I don't know."

The reverend is in no rush to return, and I wonder whether he has forgotten. But just as Jim leaves my side to get another couple of teas and a plate of cakes, Thomas Sidney approaches the table.

"I say, is anyone sitting there?" he asks.

"No," I reply, hoping that Jim will understand.

"I thought I was getting used to the sun," he says, pulling out a white handkerchief and mopping his brow. "But these English summers are fiercer than I remember."

"Is that an American accent?" I ask, feigning ignorance.

"Can you tell? Oh dear, I didn't realise," he says.

"It's very nice, and it suits you," I reply.

Tom grins. "Why, thank you. I'm Tom Sidney." He extends his hand, and I lightly shake it.

"I'm Constance," I say. "Connie to my friends."

"And I'm Jim Douglass," says Jim, placing saucers on the table. "I'm going back for cake. Can I fetch you anything?"

"Is this your seat?" asks Tom Sidney, about to stand.

"No. I've been sitting down all afternoon, and I need to stretch my legs. Please keep it. Would you like a cup of tea?"

"Yes, please, unless you can rustle up something stronger."

"I wish," says Jim and returns to the tea stand.

Tom Sidney leans back, straightens his legs and cups the back of his head. "This is nice," he says. But before he can enjoy the sun, a middle-aged woman bustles towards him.

"What are you doing here?" she asks sharply.

Tom removes his hat and stares quizzically into her face. "Do I know you?"

"Caroline Caldwell," she says. "Grace's friend."

"Pleased to meet you," says Tom. The woman returns a scowl. "I wish I could say likewise, but you did a real number on Grace. No wonder she left."

Tom looks nonplussed. "I don't know what you mean."

"Families should stick together," says the woman taking a few steps away. Then she turns back. "I know what you did," she says, jabbing a finger towards Tom. And then, she heads towards the vicar and disappears into the crowd.

"Charming," I say, lost for words.

Tom sighs. "It's the second time in as many days," he says. "I don't suppose it will ever go away."

I raise an eyebrow and hope he will keep talking. He does.

"I lost three members of my family to a poisoner," he says.

"How awful. When?"

"A few years ago. And now I wish I'd stayed in New Orleans, but business is business."

"What is your occupation?"

"Antiques," says Tom. "I'll be purchasing a few pieces while I'm here. That's if I'm allowed to go about my business unimpeded." He shakes his head. "Damned woman," he says bitterly.

"I take it you don't see your sister anymore?"

"No. Grace last wrote in 1930. God knows where she is now."

Jim arrives bearing a plate of cakes and another cup of tea. He places it in front of Tom.

"Mr Sidney was telling me about his family," I say. "Such a shocking tragedy."

"Ah, the poisonings," says Jim. "I remember. Do you know

who did it, or would you rather not say?"

I inwardly cringe at Jim's direct question, but Tom Sidney reacts favourably.

"Grace, of course," he says. "Who else could it have been?"

"You," says Jim and Tom Sidney chuckles.

"Good point," he says, good-humouredly. "Hedges and Morrish certainly suspected me at first. And as for Jackson, the coroner, well, he had my card marked right the way through."

"Not an ideal position," says Jim and Tom nods.

"It wasn't, and his feelings towards me did not improve at my obvious dislike of Grace's husband."

"Edmund Duff?"

"Yes. Duff was a frightful man, grubby, dishevelled and disliked by his colleagues. I couldn't get on with him at all, though my dislike was nothing compared to mother's, which was more of a visceral loathing. She detested him and would have been quite happy for Elwell to have stepped in."

"Dr Elwell?" I ask.

"Yes. Have you met him?"

"He treated me yesterday," I say, pulling back my sleeve and brandishing the bandage.

"Was Binning there?"

I nod.

"Binning is a good man," says Tom. "We've stayed firm friends, and I'll be dropping in on him while I'm back in blighty. I much prefer him to Elwell. Less slippery. Elwell's friendship with my sister was far from satisfactory, yet mother condoned it."

"Did her husband know?" I ask.

"Perhaps," says Tom Sidney. "They argued often enough. I dare say Elwell was part of the problem." Tom Sidney sits upright and places his elbows on his knees. "I thought Elwell might have poisoned him for a while," he says.

"You thought Elwell killed Edmund Duff?" clarifies Jim.

"At first," Tom replies. "But when I considered it further, it made little sense. Elwell is a ladies' man. He's not the marrying kind and would never have settled with Grace. So, why would he kill Edmund? No. Duff was about to sell their remaining life insurance policies, leaving Grace unprotected. If she was going to act, it had to be then."

"But why would she kill your sister and mother?" asks Jim.

Tom Sidney steeples his hands. "That's another good question," he says. "Grace felt that Vera lived a rather worthless life. She didn't have any children and filled her days playing golf and running around in her little car. And she hadn't spent the inheritance she received from our father's family legacies. Grace coveted her money."

"And your mother?"

"The same thing. Grace benefited from Mother's will, and so, for that matter, did I."

Tom Sidney raises his hand and waves as the Reverend Deane approaches.

"Ah, they've found you," he says.

If Tom hears, he doesn't respond.

"Nice to have met you both," he says, getting to his feet. Then he crosses the garden with the reverend, who guides him towards another group of people.

"Nice chap," says Jim.

"Yes, he was, and very open."

"It's hard to imagine him as a cold-blooded poisoner."

"But from what I remember, he had the means," says Jim. "Hedges will know. We'll be seeing him tomorrow, and you can ask him whatever you like."

CHAPTER THIRTEEN

An Unwelcome Revelation

I wake to a headache slicing through my temples and raise a hand to my damp forehead. I am disorientated, and it takes a few moments to remember that I'm asleep in the back bedroom of Fox's house in Wimbledon. I reach for my glass of water and take a sip, but it doesn't help. The pain sears through my skull, ruthlessly shocking my mind, and I open my nightstand drawer, feeling for the Bayer aspirin tablets I brought from Pebble Cottage. My hand closes over the packet, and I sit up and open the box, popping out the pills that I place in my mouth. I gulp the water greedily and lie back on my pillow, trying to visualise the headache away. But all I can see in my mind's eye is a black oil slick seeping through my brain.

123

I imagine iron shutters slamming down, one by one, but they don't stop the progress of the noxious fluid, which courses through like molten tar. I light a candle with trembling hands and peer into the darkness, fearful of what might lurk in the shadows. The flickering flame makes matters worse, only partly exposing the hidden corners of my room and setting my imagination aflame. I draw the bed covers to my throat as I peer outside. It is dark, and the wind whispers through the ill-fitting window. And then I see it – a ball of dark energy spinning outside my room like a mini-tornado. The spinning stops and clawed wings appear, followed by a rodent-like head with curved, yellowing teeth. The creature hovers outside my room for a moment, then hurls itself towards the pane, wings beating against the glass. I try to scream, but fear has paralysed my vocal cords, and I inch up the bed, trying to put as much distance between us as I can. The creature shrieks a piercing cry which melds with my headache. My temples throb, and I clutch my forehead with tears pouring down my cheeks.

The loathsome beast starts calling like a siren, luring me outside. The pain in my head is so sharp now that I wonder if my brain is bleeding. Night air can only help, and I begin to think the unthinkable. Will the pain stop if I open the window? The creature reacts to my thoughts, and its wings beat more softly, its cry turning into a beguiling whisper. It is still hovering, head turning this way and that, but it moves half a foot away, leaving a space to unlatch the pane. I throw back the bedcovers and place a cautious foot on the floor. Then, grasping my stick, I limp towards it, closer and closer until I am almost in touching distance.

Then from nowhere, my bedroom door flies open. Oliver Fox bursts into my room, lantern in hand, brandishing the light towards the creature, which vanishes with a shriek. But he is too late. By the time I see him, I am already floating above, watching my body fall to the floor. I barely have time to understand what has happened before I am pulled back into the darkness, into the other world.

#

I do not emerge on the astral plane. When the stars settle, and the darkness fades, I find myself outside an elegant townhouse in Albermarle Road. I think I'm in London, but I can't say with certainty as I've never been there before. It is pitch black outside, and I see the street sign beneath a lamp post which also illuminates the front door. Several letterboxes sit, one on top of the other, down the left-hand side. Someone must have converted the building into flats.

I approach the door with trepidation. I am here against my will, summoned by dark forces. But the monster bat is nowhere to be seen, and my headache has gone. Whoever dragged me here has lost control. If I go inside, it will be through my agency, by my choice. And knowing this, I am no longer afraid. I walk through the door and ascend the sweeping staircase to the top-floor flat, where I see a chink of light from under the door. It is late, but the occupants of the apartment are still awake. And judging by the low murmur of voices, there are several of them.

I ease myself through and make my way towards the sounds coming from a room off the hallway. I slink inside, immediately ducking behind a couch as I see Crossley reclining on the opposite sofa with three of his disciples sitting on the floor beside him. All four wear the purple robes of Calicem Aureum. Crossley is holding a half-empty glass of wine, which he gulps greedily before wiping his hand over his mouth. He belches, then holds out his glass. "More," he says impatiently. One woman rises, walks to the sideboard, and pours another drink from a cut glass claret jug.

He takes it from her and knocks it back while I contemplate the sight before me. I've been this close to Crossley before, and although he couldn't see me, he felt my presence. This time, he's summoned me, yet he's lost control, and the reason is becoming clear. Not only is Crossley drinking heavily, but he's smoking something from a pipe. I watch as his half-glazed eyes flit sleepily around the room, noticing for the first time a painted pentagram in the centre. Someone has carelessly shoved several burnt-out candles into the fireplace next to a red-bound book. A ceremony took place here earlier tonight, and I suspect it involved summoning me.

"Where's my new woman? Where is Aristarte?" asks Crossley, running his fingers through the nearest girl's red hair.

"Fetching more wine," she says.

"I only wanted her to get it, not to brew it." Crossley curls his lip, dips his fingers into the wine glass, and flicks red droplets at the raven-haired woman.

She wipes the liquid from her face. "Wake up," says Crossley. "And get some of this down you. I hate drinking alone."

He waves towards the claret jug, and the woman gets to her feet and totters towards the sideboard. Her robe slips open. She is naked beneath but does nothing to cover her exposed breast. I instinctively look away.

"Boring, boring, boring," says Crossley, through gritted teeth.

"What do you want, master?" asks the dark-haired girl, taking a seat on the sofa and draping herself over his recumbent form. He shrugs her off. "Nothing from you," he says cruelly. She stalks off into the corner of the room while Crossley resumes caressing the red-haired girl. He starts gently, then after a few moments, he clutches her hair and viciously pulls it. She struggles free. "What was that for?" she asks.

"For not bringing me Aristarte. What's the point of you?"

Crossley is slurring and hisses his hurtful words through wine-stained teeth. He is an unattractive, unappealing man to whom these pretty girls seem drawn like moths to a flame. I wonder what they see that I cannot. To me, he is utterly repugnant, and I shudder at the thought of his podgy hands running through my hair.

The door opens, and Crossley looks up expectantly. "Aristarte," he murmurs, patting the seat beside him.

I stare in horror at his new companion. I was expecting another young and nubile woman like the other two. Though willowy and elegant, this one is much older. But fear and disappointment spike through my heart at the sight of her. The woman who slides beside him, cosying up to his portly body, is none other than Cora Pennington.

#

I wake up sobbing as the shock of seeing Cora yanks me back to my body so quickly that I can't be sure if I ever left it. But after a few moments, I hear Fox's voice, removing all doubt.

"Thank God," he says. "I thought I was too late. What happened?"

I open my mouth to speak, but tears are still coursing down my cheeks, and I choke on the words.

"Hush now," says Fox. He is about to continue when there is a rap at my bedroom door. I stare at Fox with my mouth hanging open in shock.

"Yes?" he asks uncertainly.

The door opens and Hilda, the Amazonian domestic, is standing there clad in an olive-green dressing gown that has seen better days and slippers that would fit Fox's feet twice over.

"Is everything alright?" she asks, raising the night light in her hand and peering at me across the pale beam.

"Quite alright," says Fox.

"It's just that I heard noises – loud noises."

"Miss Maxwell was having a nightmare."

"Do you want a hot drink?" She ignores Fox and turns to face me. I flush bright red as I understand her concern. She thinks Oliver Fox is forcing unwanted attentions on me while his wife is away.

"No, thank you," I say. "As Mr Fox says, I was having a nightmare. He's been very kind. You've both been very kind, but I'll try to get some sleep now."

"As you wish." Hilda stands in the doorway, light still raised in the air. She does not move.

"You can go now," snaps Fox.

She purses her lips as if to argue, then thinks better of it and slouches away.

Fox stands and walks to the door. He opens it quietly, peers down the corridor and returns to my side. "I know you're tired, and this ought to wait until tomorrow, but I'm worried about your safety. And mine too. Please tell me what happened."

"It was Crossley," I say.

"I guessed as much when I saw the creature." Fox's lip curls in disgust.

"You arrived just in time," I say, shuddering. "I was about to open the window."

"I know. Thank God, I stopped you."

"What would have happened?"

"I don't know."

"Does Crossley know where I am?"

Fox shakes his head. "I don't think so. I believe the creature is a physical manifestation of Crossley's attempts to reach you. It is a representation of your fear made real, making you weak and vulnerable. But I don't think he sends it to a geographical location. Let's not beat around the bush. He wants you, and we don't know why. But if he could easily find you, he would have done so by now."

"How did you know I was in trouble?"

"I've been on guard for days. My abilities to travel are weaker than yours, but I've attuned my mind to psychic disturbances. I was awake, and I heard the bat scream."

"That man's revolting," I say, thinking of Crossley and feeling the bile rise in my throat.

"What was he doing?"

"Cavorting with women. He was drunk and probably drugged."

"In Berlin?"

"No. In England. Perhaps London."

Fox stands and walks towards the window, then places his hands on the sill and peers through the darkness. "I'd send you away," he says. "But as close as we are to London, you're no safer anywhere else. We must work on strengthening your mind against his. I'm sorry you were so distressed."

"It wasn't Crossley who upset me," I say.

Fox turns to face me. "Then who?"

Tears prick my eyes again. "My guardian's friend, Coralie Pennington – she was with Crossley. He called her Aristarte."

"Oh, dear God."

"What does it mean?"

"She's one of his scarlet women. They participate in the darkest of his rituals. Do you know her well?"

I nod. "I know and trust Cora. She's my friend, and she's known Mrs Ponsonby since they were girls."

"Are you expecting her to return to Cornwall?"

"Yes, but not yet. Cora must stay in the capital until she settles her divorce."

"Good. I'm afraid you can't trust her any longer. Now, you may have noticed that I left the house earlier this week and didn't go to work."

I nod. "Yes. I didn't like to ask."

"I went to see an old friend," says Fox, "by the name of Anthony Bridgewater, and like me, he writes for The Occult Review. He's an acquaintance of Stella McGregor."

"Her name sounds familiar."

"It should. I mentioned her last year. Stella McGregor leads The Cult of the Shining Path."

I pull my blanket tighter around my shoulders as they begin to shake. "I don't like the sound of this," I say.

Fox takes my dressing table stool and drags it to the end of the bed. He sits down diagonally opposite and stares grimly. "I'm not keen either, but I've reached the limit of my ability to help you," he says. "I've said little to Bridgewater. He doesn't need to know, and I'm not sure he'd believe me anyway, but

I've asked for an introduction to McGregor, and I'm going to see her on Monday. I want to ask for her help."

"What can she do?" I ask.

"Psychic defence," says Fox. "It's their principal tenet, and all Shining Path initiates are taught this vital skill. They are at war with Calicem Aureum, and as the old saying goes, your enemy's enemy is your friend."

"I just want a normal life," I say, thinking of Jim and tomorrow's planned visit to Hedges.

"And you will, in the fullness of time. For now, we must find out what Crossley wants with you and establish how best to protect you."

I reach for my water glass and take a sip. "There's something else you should know," I say.

"Yes?"

"I don't know who my parents are."

"I know. You've mentioned it."

"At first, I thought Mrs Ponsonby might be my mother, but then I wondered if it might be Coralie Pennington."

Fox purses his lips. "Oh, I see. And Crossley may have an attachment to you through her? It's a shame we don't know how long they've been acquainted," he says.

"Oh, I do. When Crossley asked for her last night, he referred to her as my new woman. And anyway, he was in Berlin only a few days ago."

"So, you think they've only just met?"

"I expect so."

"Is there any evidence that Mrs Pennington is your mother?"

"No. Just a feeling. And we get along or rather did get along, so well. How could Cora lower herself to befriending such a man?"

"He's very persuasive," says Fox.

"There's no excuse. She was wearing a robe and must have been part of the ceremony. Oh, my goodness, I wonder if she knew that Crossley was trying to summon me?"

"You must stay away from her," says Fox.

"She doesn't know I'm here."

"Good. I suggest you stay close to the house for the next few days."

I gaze at my bedside clock. "I'm seeing Jim in eight hours," I say sleepily.

"I wouldn't advise it."

"He's a policeman. I'll be safe with him."

"You're not a prisoner. It's up to you," says Fox, tucking the stool back as he leaves the room. I snuggle below the blankets, my heart still pounding in anticipation of a wakeful night. But sleep takes me within moments, and it's after eight when I wake the following day.

CHAPTER FOURTEEN

Inspector Hedges Remembers

Saturday, July 2, 1932

"The thing about Hedges," says Jim, "is that he doesn't know when to give up."

It is a little after nine thirty, and we are travelling to Thornton Heath. Jim collected me after an awkward breakfast where Hilda Grady stood in the corner of the dining room, beady eyes watching like a hawk as I devoured a bowl of gloopy porridge. I didn't know what to say when she plonked the offering in front of me while brandishing a spoon. But though coloured an unhealthy tinge of yellow with a consistency not dissimilar to wet cement, the porridge was delicious. Hilda snatched the bowl as soon as I'd finished and asked about my plans for the day, seeming disappointed when I said I was going out. "Mr Callaway's already gone," she said accusingly as if it was my fault. Fortunately, Jim arrived and tooted his horn while I made my slow escape to the car, trying not to look excessively pleased to see him.

"You mean he's persistent?" I ask.

"Hedges. Oh yes, and once he's made his mind up, there's no going back. Anyway, what's wrong with you today? You look frightfully pale."

For a moment, I consider telling him. I miss having someone to confide in, but if I reveal the stranger parts of my life, I'll scare him away. He won't believe me and will think I'm batty. So, I hold my tongue. "I didn't sleep very well," I offer instead.

"Poor you," he replies sympathetically. We drive in silence for a few moments, then Jim pulls the car up outside a red brick terraced property in a road of similar houses, a world away from the more elegant residences in Birdhurst Rise.

"I think this must be it," he says, peering at the number on the door. "Yes, number nineteen Trafford Road, and look, there's Inspector Hedges."

He waves towards a man standing in the front window, who nods and raises his hand. Moments later, the front door opens, and the man steps forwards.

Jim helps me from the car, then rushes to greet him and shakes his hand while I make my way towards the house.

"Good to see you again, young man," he says, clapping Jim on the shoulder.

"And you, sir," says Jim. "I hope you're keeping well."

"No need for formalities," says Hedges, appearing pleased that Jim has extended the courtesy. "Call me Fred. Now, come in and sit down. Kate has made us a pot of tea." He gestures towards the kitchen, where a middle-aged woman is bustling towards the back door. "Can't stop," she says over her shoulder. "Make yourselves at home."

"This is Connie," says Jim as Fred Hedges shows us into the living room. It's his first opportunity to effect an introduction, as Hedges showed us through so quickly.

"Delighted to meet you," says Hedges. "Now sit down. It sounds like there's much to discuss."

Jim and the ex-inspector spend the next five minutes gossiping about police matters as we sip our tea, and I listen in bored silence, smiling now and again, so they don't think I've gone to sleep. Then Hedges places his cup in the hearth, leans back and crosses his ankles. "That's enough of that," he says. "Now, Jim. You surprised me with your message. Weren't you involved in the poisonings yourself?"

"Barely," says Jim. "I was working with Heath on the Park Hill burglaries at the time. We were on nights and mostly away from the station."

Hedges clicks his fingers. "Of course, you were," he says. "Well, I'll tell you anything I can, but I'd like to know why you're interested."

"It's Connie," says Jim, nodding towards me. "She's recently arrived in Wimbledon and took quite an interest in the murders when she first heard about them."

"Did you now," says Hedges, smiling broadly. "The damn things quite defeated me."

"Sorry to hear that," I say. "I suppose I'm interested because we had a similar murder in Cornwall where I live."

"The Hearn woman?" asks Hedges.

"Yes," I say. "Annie Hearn. I went to her inquest last year."

"Hmmm. They didn't convict her either," he remarks. "What do you think? Guilty or innocent?"

"Guilty," I say firmly. "Annie Hearn got away with murder."

Hedges leans forwards. "That's exactly what I think about Grace Duff," he says.

"Why?"

"Now, there's a question," says Hedges. "How much do you know about the case?"

"Not much," I admit. "I saw, I mean, I know what happened to Violet Sidney, but I've heard little about Grace's husband's murder."

"Let's start there, then," says Hedges.

#

"Edmund Duff was the first of the family to die," he continues, pulling out a pipe from the top pocket of his jacket. He lights it, throws the match into the empty grate and sucks the stem. "It happened in April 1928 after he returned from a fishing trip. Now, a bit of background for you. Duff was an ex-colonial-type living off his pension. The family wasn't penniless by any stretch, but Duff liked to live comfortably and a little beyond his means. He'd made some rather unwise investments and lost several thousand pounds of Grace's inheritance from her father's family. Now, I never met the man, but I have it on good authority that Duff was rather boorish. He lacked the social refinements that came naturally to the Sidney family. In short, he wasn't one of them."

"Did they get on?" I ask.

"Not really," says Hedges. "Tom Sidney tolerated him, and his mother detested the man. His wife allegedly took lovers, and his conduct towards her was unsatisfactory according to some, though opinions were so varied that it's a moot point."

"What do you mean?"

"The servants said the marriage was a good one and that it was a peaceful, happy home. But others, including Tom Sidney, say otherwise."

"We met him yesterday," says Jim.

"Who?"

"Tom Sidney."

"I thought he was in America."

"He was. He's back on business."

"Well, well," says Hedges. "What a small world. Anyway, back to Duff. He took the train back from his fishing trip, and Grace Duff met him at the station and walked back with him. Now, he was feeling ill before he even arrived home, and by

135

the time they reached the house, he was complaining so much that Grace called the doctor out."

"Which one?" I ask.

"Elwell," says Hedges. "He was always around their house."

"We've met him too," says Jim.

Hedges raises an eyebrow. "Sidney and Elwell," he murmurs. "You're not involved in off-duty sleuthing, are you?"

"Not at all," says Jim. "Connie fell over, and Elwell saw to her injuries."

"In Wimbledon?"

Hedges is looking puzzled, and I don't want him offside, so I dive in with another question to change the subject. "What happened next?"

Hedges drums his fingers on his chin, then sucks his pipe again. "They ate," he says. "Their maid brought Duff some supper and handed him a bottle of beer. Grace left to put the baby in his cot, and an hour later, the doctor arrived, prescribed aspirin and quinine, and sent him to bed. Now, the Duffs slept in separate rooms, and all seemed well, although Grace Duff heard her husband get up once or twice in the night. She woke as normal the next morning and sent a cup of tea upstairs to her husband. He couldn't keep it down and stayed in his sickbed for the rest of the morning, vomiting and suffering from severe gastrointestinal pain. Grace rang for the doctor again. Elwell was on his rounds, so Dr Binning attended instead. Binning wasn't unduly concerned and left after a quick examination, but Edmund's condition deteriorated through the day, and the poor man suffered from painful cramping. Both doctors visited again, with Binning arriving around six in the evening. He immediately noticed a significant and concerning change in Edmund Duff and began to suspect food poisoning. A distressed Duff said his limbs were cold, and Binning recorded a fast pulse rate. His abdomen was painful despite the application of turpentine strips in a vain attempt to relieve the worst of it. Nothing worked. The doctors came and went for the rest of the evening, but Duff breathed his last before midnight."

"How awful," I say, unable to suppress a shudder.

"It was hard listening in court, I must admit," agrees Hedges. "The man suffered dreadfully. And of course, his death was so wholly unexpected that the doctors couldn't write out a death certificate, and the coroner recommended an inquest."

"I thought they exhumed his body," says Jim.

"They did, of course. But that was because the first autopsy yielded no conclusive evidence. God knows how, but Dr Bronte couldn't find anything except for a weakness in the heart muscle. So, they wrote off his death as myocarditis; in other words, he died naturally."

"Unbelievable," says Jim, shaking his head.

"Not to me," I say, remembering the Lewannick exhumation. "Annie Hearn poisoned her sister and aunt. Their bodies were riddled with arsenic, but she got away with it because of the traces left from Cornish tin."

"Be careful what you say, young lady," says Hedges. "Some might see that as slanderous."

"It's no different to the way you feel about Grace."

"I know," says Hedges. "Just be careful where you say it."

"Why do you think Grace did it?" I ask.

"Because when all is said and done, she was the only person who had something to gain from every death," says Hedges.

"How?"

"She received a small death benefit when Edmund died," Hedges continues. "And if the reports of her marriage were true, she was probably relieved to see the back of her husband, especially if she had designs on Elwell."

"Was she financially better off after her husband's death?" asks Jim.

Hedges frowns. "No. She wasn't. There was little

difference, but overall, her income dropped."

"So, she didn't benefit financially, and she didn't marry Elwell," I say. "I don't see the purpose of killing Edmund at all."

"There were rumours that he ill-used her," says Hedges grimly. "At least that stopped."

"If it ever happened," I say. Hedges ignores me.

"Grace Duff received considerable financial benefit from her mother and sister's deaths," he says.

"Didn't Tom Sidney receive an equal share?"

"Yes, but unlike Grace, he wasn't short of money. Mr Sidney was a high-end entertainer and was making a decent living," says Hedges. "And there was no benefit to him in making away with Edmund Duff."

"Except that, he didn't like him," says Jim.

"Lots of people are disagreeable," Hedges replies, "but it's not enough to get them killed."

"Are you certain Grace did it?" I ask.

Hedges leans forward and knocks the remains of his burnt-out pipe into an ashtray. He places his hands on his knees, sighs and looks me in the eye. "Not certain, no. It could have been anyone, for all the evidence we found," he says. "But circumstantially, nobody else benefited unless someone held a grudge against the family. But if so, why not finish them all off? No. It boils down to money, and only Grace Duff and Tom Sidney received any."

I sigh without meaning to, and Hedges flashes a sympathetic smile. "You'd rather I thought differently?"

"No, not at all. It sounds like such a complicated story, but if money is the motive, you must be right. But having met Dr Elwell, and especially Dr Binning, I can't help but think they were involved."

"They might be, for all I know," says Hedges. "Elwell had a motive, but I can't think of one for Binning."

"I found him a little unusual," I say.

"Hmmm. Playing detective is unwise," says Hedges. He

turns to Jim. "I'd keep an eye on your young lady if I were you. If there were anything to find, we'd have done it by now, and you won't make yourselves popular poking into matters best forgotten."

"We're not, sir," says Jim. "It's more a passing interest."

"I'm not telling you off, young man. Your curiosity is admirable, and I'm well over any disappointment from our failure to convict Mrs Duff. But it's only been a few years, and these people have suffered enough. Just be mindful of their feelings."

"We didn't distress Tom," I say. "And I don't believe Grace lives here anymore."

"No. She's in Australia if the rumours are true," says Hedges. "And that's another reason for doubting her innocence. She couldn't get away quickly enough and didn't tell anyone where she was going."

"Is there anyone left who isn't family?" I ask. "Someone detached enough not to be hurt by answering a few more questions."

"There is," says Hedges. "But I still can't work out why you want to."

"Call it a feeling," I say. "Something drew me to the Lewannick poisoning, and now within days of moving to Wimbledon, I practically fall over an almost identical case."

"I understand, but what do you expect to achieve without police resources at your disposal?"

I open my mouth to reply and end up catching flies. No amount of words could convey my unusual abilities without making me look like a deluded fantasist.

"Kathleen Noakes," says Hedges, filling the void.

"Who is she?"

"Violet Sidney's domestic servant," Hedges replies. "She was present during the last two murders, and although I do not doubt that it affected her deeply, she only worked there for six months and had given her notice. It won't break her heart to recall the events, and she was very cooperative on the many occasions I spoke with her."

"Do you know where she lives?" I ask.

"Oh, yes. Give me a moment." Hedges gets to his feet and leaves the room.

"He's so nice," I say. "Not at all what I expected."

"A great deal more so than when I worked with him," says Jim. "It's amazing what retirement does for one's temperament. Is it worth it, though?"

"What?"

"The information. What are you going to do with it?"

I don't have time to reply before the door opens, and Hedges emerges, thrusting a lined card towards me. "Take this," he says.

I peer at the document. "Forty-four Scarsbrook Road," I say.

"That's only a few streets away from the station," says Jim. "I could take you tomorrow," he continues. "Does she work?"

"She didn't," says Hedges, "but that's going back a few years. And it's bad form to call by on Sunday. I'd leave it until next week if I were you."

Hedges gets to his feet, hinting that it's time to go. I reach for my stick, but Jim is there first. His manners are impeccable, just like Peter's. We head for the door, then Jim turns and extends his hand. "It was good to see you again," he says. "It's not the same without you."

"Away with you," says Hedges, good-naturedly. "And you, be good," he says, pointing at me. His tone is sharp, but he's wearing a broad smile.

We wave and get into the car. Jim starts the engine, and we pull away. "Of course, nothing is stopping us heading there now," he says.

"Are you sure?"

"Certain. I've got to pop into the station anyway."

We chat during the short drive, and I feel so easy in Jim's company that I can hardly believe I've only known him for a week. He is self-assured, intelligent and funny. I can't remember laughing as much as I have while we've been together. We pull up outside a square, red brick building on the corner of Mint Walk and Fell Road. The handsome property with its tall ornate gabled roof fits my expectations of a police house – solid, regimented and authoritarian.

"I'll only be a moment," Jim says, and he is right. Less than five minutes later, he emerges with a brown holdall and stuffs it in the boot.

"Don't ask," he grins. "It will all need a good wash."

No more than a minute later, he stops the car outside an unprepossessing terraced house in Scarsbrook Road. The curtains are drawn, and the house is still and quiet.

"Not promising," says Jim. "Don't get out. I'll go."

He slams the car door shut and raps on the front door, then waits. A minute and two further knocks later, Jim is still standing there. He shakes his head and returns to the car. "Best laid plans," he says. "Never mind. We can do it another day."

"But you're back at work on Monday," I say.

His face falls. "You're right. I am."

I look outside and notice a bus stop as we pull away. "Is there a bus from Wimbledon to Croydon?" I ask.

"Yes. You can catch it on Worple Road. I expect it will run straight through, but I'm sure the conductor will let you know. Are you up to it?"

"Of course," I say, feeling unusually confident in my ability to cope. I don't tell Jim that I've never travelled alone before and that I'm not allowed out of Porth Tregoryan without supervision. I've walked past the Worple Road bus stop a few times, and if it's the right one, then it's close enough for me to reach without undue exertion. The distance from the Scarsbrook stop to Kathleen Noakes' house is even closer. I should be able to manage, and I'm willing to try. Oliver Fox has given me my first week's pay in advance, and, unusually, money is no object. I just need to make sure that Fox doesn't find out.

I run the plan through my head as we drive back to Wimbledon and park outside Jim's house. "I'd ask you in for a coffee if mother was here," he says, and a thrill courses through my body. It's disappointing not to go inside, but if Jim is considering my reputation, he must see me as any other young woman. But then, he's never met Mrs Ponsonby and doesn't know the extent of her overprotectiveness. She'd bite his throat out if she thought he was getting over-familiar.

"Would you like to go for a walk tomorrow?" asks Jim.

I badly want to say yes, but I've already promised Oliver Fox that I'll devote the whole day to him. Fox isn't keen on me going anywhere at the moment, and I'll need to be careful. Or, more to the point, I'll need to restrict going out to the days he is working.

"I'm sorry, I can't," I say.

Jim raises a weak smile. "Don't worry," he replies.

"No. I'd like to, really I would, more than you can know," I say unguardedly, before feeling the burn of embarrassment as my brain catches up with my words. I squeeze my eyelids tight, mortified with shame, then feel a gentle hand on my chin. I look up and right. Jim has tipped my face towards him. "How about a trip to the cinema on Monday night?" he asks, hand still cradling my face.

I nod wordlessly, then Jim leans towards me and plants a soft, slow kiss on my lips. "I'll pick you up at six," he whispers. I collect my stick and glide up the pathway, lighter than air. I hardly notice as I ascend the stairs and throw myself on the bed front first, legs in the air, grinning fit to burst. "Oh, my goodness. He likes me. I mean, he likes me," I say aloud. I roll onto my back and spend the next half hour reliving the moment before remembering what Fox has employed me to do. I go downstairs and spend the rest of the day hard at it in the study.

CHAPTER FIFTEEN

A Reliable Witness

Monday, July 4, 1932

I stand at the Worple Road bus stop with a fluttering heart and
shaking legs. I might be taking too great a risk, but I will
never know whether I could have made my one and only
independent trip if I don't give it a go. Although the walk is
well within my limits, it has sapped my energy. I'm fighting a
battle not just with my damaged leg but with my fragile
confidence. The distance from Fox's house to the bus stop
added to the shorter length at the other end is less than the
half-mile stretch along Porth Tregoryan beach. But I'm
trembling from head to foot and feeling horribly self-

conscious about this unfamiliar journey. The woman to my right keeps peering at me whenever I turn away. She is one sentence away from asking if I'm alright, and if she does, it will be enough to sap my willpower. I turn away from her. The last thing I need is a well-meaning stranger. I grit my teeth and think of Jim and can't help smiling. If everything goes according to plan, we will go to the cinema tonight. I've never been before, let alone with a man who seems to be interested in me. Thinking of Jim buoys my spirits, and I decide to confront my fears.

"Does this bus go to Croydon?" I ask brightly.

The woman turns, and her face relaxes into a smile that reaches deep into the crow's feet around her eyes. "Yes, my dear," she says. "It shouldn't be long now." And sure enough, within a few moments, the bus appears, and I prepare to clamber aboard. The conductor sees my stick, jumps down and offers me his arm. I purchase a ticket with ease and take a seat near the front, feeling thoroughly proud of myself. All my life, people have told me what I can't do without balancing it against what I might achieve. I know I couldn't board a train and travel miles with luggage, but there isn't any reason why I can't go a short distance if it's within my comfort range. I've allowed Mrs Ponsonby to restrict my movements, but what could she do if I simply took the bus to Newquay? Well, she'll never know because I'm here now. Here, and making something of myself.

I spend the trip daydreaming about Jim, but as we arrive on the outskirts of Croydon, I start worrying about getting off at the right place. Nothing seems familiar, and I'm not sure whether the bus will stop in Scarsbrook Road. I beckon the conductor over, and he confirms my worst fears. The closest stop is a lot further than I expected, and even with his clear guidance, the distance is on the edge of my limits. But with no choice, I must try. I make him repeat the directions twice, knowing that I can ill afford a wrong turn, and set off for Scarsbrook Road. I take it slowly, and I am tired when I reach my destination, but as long as Mrs Noakes is at home and I can take at least a few minutes' rest, I should be alright. But when I find myself outside the door of number 44, I am paralysed with fear at the thought of the task ahead. I don't mind asking questions with Jim by my side, but I don't know whether I'll easily fall into conversation with a stranger alone. For a moment, I consider walking away. But I'm exhausted, and I'll need to rest somewhere, even if not inside this tiny, terraced house. I think of Jim confidently striding towards the door on Saturday and emulate his firm knock, waiting with bated breath for the door to open.

It does, and a woman emerges and stands silently, waiting for me to speak. Her mouth rests in a frown, and her short hair sits untidily around a pale face. Her chin is weak, her bottom lip full and moist. She is looking at me through half-closed eyes as if she suspects my motives. I open my mouth to speak, then feel a wave of tiredness wash over me. My legs feel wobbly, and I fight to keep my composure. I swallow and try to speak. "My name is Connie," I say. "Inspector Hedges sent me."

"Oh, yes?" she says suspiciously.

"Yes. He thought you might agree to help. I'm interested in, that is to say, I hope to learn more about the Sidney family poisonings."

Mrs Noakes sighs. "That's all in the past," she says. "Hedges is wrong. I can't tell you anything that isn't a matter of public record. Please leave me alone." She flashes an insincere smile, then closes the door.

"Please don't," I say, shoving my stick across the doorjamb.

Her eyes narrow again. "How dare you," she says.

"Sorry. I mean nothing by it. I've come a long way, and I feel, I feel…" I don't get to tell her how I feel. My legs buckle, and I fall to the ground.

#

"Wake up," whispers a voice. "Here. Breathe in. Quick now."

Something tickles my nose, and I jerk my head back at the whiff of ammonia. I slam my hand to my mouth, almost knocking the smelling salts away.

"You've given me a proper shock," says Kathleen Noakes, staring at me sympathetically. She is crouching beside me and, as I turn my head, I realise that I am lying in a crumpled heap on her front doorstep.

I try to sit up, and she takes my hand. "Slowly does it," she says, hauling me to my feet. I reach for my stick, but I can't see it, and panic flashes through me.

"It's over there," she says, nodding beyond the doorstep. My stick has rolled onto the pathway and is lying near a large swan-like garden ornament. "Steady now, and I'll fetch it for you."

I clutch the door frame as she squats over the stick and picks it up. "Here," she says, handing it to me.

I lean into it. I can walk, but I don't think I can make it to the bus stop. Kathleen Noakes sees my discomfort and rolls her eyes. "You'd better come in," she says.

I follow her over the threshold into a small parlour. The sofa has seen better days and the antimacassars are threadbare. A one-eared cat is cleaning itself by the fire. I sit down and reach towards it, but the cat hisses and bares its teeth.

"He doesn't like strangers," says Kathleen Noakes. "Do you want a cup of tea?"

"No, thank you. But a glass of water would be lovely."

She shuffles off to the kitchen in slippers that look one size too big, and when she returns, she passes me the glass and sits in the chair to my left.

"I was going to the market," she says.

"Don't let me stop you. I'll drink this and go."

"No, you won't. I'll have to wait for the next bus anyway. Besides, I'm a great believer in fate. Now that you're here, I might as well talk to you. Go on then. Tell me what you want to know."

I exhale with relief. I'd been bluffing when I said I would

146

go once I'd finished my tea. I am exhausted and need to prolong my stay for as long as possible.

"I'd like you to tell me everything," I say. "Who you think poisoned the family, how did Vera die, and why didn't they catch the killer?"

"What makes you think I know all that?" she asks.

"You were there. Your impressions count for a lot."

"Shame the judge didn't agree," she says, scowling. "He didn't believe a word I said, just kept questioning me about the same thing in so many ways that I didn't know whether I was coming or going." Kathleen Noakes sighs and holds her hands out. "I don't know where to start. Ask me a specific question."

"Did you like Mrs Sidney?"

"Violet? Yes, I liked her well enough."

"And Vera?"

Kathleen's features soften, and she gazes into the distance with a half-smile playing over her lips. "Oh, yes," she says. "I loved Miss Vera. A proper lady, she was."

"How did she die?" I ask. "I mean, I know someone poisoned her but was it peaceful or prolonged?"

"She died horribly. Nobody deserves an end like that, but especially not Miss Vera. A more kind-hearted and even-tempered woman you couldn't wish to meet."

"Tell me about it," I say, hoping she will oblige. Even sitting down, my legs feel like jelly. And worse still, I've sensed a gentle pull on the back of my scalp. It's nothing I can't control at the moment, but I'm weak, and it makes me vulnerable. Still, it's a different sensation from those I've experienced when Crossley is trying to infiltrate, so I am not frightened. I scratch the back of my head, trying to distract myself.

"The poison was in the soup," she says, fiddling with the top button of her high-necked blouse.

"So, I hear."

"I brought the soup in and put it on the table, so you could say I gave it to her."

"Not with any malice," I say. "You're not responsible for the contents of the soup tureen unless you deliberately put something in there."

"Of course, I didn't," she says. "But I still feel guilty."

"You shouldn't."

"I don't just mean for bringing it in. I could have made a fresh batch, but Mrs Sidney didn't like waste, so I stretched it out for longer than I should have."

"Oh, I see. I suppose you thought Miss Vera had food poisoning?"

"Yes, and I naturally assumed it was my fault. It wasn't until the inquest was over that I realised I had done nothing wrong."

"No wonder you didn't want to talk to me," I say. "You poor thing." She smiles for the first time at my sympathetic words. "Now, Mrs Noakes, was Vera generally in good health?"

"Call me Kate," she says.

"Thank you."

"I only worked at Birdhurst Rise for six months," she continues, "and Miss Sidney was in excellent health at the start. But the new year brought nothing but problems for her. From the first day of 1929 until the day she died, she ailed with one thing or another."

"Oh. Could someone have poisoned her over a long period?"

"I don't think so," says Kate. "She was just run down and tired all the time. No amount of sleep seemed to help, but it wasn't until the end of January that she started feeling worse. I think someone took advantage of her poor health."

"Did it come on suddenly?"

"Yes and no. Vera had been sick a few times before but always got over it. Then she came down to breakfast a few days before she died, with a terrible cold and feeling seedy. She took it easy for the rest of the day but was back on the golf course the next morning. She was out in the afternoon for a rubber of bridge, I believe, and came back in time for supper."

"Did you make the meal?"

"Of course. I can't remember what I served after all this time, but it would have been meat or fish and a pudding, and the soup, of course. Mrs Sidney didn't bother with it, but Vera always had a bowl of soup before her main meal."

"Which you made?"

Kate Noakes nods. "Yes. It was always the same: vegetables, onions, Symington's soup powder and tap water. Nothing fancy."

"What did you do with it?"

"After I made it or after I served it?"

"Both."

"I would leave it in the larder," she says. "Often for several days. But on this particular night, I wasn't feeling well either. Mrs Sidney had her peculiarities and didn't like the domestic help eating certain foods, particularly soup. But as I was suffering from a cold, I thought a little warm bowl of it might set me right. So, I helped myself to a ladle of soup and poured it into a cup. There was a tiny bit left, and Bingo, Miss Vera's cat, was weaving around my feet, crying for food. I popped the rest in a saucer and gave it to him."

"What happened next?"

"The soup tasted alright, but it made me feel funny inside. And while I was washing up, I began to feel nauseous. You know, bile was rising, and I needed something sweet. I had an orange upstairs, so I went to fetch it and passed Miss Vera on the stairs as she was rushing down with her hand over her mouth. Anyway, the long and short of it was that we were both sick. I'd not long had a slice of rich iced cake and thought it must have caused the vomiting, but Miss Vera didn't know why she ailed. And you know what else?"

"What?"

"Bingo was sick too."

"The cat?"

"Yes. He vomited everywhere and cleaning up cat sick when you're feeling ropey isn't at all pleasant." Kate Noakes grimaces as she speaks.

"I can imagine," I say sympathetically.

"Well. It was enough to start me off again," says Kate. "And it continued all evening. Mrs Sidney called me a few times, and Vera was up all night with it too. But I simply couldn't deal with either of them. Paid help or not, I was too unwell."

"But you recovered?"

"Yes. I still felt queasy for a few days after, but I was over the worst of it by the following day, which is more than I can say for Miss Vera. She took to her bed and couldn't eat at all. She only managed tea and Oxo. Grace visited her that day. It was Tuesday, I think," she continues, her eyes darting to the ceiling as she remembers. "Yes, Tuesday. Mrs Duff, Grace that is, said that Vera was lying in a darkened room. She couldn't tolerate the light, you see. But you'll never guess what happened the following day."

"She died," I suppose, I say.

"No. Quite the opposite. She got up and had breakfast. Vera was no idler and was worrying about her car. She'd stopped being sick, and despite feeling seedy, she rang her mechanic and went to meet him. When Grace came by to visit, she was shocked to hear her sister was out. Miss Vera had been so ill the night before that Grace didn't think it was possible. She actually went upstairs to check her bedroom, you know. Didn't trust me, I suppose."

"Was Vera out all day?"

"No. She returned before lunch, and I let her in. She'd been to see Mr Tom and his wife on the way back from the garage."

"His wife?"

"Yes, Margaret Sidney. She and Vera were friendly, and she was the only person who got on with Edmund Duff. They were both outsiders, so I expect that's why."

Kate Noakes stops and takes a breath, and I smile

encouragingly. A torrent of words has replaced her initial reluctance to talk, and they are now spilling out as if calming a guilty mind. She licks her lips.

"I'm parched," she says. "Shall I fetch a pot of tea?"

I hesitate, reluctant to stop the conversation, but she is half out of her chair and heading for the kitchen. I wait for her to return, looking around the room at a framed photograph of a short man, with a receding hairline and boyish smile. I wonder if it is her husband, but I don't get up to look. I'm still feeling fragile, but I've stopped shaking. Five minutes pass before she returns, carrying a small, round tray, two cups and a bowl.

"I won't ask if you want it," she says, spooning sugar into my cup. "It will give you strength. I don't resist and sip the hot, sweet liquid while she blows across her cup and drinks.

"That's better," she says. "All that talking. I'm not used to it during the day. Anyway, where were we?"

"Tom and Margaret," I say. "I met him yesterday."

Her eyebrows arch. "Mr Tom?"

"Yes."

"But he's in America."

"He's here on business. I met him at a church fete in Wimbledon."

"Well, I never," she says. "That's a turn up for the books."

"It's a shame they're so far apart," I say. "The only surviving members of the family and on different continents."

"I don't know what you mean."

"Tom in America and Grace in Australia."

"Who says Grace is there?"

"Inspector Hedges."

"Well, she wasn't last summer," says Kate. "I saw her catching a train at Victoria station."

"Really?"

"Yes. Mrs Duff was on the other side of the platform, but I'd recognise her anywhere. I waved, but she didn't see me."

"I wonder what Hedges would say to that."

"He'd want to lock her up," says Kate. "He was always

more partial to Mr Tom and got quite friendly with him in the end, if you know what I mean."

"He never said."

"Well, he wouldn't."

"Anyway. You were telling me about Vera," I say, guiding her back on track.

"Oh, yes." Kate drinks deeply from her cup and places it on the tray. "Poor Miss Vera. She wasn't right when she returned and said that she was cold and didn't think she would ever be warm again. I suggested she go to bed, but she wouldn't because Mrs Greenwall was coming for lunch."

"Mrs Greenwall?"

"Vera's aunt and Mrs Sidney's sister-in-law. Grace collected her from the station and brought her to the house. She bowled in with a large pineapple under her arm as a gift which, of course, they handed straight to me. I like pineapple as well as the next person, but it's a lot of work chopping the thing up, and I didn't get any of the benefit. Anyway, I was feeling much better and prepared a meal for the three of them."

"Three?"

"Mrs Duff didn't stay. She went home to cook a midday meal for her children but invited her aunt for tea later, and I got on with serving."

"I suppose pudding was fresh pineapple?" I ask.

Kate Noakes frowns. "It wasn't. I was far too busy to mess around with that. No. I can tell you exactly what they had, even after all this time. Repeating it at the inquest, trial, and countless times for Inspector Hedges has fixed it in my memory. They had boiled chicken, potatoes and sprouts with pears and baked custard for pudding. But the poison was in the soup, so they say."

"Again?"

Kate Noakes nods. "Again. But this time, it was a different batch. I'd only made it the day before; the same recipe as usual, but with a leftover knuckle of veal. It was in the tureen in the larder, as usual, but somebody got to it."

"Who could have?"

"Anyone who knew the house," she says. "We kept the back door open, and the larder was only a few steps inside. It wouldn't have been difficult."

"Yet only Vera Sidney ate soup."

"Not this time," says Kate. "Mrs Greenwell had a few spoonful's but didn't finish it. Vera had more but said it had made her ill earlier in the week. Well, Mrs Sidney stared daggers at her. She didn't want Mrs Greenwell questioning her household management, and any talk of food poisoning reflects badly on the mistress of the house. So, Miss Vera pushed her bowl away, and I left the room. As far as I know, she had very little else."

I sip the last of my tea and reach for the table, but it's too far away. Kate Noakes stands and takes the cup, stacks the saucer on hers, and tidies the tray.

"By the time I returned to clear the table," she says, sitting heavily back in her seat, "both Vera and Mrs Greenwell had started vomiting, and Mrs Greenwell was suffering from diarrhoea. When Vera had recovered a little, she came into the kitchen and inspected the saucepan. I was quite put out that she didn't trust me to keep things clean without checking. It hurt my feelings a great deal, but when she had finished examining the pans and cookware and saw how clean they were, she apologised. The next time I saw her was later in the hallway. She'd just telephoned Mrs Duff to tell her that she was too ill to come to tea, and half an hour later, Grace came back to the house instead. I opened the door to her, and she stood there, looking tragic and asked what had happened to her family. I explained that they'd all been sick, which I'm sure Miss Vera had already said during the earlier call. When Grace asked why they were ill, I said it was probably the veal. It was leftovers, you see. So, I was worrying, yet again, that I'd given them food poisoning."

"Who would want to be a cook," I muse aloud.

"Exactly. There wasn't a day that passed that week where I didn't feel guilty about something. Mrs Sidney encouraged frugality. She hated waste of any kind, so I had to use food well past its best. I wish I'd just upped and left. I was working my notice at the time and only had a few weeks to go."

"Did Grace join them?"

"Yes. She went into the drawing room where they were sitting looking like death warmed up. And not long after Grace arrived, Mr Tom's wife joined them. Mrs Greenwell was still sick, and Grace drove her back to her hotel. Vera went to bed, and that was that until Dr Elwell arrived."

"How did he know about the illness?"

"Grace telephoned him. He came late in the evening and stayed for several hours. Vera was not only sick but in a great deal of pain. The doctor returned and gave her some morphine, but it didn't help. He sent for a nurse to minister to Vera while Grace fetched Tom Sidney. Doctor Elwell called a gastrointestinal specialist in to examine Miss Vera, but she was fading fast. Dr Binning took over from Dr Elwell and stayed with Vera when the nurse went to bed. By now, Miss Vera was distressed. I could hear her cries from my room on the top floor. I put on my dressing gown and crept down to check on her. The bedroom door was ajar, and I could see Binning wiping her forehead as Miss Vera tossed from side to side in agony. Her face was grey, drained of colour. She didn't look like herself. Mrs Sidney joined me on the landing, tears streaming down her face. Dr Elwell returned with a nurse, and they tried to close the bedroom door to us, but Mrs Sidney couldn't bear the thought of it. So, we stood there until a little after midnight and watched as Miss Vera's body arched for the last time before her features softened, her suffering over. It was the worst thing I have ever seen or ever will see."

I shake my head as I watch a tear trickle down Kate's cheek and blink to stop my eyes welling up in sympathy. There is no doubting Kate's sincerity or how much she cared. Pain is etched over her pale features.

"How awful for you," I say, reaching towards her. She hesitates, then raises her hand and briefly brushes mine. And as her fingers touch my palm, I know without question that this woman is telling the truth.

"Did your employment end with Violet Sidney's death?" I ask.

She nods. "Yes. I was already working my notice when Miss Vera died, but Mr Tom begged me to stay on. Mrs Sidney was distraught at Vera's loss, and they couldn't leave her alone, so I agreed to stay until they found somebody else. As it happened, Mrs Sidney died three weeks later, and I left the very next day."

"Why were you working your notice?" I ask. "Didn't you like it there?"

Kate Noakes visibly stiffens. She sits straight-backed and looks away from me.

"I'm sorry. It's none of my business," I say.

"It doesn't matter now," says Kate. "But it's yet another thing I feel bad about. I lied to Mrs Sidney and told her I was a widow, but I wasn't. My husband was a sailor. He was never around, and when he was, we weren't happy together, so he petitioned to divorce me, and it did not bother me because of Harold."

Kate nods towards the framed photograph.

"He looks handsome," I say.

She smiles. "He is, but Harold isn't mine. He is in an unhappy marriage too, but he won't leave her. They have children, you see. We are friends, and it will never be more than that, but it's enough for me."

"You shouldn't feel bad about your marital status," I say. "It's a personal matter and nobody's business but yours."

"That's what I thought," says Kate, "but Miss Vera got talking about being single one night and asked me if I minded being a widow. I could have told her the truth, but I didn't."

"Was she lonely without a husband?"

"Not in the least. Men meant nothing to Miss Vera. She

didn't dislike them, but she didn't have time for them. Still, it didn't stop the gossips."

"Gossips?"

"They said that Mr Edmund Duff liked Vera more than he should have done."

"But she didn't reciprocate?"

"Mr Duff was dead long before I arrived, but I can tell you now as I live and breathe that Miss Vera wasn't the kind. She would never throw herself in the path of any man, much less her sister's husband."

"It's odd that both Margaret and Vera Sidney were linked to Edmund."

"Not really. I've heard every piece of gossip under the sun regarding this poor family. And I'm still none the wiser."

"Did you like Tom Sidney?"

"He was alright. I didn't trust him though, and I'm sure I saw him in the house the day Mrs Sidney died. He denied it, of course, and they tricked me into saying all the wrong things in court. I got confused, but that's hardly surprising considering how often the family were in and out of each other's houses. Mrs Duff and Mr Tom came almost daily, Mrs Margaret Sidney visited several times a week, and Mrs Violet Sidney spent time at her children's houses and borrowed things from the shed. So, it was no good her grumbling when Mr Tom's children occasionally came in through her back garden. Poor manners, said Mrs Sidney, and she didn't like it, but she was as bad as they were."

"And Grace Duff. How did you feel about her?"

Kate pauses. "I didn't like Mrs Duff, if I'm honest. She could never look me directly in the eye."

I nod and change the subject. "Inspector Hedges mentioned arsenic a few times during our conversation, but it was confusing. Everyone seemed to have weedkiller in their possession."

"Yes. Mrs Duff had some, Mr Tom had some and Mrs Sidney borrowed some from Mr Tom. All three households had access to it. It got so confusing during the trial that I nearly fell asleep."

"You've been very accommodating," I say. "But I really should leave you to it. Before I go, who do think did it?"

Kate Noakes shakes her head. "Not a day goes by when I don't wonder. I just don't know. Inspector Hedges thinks it was Mrs Duff; other people say Mr Tom did it, but I wouldn't rule out either of the doctors. Dr Elwell was all over Mrs Duff, but there was something odd about Dr Binning too. And he was always around when bad things happened. Mark my words, whoever did it, these murders were not straightforward, and the answer, if they ever find it, won't be obvious."

I rise and limp to her front door.

"Stop," she says, jamming a hat on her head. "I'll walk you to the bus stop."

Kate Noakes stays with me until the bus arrives, chatting about mundane matters. She waves as the bus pulls away, and I know without a doubt that I can trust her.

CHAPTER SIXTEEN

Paradise Lost

It is late afternoon when I stumble through the door to Worple Road, utterly exhausted. I slump on the sofa, lacking even the energy to remove my shoes. I must have fallen asleep, and I wake to the clock chiming five o'clock. I sleepily rub my eyes and look outside to see a car pulling up in front of the house. I think nothing of it and rise unsteadily to my feet before proceeding towards the stairwell where a delicious smell emanates from the kitchen. I am about to ascend the stairs when the doorbell rings, and I jump half out of my skin. Moments later, Hilda appears and strides towards the door before yanking it open. I hear a familiar voice and stand stock-still in shock.

"Is Connie here?" asks Peter Tremayne breathlessly.

"Yes," says Hilda.

"Can I come in? I must see her urgently."

I don't know what Hilda says, but I hear the door close, and when I turn around, Peter is walking towards me.

"Thank God," he says.

"Oh, no."

Peter scowls. "Charming. That's a lovely reaction when I've come halfway across the country to find you."

"But why? Oh, never mind. Come through here. Sit down."

"We haven't got time."

"We must. I've been on my feet all day, and I'm beyond weary. Sit down."

Peter follows me back into the living room and perches on the edge of a chair. I slump back on the settee, still desperately tired from my earlier exertions."

"Pack your bags," says Peter.

"I beg your pardon?"

"Pack them. Now. How quickly can you be ready?"

"I can't. I'm not going anywhere. I've got a job here. This is my new home."

"You can't stay here, Connie. Mrs Ponsonby is on her way. She could arrive any time."

"But why? How does she know I'm here?"

"By process of elimination," says Peter. "She's been out of her mind with worry since you left. It took a while, but eventually, she thought to check with the hotel and spoke to Dolly, hoping she'd know where you might have gone. Dolly suggested Bosula and Mrs Ponsonby contacted your friend Mary, who said she didn't know. It didn't stop Mrs P from going down there to check, for all the good it did her."

I sigh with relief. Good old Mary – she didn't cave in under pressure, and Mrs Ponsonby won't be able to hold her responsible for my disappearance.

"Then, how does she know where I am?"

"Dolly also said that you often talked to Oliver Fox when

he visited last year, and Roxy Templeton agreed. She searched through the register, found his address and gave it to my mother. And that's how I knew where to find you. Mother agreed to drive Mrs Ponsonby to meet you, but I persuaded her I needed her car to transport books for the reading room. She agreed on condition that I drove them to the station, which is where I left them earlier this morning. I drove like a demon to get to you in time, but they won't be far behind. About an hour, I expect, unless something has held them up. So, pack your bag and come with me before we all get in trouble."

"But, Peter. I'm a grown woman with a job. And I can't go back to Porth Tregoryan. It's not safe. Cora Pennington is one of them."

"One of who?"

"She's a member of Calicem Aureum and disgustingly close to Felix Crossley. Mr Fox thinks she's one of his scarlet women."

"No. Not Coralie."

"Yes, Coralie. I'm devastated. But there's no doubt. I saw them together."

Peter doesn't ask me to explain. He knows how things work now and trusts my judgement in that respect.

"Where is Cora?"

"In London, with Crossley."

"Then you're safer back in Cornwall."

"But I don't want to go. I have a life here, a job, a home and – and Jim."

"Who's Jim?"

"A friend," I whisper.

"You've only been away for a week," Peter says. "Do you want your new friends embroiled in this thing?"

"It's my life," I say.

"Mrs Ponsonby won't give up," says Peter. "It will be horribly embarrassing for you, not to mention Mr Fox. She's already contemplating involving the police."

"But I'm old enough to do as I please," I say. "Mrs Ponsonby needs to leave me alone to get on with my life."

I hear the door open, and Peter and I sit up straight, listening intently. "Oh, no," I say, as tears fill my eyes. But when I blink them away, I see Oliver Fox standing in the door frame.

"Oh, thank goodness," I say. "This is Peter."

"I know. We've met several times," says Fox, striding towards Peter with an outstretched hand.

Peter shakes it firmly. "I'm here to fetch Connie," he says. "Her guardian is on the way to collect her."

"But I'm not leaving," I tell him. "We're too busy, and there's a lot of work left to do."

Fox sits next to me and takes my hand. "I think you should go with Peter," he says.

My heart drops like a stone, and I recoil. "No. I don't want to."

"You're not safe here," says Fox.

"I'm not safe anywhere, but at least you're close."

"That's the problem."

"I don't know what you mean."

"He's found me."

"Who?"

"Crossley. He came to me in my dreams, the night before last."

"Are you sure?" asks Peter. "Don't you mean you dreamed about him?"

"Yes and no. I was already in a waking dream when he drew me from my body though God knows, I fought against it and struggled hard, but he pulled me from the astral plane, and though I only saw him from a distance, I know it was Crossley. I escaped this time, but I'm not as strong as Connie, and it's only a matter of time before he tracks me down to this house."

"What difference does it make?" I ask. Tears are streaming down my face, but I don't care who sees. "Coralie Pennington is working with him. All he needs to do is ask, and he will find me. She doesn't know I'm here, but she's familiar with Pebble Cottage."

"Connie's got a point," says Peter.

"I'm a liability," says Fox. "And if Coralie Pennington had told Crossley where you lived, he would have come to your cottage in Cornwall. He didn't so you're safer there than here."

"But you said you would speak to Stella McGregor and ask her organisation for help."

"I have, and they will," says Fox. "You should go. It's for the best." Fox rises and walks towards the door. I sit trembling as he yells for Hilda Grady. She returns his call and arrives, dressed in a flour-covered housecoat.

"Yes?"

"Pack Miss Maxwell's bags at once," says Fox.

"But I'm in the middle of making dumplings," she says.

"At once," Fox demands.

"I can't believe you," I say, shuddering with disgust at his decision. "I trusted you."

Fox turns and gazes at me with sad spaniel eyes. "I wouldn't be doing it if I didn't truly believe that it's for the best," he says. "Your safety is paramount."

"I don't care whether I live or die," I say, thoughts of Jim and the cinema dissolving into a black hopeless void. I want to scream at the unfairness of it. I've been happily independent here. And just as my burgeoning friendship with Jim is growing into something important, I'm being dragged back to the hell of life under Mrs Ponsonby's strict guardianship.

"At least let me tell Jim?" I beg.

Oliver Fox and Peter exchange glances. Fox nods.

"Make it quick then," says Peter, and at that moment, I truly hate him.

He follows me to the door and watches as I walk down the pavement towards Jim's house. Peter takes no chances, and by the time I arrive at the foot of Jim's drive, I feel him watching just feet behind me. I flash a glare of undisguised anger behind me as I knock on Jim's door.

"You're early," he says, swinging the door open. Jim is still in his uniform and stands there straight-backed and handsome. My heart does little flips as I gaze into his eyes.

#

"Come in," says Jim, smiling disarmingly. I bite my lip as I step across the threshold.

"Cup of tea, or something stronger? I've got the key to mother's sherry cabinet."

Jim is all smiles as he offers me a drink, but his face drops as he notes my expression for the first time.

"What's wrong?" he asks, taking my hand. "What is it, old girl?"

I feel my lip wobbling and open my mouth to speak, but the words won't come. Instead, tears prick my eyes, and I stifle a sob.

"Sit down," says Jim, guiding me to the settee. "Here, tell me all about it." He puts a protective arm around me, and Teddy, the cocker spaniel, rests his head on my knee. I scratch his ears, glad of the brief distraction, then pull myself together and take a deep breath.

"I have to leave," I say in a shaky voice.

"But you've only just got here."

"I mean, I must go back to Cornwall."

"When?"

"Now. At once."

Jim strokes the top of my hand. "Was it something I said?" he asks.

I forgive his ill-timed humour. "No. Of course not," I say.

"May I ask why?"

"I don't think I've got time to explain. And anyway, I'm not sure I can."

"You don't have to tell me anything."

"It's not that I don't want to. My complicated life is unravelling."

Jim nods his head. "Then off you go with my blessing," he says, flashing a smile that doesn't reach his eyes.

"That's just it. I don't want to go. She's making me."

"Who?"

"My guardian, Mrs Ponsonby."

"How old are you?" asks Jim, incredulously.

"Twenty-five, as I told you."

"Your guardian has no legal authority to take you against your wishes."

"I know. It's a question of safety." And as soon as the words leave my mouth, I know I've said the wrong thing.

"Are you in danger?"

"Not in the way you might think."

"I'm a policeman. I can help. Say the word, and I'll arrest this, Mrs Ponsonby."

"Oh, Jim," I say. "I believe you really would, but there's so much I can't explain."

"I wish you would try, Connie."

"I will, I promise, but not now. Do something for me, and don't ask why. After I've gone, write me a message and put it there," I say, pointing to the side table by Jim's usual armchair.

"There, where everyone can see it? The sort of message I'd want to write wouldn't be fit for public consumption." Jim stares deeply into my eyes, a long, languorous look that makes me flush scarlet. He touches my cheek, strokes it and moves a wisp of hair from my eyes.

"On your bedside table then," I whisper, never moving my eyes from his.

"What sort of message?" he asks, kissing me gently on the end of my nose.

"Anything."

"Anything?"

I open my mouth to answer, but he covers my lips with his.

"Don't go," he says when he comes up for air.

"I'd do anything to stay," I say. "I can't, but I'll come back,

I promise."

Jim sighs and pulls away. "Stay here for a moment," he says, getting to his feet. Teddy follows as he leaves the room, returning a few moments later with a page torn from a notebook.

"This is the telephone number for the police station and the one for our house," he says, pointing to the page. I glance around the room. I hadn't noticed before, but a tall, black handset sits in the corner of the room.

"And this is my address."

"I'll write as soon as I can," I say. "I'll explain everything. Just don't forget to write my message, and then you'll understand."

Jim shrugs as if he is humouring me. "I will," he says. "I suppose we can forget about the poisonings now."

"Oh no," I say. "I think we're making progress. I haven't told you what Kathleen Noakes said, but I'll write it in the letter."

"Any clear suspects emerging?"

"They could all have done it," I say.

"And that's why they didn't arrest Grace," says Jim.

"It doesn't mean we're not making progress," I protest. "And Grace isn't in Australia either."

Jim frowns. "Are you sure?"

"Yes, I'm certain," I say before a loud rap at the door interrupts our conversation.

"I'll get it," says Jim and strides from the room. I follow behind him, knowing from the urgency of the knock that it can only be Peter.

"Yes?" says Jim.

Peter tips his hat but otherwise ignores him. "We've got to go now," he hisses.

Jim raises an eyebrow.

"This is my friend Peter," I say, feeling as if my heart will break. "He's driving me home before Mrs Ponsonby catches up with us."

Jim takes my hands. "It doesn't have to be this way."

"I'll be back," I whisper.

"I'm sorry about this," says Peter, grabbing my elbow. "Nice to have met you, but time is not on our side." He offers his other hand to Jim, who drops mine and accepts it uncertainly.

He shakes Peter's hand. "One more minute?" he asks.

Peter opens his mouth to decline.

"Man to man – one private minute." Jim is firm and authoritative.

"Just one," says Peter turning his back as he walks away.

Jim tips my face towards his and plants a gentle kiss. "Until we meet again," he says. "And we will, soon."

I can still feel his soft lips as I stumble towards Peter's car.

CHAPTER SEVENTEEN

Return to Pebble Cottage

Tuesday, July 5, 1932

The sun streams through my bedroom window when I awake the following day. Ordinarily, it would fill my day with promise, and I'd be on the beach before breakfast. But my heart is heavy with disappointment, and it might as well be blowing blizzards outside. I am already trapped in my old life, though I left Croydon with a week's wages, less a bus fare, and at least I'm not entirely reliant on my captor for money. But here, in the back of beyond, it's much harder to gain independence. Sure, I can physically hop on a bus to Newquay, but Mrs Ponsonby would follow, or worse still,

167

insist on joining me. I wonder if she's back yet? I didn't hear her arrive in the night, but then I didn't hear anything. And, more importantly, nobody knew of my presence. Elys must have been in the kitchen when Peter dropped me off yesterday evening. He didn't want anyone to see him and sped away as soon as he'd dropped my case by the door. I dragged it inside and stashed it behind the settee. So, unless Elys has been particularly scrupulous in her cleaning, she may not have noticed it, which begs the question – has she realised I'm back?

I stand up and sit on the end of my bed, staring out to sea as memories of Jim and our last kiss swirl around my mind. My heart feels leaden and empty. I miss him already, and the promise of what might have been, or perhaps could still be if I can find my way back to Wimbledon, assuming that I can convince Oliver Fox that I'm safe there. I glance at my bedside table. Resting on top is the page of telephone numbers that Jim gave me. I pick it up and search for a hiding place. I can't trust Mrs Ponsonby, and I think she'd confiscate it if I left it in plain view. I peel back the rug and place it behind the tear in the back covering to join the other piece of paper already hidden there. The one I'd hastily scribbled when I found the house deeds concealed in Mrs Ponsonby's closet. Written upon it is the address of Netherwood, Bury St Edmunds, so I don't forget it. I lean back and fantasise for a moment. In my dreams, Netherwood is a large family home. Jim is the master, and I am his wife with three little girls running around outside, none of them limping.

I hear a noise on the landing. Someone is home. I'm dreading my first confrontation with Mrs Ponsonby and hope that it's Elys. I slowly get dressed, lacking the vigour for a quick change, then haul my tired body downstairs with all the enthusiasm of a floundered turbot. I hear singing, a discordant dirge with an overarching air of despair. It's Elys, and judging by the mournful sound, things have not improved vis-à-vis her relationship with Jory.

I fling open the kitchen door. "Surprise," I say in a monotone voice.

Elys clutches her neck. "Areah! You daft maid, creeping up on me like that."

"Creeping?" I exclaim. "I made plenty of noise."

"Where have you been?" demands Elys, dropping the slang. "And where have you come from?"

"Upstairs," I reply.

"Just now?"

"Yes, I just got out of bed," I say.

"You've been upstairs all night?"

"That's what I said."

"I've been sleeping in a house thinking I was alone, and you were here all the time?"

"She's not back then," I ask.

"If by she, you mean Mrs Ponsonby, then you've got a nerve, Connie."

Elys scrunches her forehead into a frown, and her neck turns blotchy red.

"What do you mean?" I ask unnecessarily. Elys is showing all the signs of unsuccessfully containing pent-up rage.

"I mean, you didn't just leave Mrs Ponsonby high and dry. You left us all wondering if you were dead or alive. Half the town was out searching the beach the day after you left, fearful that you'd got into difficulties in the water. It wasn't until Mrs Ponsonby thought to check your wardrobe that we realised you'd taken a suitcase. And not a word from you for days. You could have been dead in a ditch for all we knew, selfish girl."

I stare at Elys aghast. I'd been so smug at the success of my plan that it hadn't occurred to me that they wouldn't know I'd left by choice.

"But it was obvious," I say.

"So obvious that every fishing boat from here to Newquay was out on the water, was it?" fumes Elys. "And it was squally that day. How would you have felt if someone had died while looking for you?"

I sit down on the kitchen chair and consider her words. "I didn't think," I begin.

"You never do," says Elys, turning her back and grabbing a cloth from the draining board. She drenches it under the tap, wrings it out and aggressively wipes down the kitchen cupboards. "Jory rallied the fishermen," she says, "and Kit Maltravers led the search towards Newquay while the girls and I went north. We know you can't walk far, and we dared not take any chances."

"I am so sorry," I say as a tear spills down my face.

"Oh, stop feeling sorry for yourself," Elys replies. "And where's Mrs Ponsonby? I assume she caught up with you."

"No," she didn't, I say, trying to stifle the tears. Elys is fresh out of sympathy, and prolonged crying will only annoy her further.

"Then why are you back? A guilty conscience?"

I stop short in my reply. I cannot tell Elys about Peter without getting him into trouble, and I can't risk anyone knowing where I've been. At least Oliver Fox will not suffer for having accommodated me, and his house may yet be a potential refuge in future.

"I thought I'd better come home," I say lamely.

"You mean you ran out of money or goodwill," says Elys.

"Something like that," I lie.

"Well, good for you. I'm not sure you'll be getting the welcome you expect."

She intends her spiky words to wound, and they do, but their pain gives rise to anger. "Now, hold on a moment," I say, feeling a surge of fury. "I left here friendless and accused of something I didn't do. I am not a thief, and I couldn't clear my name. And if I've come back to the same level of loathing, then what difference does it make?"

"We were on your side."

"Oh yes. I well remember you and Mrs Ponsonby heading to the hotel to tear a strip off the staff for accusing me of theft."

Elys scowls. "I'm a housemaid," she says. "A domestic. I may be your intellectual equal, but if you think anyone would pay the slightest attention to an angry servant, you're daft. They don't care what I think."

"Mrs Ponsonby could have," I say.

"After you swore at her and invaded her privacy?"

I put my head in my hands. She is right. I've behaved dreadfully, and for what? I am back almost exactly where I started.

"I'm sorry, Elys," I say again. "Truly sorry. But I couldn't tell you then, and I can't say much now."

"A note might have helped," says Elys. "It would have saved a lot of trouble and upset."

"I'm sorry I embarrassed you."

"Not me," says Elys. "You're the one who will have the explaining to do. All kinds of rumours are doing the rounds. The last I heard, you had eloped, leaving poor Mrs Ponsonby mortified. If not already determined to leave, the humiliation would drive her to it."

"Does she still intend to sell Pebble Cottage?" I ask.

Elys nods.

"Perhaps it's for the best," I say, thinking of Coralie Pennington.

"Thinking of yourself again," says Elys drily. "Don't worry about me being out of a job or Mrs Ponsonby leaving her friends."

"She's the one who wants to uproot us."

"Hmmm, I wonder why?"

"I don't know," I shout. "And if you do, then stop judging me over my ignorance. You're content to criticise me, Elys, but how do you think I feel about being the only one who doesn't know whatever it is that makes me different? I wish I were dead. I wish I had drowned." I stand and clutch my stick, but it falls to the floor. I stoop to retrieve it, hoping Ely's won't see my tear-filled eyes, but as I rise, she grabs my arm.

"Sit down," she barks.

"No. You're as bad as Mrs Ponsonby."

"Sit down."

I wrench my arm away and make for the door.

"Connie. I'm sorry too. You're right. I'm not perfect either. But you can't imagine how worried we were when you went away, and I'm angry now but also relieved. I didn't think I'd ever see you again."

I turn, and Elys rushes towards me and envelopes me in a bear hug. Her impulsive act of friendship sets me off, and I sob against her shoulder, waves of regrets coursing through me. "It's all such a mess," I say through my tears.

"I know, but you'll find a way through it."

"What shall I say to Mrs Ponsonby?"

"Tell her the truth."

"I can't. I wish I could say why, but I'd be exposing too many others to danger. Please trust me when I tell you that, for once, I'm not just thinking of myself."

"Do you want a cup of tea?"

I smile and nod. The small gesture means Elys has forgiven me. I have a long list of things to put right, but at least I've dealt with one of them.

Elys spoons tea into the pot then turns to face me. "Wait a moment," she says. "I've just remembered something."

She disappears into the hallway then returns seconds later, carrying a brown paper parcel. "I think it's from your friend," she says.

I examine the postmark. "Yes, it's from Bosula, but why is it addressed to me care of you?"

"Because she didn't want Mrs Ponsonby to see it, I suppose."

I flash Elys a grateful smile. It would have been the work of a moment for an angry Elys to give my package to Mrs P, but she didn't. I rip it open as Elys stirs the teapot and places it on the kitchen table. She disappears into the larder, and I feel a familiar sensation across my leg.

"Mr Moggins," I smile as the cat weaves past before leaping into my lap. I bury my nose in his soft fur as I stroke him, feeling a pang of split loyalties as competing thoughts of Teddy flash through my mind. I wonder if Jim will take him to the station today or he'll be home alone? Mr Moggins jumps on the table and treads carelessly through the discarded packaging as I examine the contents. Mary has sent me part of a book – a journal exposed to severe fire damage. She's done her best to clean it, but charred fragments drop into my lap. I gaze at the journal, perplexed, then open the front cover. Inside is a note folded into four. It is from Mary.

Dear Connie

I am sending this to Pebble Cottage as I don't want to risk it falling into the wrong hands. You might still be in Worple Road, but I don't know how much longer you will remain undisturbed. Your guardian left here the day before yesterday, having turned up unannounced. She was looking for you, and although I haven't said a word to her about my part in your disappearance, her determination to find you and bring you home makes it too risky to post this to Wimbledon. I hope you continue to live life your way, but I fear that you will be back in Cornwall by the time you read this. I know you trust Elys, and I have addressed the package to her, hoping she will protect it until you return.

Laura found this book in a firepit behind Crawford's workshop and passed it to me. It's tricky to read, and little has survived the flames, but what remains is concerning. The book is full of symbols, and I don't understand what they mean. My brother's writing style is familiar enough to know he was distressed when writing the last few pages. Alarmingly, Mother mentioned the book during a commune meeting, and when I got back to my room, it was lying on the floor. I think someone was reading it and left in a hurry when they heard me coming. Boo thinks I'm being silly, but it's making me nervous. I remember our conversations about Crawford, and your percipient questions about his mood gave me much food for thought. The book is safer with you than with me. Please read it, keep it out of sight and when you can, contact me and tell me your thoughts.

In the meantime, I am yours ever. Mary.

I close the letter, open the cover and turn a few pages. Most are too fire-damaged to read, but the symbol on the first clear page is horribly familiar. It is the unmistakable unicursal hexagon above a rudimentary wine glass, the sign of Calicem Aureum.

CHAPTER EIGHTEEN

Matchmaking

No sooner have I stashed the book upstairs beneath my smalls than a cab brakes loudly and I glance out of the window just in time to see Mrs Ponsonby sweeping from the vehicle and into the cottage.

"Elys," she barks.

I creep towards my bedroom door and peer downstairs to see her placing her handbag by the coat stand.

"Oh, you're back," says Elys. "Do you want a cup of tea?"

"Yes," sighs Mrs Ponsonby. "Another wasted trip," she continues. "I saw neither hide nor hair of Connie, and I've exhausted all possibilities."

"Oh, but you don't need to worry."

"I'll be the judge of that," snaps Mrs P.

"I mean, she's back. Connie's back."

Mrs Ponsonby audibly gasps.

"Back here?"

"Yes. She arrived last night."

"And you didn't think to send me a telegram?"

"I didn't know. She surprised me this morning."

"Where is she?"

I sigh and prepare myself for the inevitable confrontation. I'd rather it happened in front of Elys where Mrs P might show a modicum of restraint, so I slowly descend the stairs.

"Connie," exclaims Mrs Ponsonby, gaping like a guppy.

I nod.

She doesn't respond. For once, Mrs Ponsonby has nothing to say. She stares at me as if I am a figment of her imagination, and tilts her head, peering at me from a different angle. Still, she remains silent.

"I'm back," I say lamely.

Her eyes fill with tears, and for a dreadful moment, I think she is going to hug me, but instead, she licks her lips. "Where the devil have you been, young lady?"

"I can't tell you."

"Can't or won't?"

"Both."

"How did you get back?"

I shrug.

"You can't come wandering back in here as if nothing has happened. What have you got to say for yourself?"

"Only that I'm dreadfully sorry, and I now realise how selfish I've been. Please forgive me."

Mrs Ponsonby reverts to guppy mode, taken aback by my apology.

"I don't know what to say, Connie. I've been so worried, and I've travelled all over the country looking for you. I went to Wimbledon yesterday, hoping to find you there, but nobody knew anything about your disappearance. I must have looked so foolish."

"I know. I was thoughtless. I didn't foresee that you might think I was in danger and go looking for me."

"You're always in danger, Connie."

The words escape her lips before she realises what she's said.

"What do you mean?"

"Nothing. I mean, any girl out in the world alone faces potential perils."

A bloom of red settles on Mrs Ponsonby's neck, betraying her discomfort, and I mentally bank the moment for future dissection.

"I suppose you felt you couldn't stay here after what happened at the ball?" she asks.

I nod. "That and what passed between us the following day. Please don't sell Pebble Cottage."

Elys turns and leaves us to it, and I seize the moment. "I hate being under suspicion, but I don't want to go either."

Mrs Ponsonby's face softens. "Now is not the time, Connie," she says.

"It never is," I protest. "You never tell me anything."

"There's nothing to tell."

"You're lying to me again. You expect one standard of behaviour from me and quite another of yourself."

Mrs Ponsonby opens the living room door. "Sit down," she says.

I follow her through and shrink into the armchair.

"You're right, of course," she says, taking a seat on the sofa. "There are one or two things that perhaps I ought to have told you, and it must be upsetting to know so little of your background."

"It's horrible," I say. "I feel rootless."

"I know," she replies. "I can't promise much, but we'll chat about it soon."

"Why not now?"

"It's not that simple," says Mrs Ponsonby. "I'll need time to prepare."

"When?"

"Don't tie me to a date, Connie. Just accept that we'll talk more soon."

"What about Pebble Cottage?"

Mrs Ponsonby closes her eyes as if she is in pain. "I think we'll have to move. I can't see what else we can do."

"I'll apologise," I say. "I'll tell everyone it was my fault. I'm sorry I embarrassed you, and I won't let anybody think that my behaviour reflects my upbringing. I'll even say I took the ring if it helps."

"But you didn't," says Mrs Ponsonby, and her quiet sincerity leaves me in no doubt that she believes me.

"No. Of course, I didn't. And even I have reasons for thinking I might be better off living somewhere else, but I don't want to. I can't imagine leaving Pebble Cottage forever."

"You've lived without it for the last week or so," says Mrs Ponsonby drily.

"And you stayed in St Austell for a week last year," I reply. "But I bet you wouldn't have enjoyed it half as much if you thought you'd never go back home again."

Mrs Ponsonby purses her lips and draws a breath, but I beat her to it.

"Tell me what you want me to do, and I'll do it," I say.

"Connie, this is not a punishment. It's a matter of your safety."

"In that case, you should know that I may not come with you if you leave Pebble Cottage, and my decision won't be from ingratitude or to make a childish point. If I go elsewhere, I will let you know in plenty of time, so I don't cause a fuss."

"But how will you live?"

"I'll get a job," I say.

"It won't be easy."

"Nothing worthwhile ever is."

Mrs Ponsonby smiles sadly. "I'll think about what you've said. No promises though."

#

I leave the room deep in thought. My conversation with Mrs Ponsonby is revolutionary. She has listened for once and accepted my concerns, even acknowledging the gaps in my knowledge. But sadness and confusion have tinged our progress. While I want a claim on Pebble Cottage, my desire to return to Wimbledon is greater. If I can never go back, then Pebble Cottage will have to do, but if given free rein, I'd be living with Oliver Fox again in a heartbeat. Which means I'm playing a duplicitous game with Mrs Ponsonby's trust. It's wrong of me, but the alternative is living somewhere neither of us wants to be. I feel sick at the extent of my deception and crave an urgent visit to the cave to find peace while staring at the sea. I head for the door and walk towards the beach, stopping to inhale the sea air as I approach the handrail. I turn right for the caves, but the beach is full of people. It's mid-morning, and I've missed the opportunity for a quiet walk. I carry on regardless, and I am ambling with my nose in the air, ignoring the holidaymakers when someone bellows my name.

"Oy, Connie. Wait." I turn to see Jory stomping towards me." It is you. I thought it was," he says. "Where have you been?"

I can feel a lengthy conversation coming on and ask Jory to join me in the cave where I can talk sitting down. He follows reluctantly, suspicion in his eyes.

"Have you seen my cave before?" I ask, looking around for signs of change. There are none.

"Only every day, while you were away," he says. "We thought you might come here."

"Sit down," I say, pointing to the trunkful of books. Jory does as he's told and sits froglike on the low case, long legs somewhat closer to his ears than he's used to.

"I'm sorry, Jory," I say before telling him as much as I dare about what I've been doing for the last week. "And I'll apologise to anyone else who risked their lives due to my thoughtless actions."

179

"No need for drama," says Jory. "It's July, and nobody sailed in a howling storm. We were perfectly safe. None of the boys thinks you did it anyway," he continues.

I grimace.

"Yes. We heard about the missing ring," he continues. "And I said to my mother, Connie never took it. She isn't the type."

"Thank you," I say. "Elys believes me too."

"I wouldn't know." Jory sniffs and turns his head away.

"She misses you," I say.

"Well, she shouldn't mess around with other men," he snaps.

"She didn't."

"Isaac Langley says she did and that they went together behind the dunes. He told all the boys, and now they think I'm a proper Charlie for trusting her."

"It didn't happen," I repeat.

"Why would he say it did?"

"I don't know. I've never spoken to Isaac, but you know Elys as well as I do. She's honest and straight. Too straight sometimes. If Elys preferred somebody else, she'd be the first to tell you."

"Not if she wanted both of us."

"Oh, for goodness' sake. Elys barely has time to see one of you. She works so hard she has very little leisure time and certainly not enough to deal with two men."

"But Isaac..."

"Does Isaac have a girlfriend?"

"No."

"Does he always tell the truth?"

"As far as I know. He likes Ruthie Blamie."

"What?"

"He doesn't have a girlfriend, but he's interested in Ruthie. She won't give him the time of day, though, at least not until recently."

"But she is now?"

"A little. They're not walking out or anything. But she speaks to Isaac sometimes."

"Well, that's your answer then. A dull young man makes himself more interesting by lying about being with someone else."

Jory pulls a face. "I suppose it's possible."

"Elys did not cheat on you. The end," I say, angry that he's in complete control of the situation and still punishing Elys for an imagined slight. "If someone cared for me the way Elys cares for you, I would never leave them," I rage, feeling a swell of longing for Jim. "Some people never get the chance to say sorry. You don't know how lucky you are."

Jory regards me through eyes wide with shock. "Steady on," he says. "You're only surmising about Isaac."

"Oh giss'on," I say, and Jory laughs, loud and long. I feel utterly foolish parroting one of Elys' slang phrases to her fiancé in the height of anger, and it sets me off again.

"Get out of my cave," I say, waving my stick at Jory. "Out, get out, now." I stand and follow him, holding my stick in front like a gnarled wooden sword. Jory strides ahead, and I can still hear him laughing long after he is out of my sight.

CHAPTER NINETEEN

The Mask Slips

Wednesday, July 6, 1932

I'm on my way to the hotel. It's nearly ten o'clock, and I've avoided Elys all morning and most of last night, barring a few moments of small talk, which amounted to a couple of disjointed sentences. I can't tell her what I've said to Jory, or she'll be furious. And it didn't do any good anyway. Hopefully, she'll never know, and if I avoid her long enough, my conscience won't guilt me into revealing our conversation. I felt an urge to travel to Wimbledon last night. Once I'd got over the humiliation of my encounter with Jory, I couldn't stop thinking about Jim, and thoughts of the distance between us left me overwhelmed with sadness. I knew it wouldn't hurt as much if only I could see him. So, I tried to settle into the dream state and go to his side, but it didn't happen. Perhaps I wanted it too badly, or my fear of meeting Crossley stood in the way of success, but regardless, I stared at that candle until the shape of the flame etched itself into my retinas, to no avail. And when I woke this morning, sadness flattened my spirits. But what I can't do one way, I'll try to do another. I'm going to see if I can get to Dolly without anyone else seeing me. Perhaps then I can phone Jim at the station and listen to his voice.

I pick my way up the short path to the hotel door passing several guests along the way. It's high season and busy. I will be lucky if I get to see Dolly at all, much less undetected, but I'm determined to try. There's nothing else for me here, and Jim is occupying so many of my thoughts, I couldn't settle if I didn't try to contact him. I wait for yet another guest to leave, then peer around the door. The view to the desk is unimpeded, and I can see Dolly. But Roxy Templeton is hovering at the rear, and there's no point in entering while she's around. I wait for five minutes, then ten. I'm tiring rapidly and will have to find a seat if I don't get in soon. I risk another glance and find the coast clear: too clear. Not only has Roxy gone, but Dolly has too. Still, I know where the telephone is, and if the office is closed, I might be able to make a call before either of them return. But I haven't got more than a few feet inside when I hear a cough and Georgio appears from the dining room.

"What do you want, miss," he asks in his heavily accented voice.

"I was looking for Dolly," I say.

Georgio waves his arm. "She's not here," he says.

"I know, but she'll be back soon. Can I wait?"

The waiter glances around then peers up the corridor. He tuts and chews his lip as if trying to decide what to do. "I don't think so," he says, eventually. "You're not supposed to be here."

"Please," I say.

"No," says Georgio. "You wait here and I'll find Dolly."

"Thank you," I say, grateful for this small concession even though it doesn't help me get to the telephone. I linger for a moment. But luck has abandoned me today and Roxy Templeton arrives before Georgio gets back. She looks me up and down and wrinkles her nose as if I'd just crept in from a sewer. "What are you doing here?" she demands.

I grit my teeth. Roxy two-faced Templeton had Charlotte Napier's ring in her drawer while still letting everyone blame me. And I can't say a word without dropping Dolly in it. I resist the urge to slap her and smile sweetly. "I'm waiting for Dolly."

"No, you're not. You're banned."

"I'm not doing any harm. I'll leave as soon as I've seen her."

"You'll leave now or I'll call the police."

I can't help grinning at the thought of Constable Maddox weaving his way from Newquay to Porth Tregoryan on his rusty old cycle to arrest me for waiting in the hotel lobby. "Feel free," I say. "Meanwhile, I'll wait for Dolly."

"I'll have you thrown out," says Roxy, just as one of the guests walks down the staircase and into the reception area. I perform my best dying swan impression and lean heavily on my stick as she passes.

"I feel awfully faint," I say, swaying ever so slightly.

"Are you alright, dear?" asks the woman. She is short and plump, with auburn hair and a pleasant, kind face.

I smile bravely. "I will be in a minute," I reply.

"Sit down," says the woman, taking charge. "Here, on this comfy chair." She snaps her fingers in the air. "Fetch a glass of water," she commands.

Roxy's eyes widen at the tone of the woman's voice, and she looks as if she's been slapped in the face.

"Yes, you, fetch this poor young girl a glass of water before she passes out."

Roxy opens her mouth to speak. But even with her rhino hide, she wouldn't dare argue with a guest and publicly remove me in my frail condition.

She snaps her mouth shut and strides to the bell, which she ferociously presses until Georgio appears. "A glass of water for Miss Maxwell," she snarls, then hovers by the desk as if she cannot bear to be any closer.

The kindly guest stares bemusedly, probably wondering why Roxy wasted time summoning Georgio when she could easily have fetched a drink herself. She pats my hand. "Not long now," she says. And she's right. Georgio bustles back with a tall glass on a salver. The auburn-haired woman takes it and presses my hands around the drink. I take a few sips.

"That's so much better," I say. The kindly woman is just about to speak again when Peter appears.

"Connie. What are you doing here?" he asks.

I smile weakly. "Is this young man a friend of yours?" the woman asks.

"Yes," Peter replies on my behalf. "What's wrong with her?"

"She's had a little turn," says the woman. "The poor girl nearly fell over." She glances at her wristwatch. "I'm playing tennis with Mabel in a moment. I must fly. Will you take care of her?"

"Of course," says Peter, and we watch as she leaves the hotel.

Roxy doesn't waste a second. "Get out now," she snarls as the door swings shut.

"Steady on," says Peter, shocked at her tone.

"She's play-acting. Now, Mr Tremayne, I don't want to have to tell Mr Brookbank that you assisted in Miss Maxwell's deceptions, so kindly escort her out of here now."

Peter raises an eyebrow. "What exactly have I done that you think requires reporting to Mr Brookbank?" he asks icily.

"Nothing yet. But if you don't remove Miss Maxwell, I'll take your inaction as a sign that you condone her behaviour, and I'll notify Mr Brookbank accordingly."

Peter adjusts his tie and glowers. "I will have a word with him myself," he says. "You've no right to speak to me this way, and you've overstepped your authority."

Roxy's eyes widen, and a worried look settles across her face.

"I'm sure that won't be necessary," she says. "But Miss Maxwell may not remain in this hotel, and it is in her interests to leave. As her friend, I'm sure you realise this."

Peter holds his arm out, and I take it, then drink the last of the water before hauling myself up.

"Are you ready to leave?" he asks.

I nod. "Yes. I think a stroll around the grounds is in order."

We walk from the hotel as if we were a pair of paying guests, heads up and pride intact. And as soon as we are out of sight, Peter speaks.

"Well, the scales have fallen from my eyes today," he says.

I grin. The visit to the hotel has been an absolute disaster in all regards, save for this. Roxy Templeton has finally revealed the extent of her loathsome personality.

"Unpleasant, isn't she," I say.

"And well hidden beneath the pretty face. I'm shocked, Connie. She truly dislikes you."

"Correct. And you don't know the half of it. Can we sit, Peter? That fainting fit wasn't as much of an act as she thinks."

Peter guides me to the flat stone near the front of the hotel.

"Go on then," he says. "Tell me everything."

Peter already knows my version of the events of the Summer Ball, a conversation that started when we left Worple Road and continued until we arrived in Cornwall. But the news about Mr Brookbank, the office phone, and the actual location of Charlotte's ring is news to him.

"I can't believe it," he says. "Nobody could be that stupid."

"Cunning," I say.

"I meant Brookbank, not Roxy. What's he thinking of by having a dalliance behind his wife's back? I've met her once or twice, and she's a lovely woman. Far too good for him, if I'm honest."

"But the ring?"

"Well, yes. Disgraceful, if it's true. But how do you know Roxy put it in the drawer?"

"It's her desk."

Peter shakes his head. "No, it isn't. She uses it, but so do Dolly and the accounts girl. And the waiters are and in and out of the office all the time, not to mention the housekeeper."

"Oh, come on. The ring was well hidden. Whoever put it there didn't intend anyone to find it, much less me."

"What are you going to do about it?"

"Ask for your help, now you know."

"What can I do?"

"Tell someone where it is. Then they'll know I didn't take it."

Peter cocks his head and smiles fondly. "No, Connie. Any interference will provoke the opposite reaction. They'll ask how I found it and might assume you told me because you hid it there in the first place. It should stay where it is until it's naturally discovered."

"But it's been over a week, and nobody can have found it, or Roxy wouldn't have tried to eject me."

"Mr Brookbank's been away," says Peter. "A domestic matter, I hear, which given what you've just told me, might involve Mrs Brookbank learning of her husband's infidelities."

I smirk. "I hope so," I say. "Do you think I should leave it?"

"Definitely. Brookbank is back tomorrow. Give it a day, and if nothing transpires, we'll reconsider."

"Thank goodness you believe me."

"I never doubted you," says Peter. "Whatever your many faults, dishonesty isn't one of them."

I hit him playfully, and we part, Peter, striding back to the hotel while I take a slower walk to Pebble Cottage. I watch the horse and trap parked in front of our home as I approach, but it takes a few minutes to realise that it's Jory's. I tiptoe through the front door and into the parlour to hear voices coming from the kitchen. I wait for a moment, then decide to announce my presence by opening and closing the front door loudly. The voices stop, and I advance towards them and open the door. Jory is sitting at the kitchen table with a glass of beer and a thick slice of cake. Elys is standing next to him, looking bashful.

"Oh, my goodness. Are you?" I ask.

Jory nods, and Elys blushes.

"Wonderful," I say and leave them to it.

CHAPTER TWENTY

In the Doctor's Lair

Seeing Jory and Elys reunited has left me with mixed feelings. I'm delighted for the pair of them. They belong together and were miserable apart. But their obvious happiness leaves me with an uncomfortable ache when I think of Jim going about his day without me. I've only known him for a week and he's probably forgotten me already, but it's time to have another go at dream walking and see if he's left me a message. An involuntary shiver sets my nerves jangling as I think about Oliver Fox's warnings. He would hate the idea of me travelling, and we didn't complete our training, which he clearly felt was beyond him. I sigh as I climb the stairs, remembering how quickly he agreed with Peter's plan to bring

189

me home. I still can't understand why Fox thinks I'm safer here. If it weren't for Jim, I wouldn't try to travel. I'd accept that it's not safe on the astral plane, and I don't need Fox to tell me how bad things could be. I've seen it myself, and if I never meet Crossley again, it won't be a day too soon. But my heart aches for Jim. I long to see him again, even if only in spirit. And it's worth the risk, no matter what.

I light a candle even though it's bright outside, and I can barely see the flame. I haven't found myself involuntarily pulled from my body since I returned from Wimbledon, and making it happen myself is the only way to make progress. So, I concentrate as I did the other night. After five dull minutes, the results are the same. I am still in my usual form and going nowhere. I adjust my position, hoping it helps, but it's like someone has turned off a switch, and I can't get into the dream state no matter how hard I try. My frustration emerges in a loud groan, and I sit up and put my head in my hands, watching the echoes of the flickering flame dancing in the backs of my eyes. I watch until the light finally dissolves, then lay down again, my pent-up disappointment dissipating as I turn my head sleepily back towards the candle. I watch, drifting in and out of that moment just before sleep. Then a tingle fizzes through my body, settling at the back of my scalp. I don't check but rise and move, knowing that my body will be on the bed when I turn around. It is, and I am finally free.

I take a moment to marshal my thoughts, more lucid in my astral form than I can ever remember. I want to go to Worple Road today and in the present. So, I set my mind on something that ought to be there. Jim will be at work, and Oliver Fox could be anywhere. Bertha Callaway is still on holiday with Jim's mother, so the only certainty is Teddy. I smile as I recall his snuffling nose as he rested his head against my knees, and I can almost feel myself ruffling his soft brown ears. It works like a dream. I feel myself hurtling through time and space, but I don't look. I keep my eyes tightly shut until the movement stops a split second later. And when everything feels right, I open them again to find myself standing by the side table in Jim's front room. My heart flips as I reach for the arm of his chair, the place he sits every night. I can't feel the fabric or the rough edge of the repaired tear as my hand goes right through, but it is enough to know he sat there. His morning newspaper lies folded across the table, weighed down with a copy of *Very Good Jeeves*. With his ready wit and humour, I should have guessed that Jim would be a PG Wodehouse fan. And the condition of the book with its torn cover and well-thumbed pages suggests he has read it often. The book covers some of the newspaper, but not enough to obscure the date, which tells me I'm in the right place at the right time. I am about to proceed upstairs when the telephone rings. It startles me, and I clutch my chest and gaze around the room in a panic. I hear steps in the kitchen and shrink against the wall as if hoping for protection. The door squeaks open, and Hilda Grady appears, carrying a bowl of chopped meat. Teddy follows eagerly behind, watching the food. She hovers by the telephone, reaches for the handset, then hesitates. She seems unsure whether to answer or not. I stand stock-still, entirely in her eye line. She doesn't see me, but Teddy does, and he bounds over. I kneel without thinking and ruffle his ears, both of us momentarily perplexed when he doesn't feel my touch. Teddy whines and paws at my ankles, but his legs go through mine, and he whimpers in puzzlement.

"Stupid mutt," mutters Hilda as she balances the food on the side table. The phone is still ringing as she finally answers, but it is too late. By the time she puts the earpiece to her head, the caller has rung off. "That's your fault," she says, jabbing a meaty finger towards Teddy. He shrinks towards me, still crying.

"What is wrong with you today?" asks Hilda, dropping to her knees beside him. I stare in horror. She is less than an inch away from me, and although she clearly can't see me, she is intrusively close. I glance at her tangled mane of hair, uncharacteristically luxuriant for a woman of her age and can't help noticing her swarthy face and pronounced chin. I register a few patches of stubble and wonder if she has a medical condition. She strokes Teddy, who is still distressed, and when he doesn't respond, Hilda gets to her feet and takes the food bowl.

"Come on now," she says. "It's time for dinner."

Teddy doesn't move, and Hilda Grady is at the door before she notices he's missing. She sighs, turns tail and grabs him by the collar before dragging him towards the kitchen. Then, she leaves, and I hear the rattle of the bowl as she deposits it on the kitchen tiles.

Banishing the thought of Teddy's puzzled little face, I return to the hallway and ascend the stairs. Jim's house isn't quite the same as Oliver Fox's. It's a similar age and was probably erected by the same builder, but the style is slightly different so I ascend in a straight line instead of the more familiar dogleg onto a landing leading to three doors and a further staircase. Though I've never been upstairs, I know without question that Jim's room is behind the second door. And sure enough, when I open it, the first thing I see is a policeman's helmet lying on the chest of drawers. Beside it is a bookcase full of police-related texts and pamphlets.

Jim's double bed is directly in front of a long window overlooking the garden. I imagine waking up here, and though it is pleasant, I would miss the cawing gulls and windswept coast. I approach Jim's bedside table with trepidation, nerves jangling at the thought of what I might find there. If he hasn't written a message, hasn't bothered, then I will know that he doesn't care and that I was a passing fancy. But when I reach the foot of the bed, I see a piece of lined paper with a drawing across it. I grin with relief at the sight of his picture. Jim has sketched a red love heart with an arrow through it. On one side, he has written J D, and on the other, C M. My heart flips at the sight of the childlike drawing and I'm dizzy with delight. His small gesture has buoyed my hopes and offers scope for the long and tricky process of explaining my travel abilities.

With a heart filled with hope, I inspect the room, exploring and remembering every detail as far as I can without touching things. I feel closer to Jim now that I've immersed myself in his surroundings. My scalp tingles as I return to the window. It's timed to perfection, and I will give in and allow it to take me as soon as I've glimpsed the garden. I lean out, head and shoulders pushing through the glass window to see a long, narrow but tidy lawn with pretty flower borders and a rose arbour. The neighbouring gardens are similar, with summer flowers in full bloom. They all look the same, except one. To the right, a few doors down, a writhing mass of airborne black bodies conceal the lawn. I lean out further still, trying to see if it's a swarm of bees. But they're too big, too shadowy and vague, otherworldly. And then it hits me with a sickening jolt. Oliver Fox is in terrible danger, his garden under siege beneath a sea of bats, swooping in a dark-winged, smoky swarm. I close my eyes, turn tail and run for the door, passing through it and running onwards in a blind panic.

#

I run until I feel safe. The tingling has stopped, but I've missed the opportunity for an easy return to my body. And if it doesn't start again soon, I may not get back at all. I slowly glance to my rear before taking stock of my surroundings, half-expecting a black mass of bats in hot pursuit. But all I see is a dull orange sun hanging low in the sky as the afternoon turns into evening. The bats haven't followed, and my first instinct was correct. They are there for Fox and not for me. But then I think back to Fox's theory. He says the bats are a manifestation of my fears, but how can this be so? I wasn't thinking about Fox when I saw them, unless at a subconscious level. But perhaps they represent his dread rather than mine. Or maybe he is wrong, and they are Crossley's creatures. I shudder at the thought of it. I've learned a lot from Oliver Fox, but experience suggests he's a theory man who knows a lot about the occult but struggles to put it into practice. His dream travel success rate is relatively low. I ponder this for a while before snapping back into high alert. I shouldn't be daydreaming when I don't know where I am.

I flit around from street to street until my surroundings become familiar, grinning as I realise that I'm back in Croydon, having run more or less the same route that I did all those weeks ago. I recall my last visit and find my way back to Scarsbrook Road and from there to the police station. I think of Jim as I gaze at the building, waiting for the familiar surge of emotion, but disappointingly, it doesn't arrive. Why is it that panic and fear flood through my astral body, yet excitement and happiness are slow to follow and much reduced in impact? It's not fair, and I am glad that I can still hop between my real and spiritual forms. I don't know what I'd do if I became stuck in this ethereal body indefinitely. My gift is more frustrating than useful.

I turn my attention to the police station, wondering if I dare go in. Physically, it's easy, and I want to see Jim more than I can say. But what if he's there and talking to another woman? What if he's chatting to a colleague about a girl he knew who's just returned to Cornwall, and it's a good thing too? I might walk in on him just as he's telling someone about his cinema trip with the second woman as the first one couldn't go. No, I couldn't bear it. As much as I want to see him, it's not worth the risk. When I wake up in Pebble Cottage tomorrow morning, I want my first thought to be of the love heart he drew, not of some half-heard and misunderstood conversation. So, I turn away and walk a few streets further, finding myself outside Birdhurst Rise more by luck than design.

I'm at the start of the road outside number 1 Birdhurst Rise considering what to do next when I see Doctor Binning emerge from the building, carrying his medical bag, face set into a fierce frown. He stomps up the street, lip jutting out while muttering under his breath. His clean-cut face is flushed, and his jaw clenched. I ought to return to my body, but his demeanour is so puzzling that I follow him instead. We walk about a mile to a pleasant tree-lined road and stop outside number 14 Addiscombe Road, where I look at the door plaque to see that we've arrived at Dr Elwell's lair. I thought the two doctors shared a surgery, but apparently, they operate from two different locations and share their patients. Dr Elwell's house is a similar size, but when I follow Dr Binning inside, I see Elwell's surgery is less formal and operates from a single room with a limited waiting area and a surly faced receptionist who looks ready to go home.

"Is he in?" asks Binning, rudely.

She nods but doesn't speak and glances towards the door as if she can't raise the energy to tell him to enter.

"Right," says Binning curtly. He strides across the room, knocks once and disappears inside without waiting for Dr Elwell's response. I follow behind.

Dr Elwell is sitting at a large, ornate wooden desk with a handsome silver pen in his hand, with which he scribbles in a leather-bound appointment book. Two carved and well-upholstered wooden chairs sit side by side in front of his desk, and a pair of oil paintings hang on each of the longer walls. A colourful Tiffany lamp sits on the side table next to a crystal jug, and a set of glasses perch upon a silver salver. The room, though functional, is dripping with opulence and shows that Dr Elwell is not short of money. He looks up as Binning enters and watches him place his medical bag firmly on the chair.

"Be careful," says Elwell, curling his lip at the sight of the battered bag.

"Funny, I was about to say the same to you."

"I'm sorry?"

"You should be."

Dr Elwell sighs. "What's wrong?" he asks.

"You mean you don't know?"

"Clearly not. Now, are you going to tell me, or must I spend the rest of the day playing guessing games?"

"Judith Parker," says Binning.

"Ah. I see. What's her problem?"

"You, quite frankly," says Binning. "How many complaints is it this year? Two or three, at least. For God's sake, man, it's unprofessional."

"It's also unfounded," splutters Elwell. "The woman is hysterical and quite off her head. She accused me of making eyes at her mother."

"Were you?"

"Don't be ridiculous. What did the Parker woman say to you?"

"Nothing I care to repeat verbatim," says Binning, smugly. "But the gist of it was that you were after her mother's money."

"Ridiculous," says Elwell.

"She's changed her will," says Binning. "One hundred pounds to you and the rest split between her three children."

"I didn't know," says Elwell. "But it's uncommonly kind of her."

"Isn't it? Especially considering the short time she's been my patient."

"You're only jealous that she didn't leave it to you."

"Not at all. I don't go in for that, as you jolly well know. But Mrs Parker senior is *my* patient. She's only lived here for a year, and I've seen her five times, so why is she leaving money to you?"

"You'll have to ask her," says Dr Elwell, closing the journal. "Now, is that all?"

"Don't bank on getting the money," says Binning. "Judith Parker is putting a stop to it. She's seeing her solicitor tomorrow to try to remove your legacy."

Elwell's eyes narrow. "It's no skin off my nose," he says. "I won't miss it, but I can tell you that it's not the money she's concerned with. The woman is jealous. She's obsessed with me."

"Tell me you haven't."

Dr Elwell arches an eyebrow but says nothing.

"You've learned nothing from Grace, have you?" snarls Binning.

Elwell stands and straightens his tie. "Jealous people surround me," he says.

"Jealous? Me?"

"Rabidly so," says Elwell. "Just because Grace wanted me and didn't give you the time of day."

"She flirted with me as she did with everyone," says Binning. "And I didn't want her. I swear she tried to poison me."

"Not that again," says Elwell.

"She did. When Mrs Sidney died, Grace gave me a cup of tea, and I tipped it into the flowerpot rather than risk it. I swear to God that there was something dangerous inside."

"Tea, and perhaps a spoonful of sugar," says Elwell. "You really ought to be on stage."

"And you ought to be debarred."

Dr Elwell examines his cufflink, sees something about it he doesn't like and removes it. Then he extracts a large, monogrammed silk handkerchief from his top pocket and starts polishing.

Dr Binning looks heavenward. "It's time we reconsidered this arrangement of ours," he says.

"I agree. I don't trust you, Binning. Not since your friendship with Tom Sidney and that awful inspector. You're not a private investigator and spreading all this tittle-tattle when our work is confidential, reflects badly on the practice. Frankly, I'd be glad to see the back of you."

Binning glowers and holds his fist. I shrink backwards as if being a few inches away might protect me from his evident wrath. Not that he could hurt me, and he certainly can't see me, but in or out of my body, instinct prevails.

"Hedges didn't trust you," says Binning.

"No doubt that was your doing," says Elwell. "I've done nothing to provoke his suspicion."

Binning snorts. "Apart from your dalliance with Grace. Though dalliance is perhaps the wrong word as it implies something short term."

"That was all gossip," says Elwell.

"Except that you've already told me it wasn't. Don't rewrite history because it's inconvenient."

"Why are you doing this? Let's go our separate ways and have done with it."

"And you get off scot-free for stealing wives, ruining reputations and taking money from old ladies?"

"Apologise," demands Doctor Elwell, coldly pressing his face close to the excitable Dr Binning.

"No. I won't."

"I asked Grace to marry me and she refused," says Elwell. "I didn't get her money or anyone else's."

"Not for want of trying," says Binning. "And as for that poor Anna Kelvey, you and Grace should be ashamed of yourselves."

"I'm going to ask you again to leave," says Dr Elwell. "And if you don't, I'll call the police."

I never get to find out whether he did. As Binning opens his mouth to reply, a long-awaited tingling settles on the back of my head, and I find myself drawn backwards. Once again, I resist the urge to open my eyes and the next thing I remember is waking up in Pebble Cottage the following day.

CHAPTER TWENTY-ONE

Letter from Seaford

Thursday, July 7, 1932

I wake, rub the sleep from my eyes and think back to my latest and, in some ways, highly successful dream travel. Though marred by the plague of bats and my uncertainty at the level of danger they represented, the trip was otherwise good. I didn't run into Crossley or feel his presence, but I kept my eyes firmly shut, which worked rather well. I am thoroughly acquainted with the contents of Jim's bedroom and delighted with the red-pencilled heart that he drew. I doubt he's in love with me unless he's the romantic type who develops powerful feelings at first sight, but things are going in the right direction. And on that basis, I will abandon any thought of visiting my cave to concentrate on the tricky task of explaining to Jim how I know what was on his side table. I rise, splash my face and get into my day dress, but instead of going down for breakfast, I pull up a chair at my dressing table and start the letter. Five minutes later, I am still chewing the end of my pen as I stare out to sea. I don't know where to start. It's one thing proving what he wrote, but another altogether expecting him to understand how I know what it says. I wish I had time to consult Peter and ask him to write to Jim independently. But Peter doesn't want me anywhere near Wimbledon while danger lurks, so I can't count on him to help or encourage my friendship with Jim. And anyway, time isn't on my side. The two doctors are fighting like rats in a sack three years after the poisonings happened; Tom Sidney is back in Croydon, and Grace is not in Australia. I can't help feeling that the case is far from over, and if I want to know more, I'll have to ask Jim. I must send this letter today, however difficult it is. I peel a piece of writing paper from my pad, unscrew the cap of my best ink pen and begin.

Dear Jim,

Please read this letter to the end, even if it seems unbelievable in parts. I will try to explain something unusual that you won't have experienced before, and I must ask you to suspend belief and hopefully let the facts speak for themselves. But before I begin, thank you for the time we spent together, for driving me around and tolerating my interest in the Croydon poisonings. I am so sorry that we didn't get to go to the cinema. I was looking forward to it more than I can say.

You may wonder why I've been so interested in the Sidneys, and it's because I'm drawn to the crime in the same way I was with Annie Hearn. It's a feeling, no – more than a feeling – a compulsion to put things right. And I am uniquely qualified to do this because I can see things others can't, in the past, present and future. Before you screw this letter into a ball and abandon me for a fool, the message you left on your bedside table contains a red heart with an arrow through the centre, and you wrote it on a piece of lined paper. I'm blushing as I write this, but you pencilled our initials by the head and foot of the arrow. I know this because I was in your room yesterday afternoon. Your double bed is directly in front of a large window overlooking the garden, and your helmet is on your chest of drawers. I arrived in your living room just as Hilda Grady was feeding Teddy, an arrangement I didn't know you had made. Hilda did not see me, but Teddy did. And so, I have learned something too. Whether it applies to all dogs is another matter, but Teddy can see me in my astral form.

I know you will hesitate as you read this. I'm expecting a lot of you to take this information at face value. But how else could I see what you have drawn and the contents of your bedroom? I have never been there before, and you drew the picture after I left Wimbledon. You might think I'm in league with Hilda Grady, and she passed on the information, but I assure you that is not the case. And I am willing to undertake whatever test or challenge you may deem appropriate to prove that I'm telling the truth, though you should know that dream walking is an inexact science, and I can't always control it.

I know we've touched on Annie Hearn, but the reason I know she's guilty is that I saw her in the future and read her diary, which doubled up as a confession. She dies, Jim. She's poisoned to death out of love. I don't know why I'm compelled to follow these crimes as I can't do anything about them. But the Croydon poisonings are so close in nature to the Lewannick crime that I don't think it's a mere coincidence that I've happened upon it. I am here for a reason, and it's to do with finding the truth. So, I will keep on investigating until I know.

Unfortunately, Jim, it will be from a distance. I cannot

return to Wimbledon for the time being for reasons that are too complicated to explain. It's not just Mrs Ponsonby, though she keeps me on a tight leash, as you know. But other, more dangerous matters keep me from re-entering Mr Fox's employ. But Jim, I aim to come back as soon as possible, and with Mrs Ponsonby threatening to sell the cottage, it may be sooner rather than later.

Anyway, I overheard a conversation between Dr Elwell and Dr Binning while I was travelling yesterday. They are at loggerheads and about to separate their practices. As you know, Dr Elwell has received at least one legacy, and from what I heard yesterday, there may be many more. Perhaps you could look into this? You may also be interested to hear that Kathleen Noakes harbours suspicions about Tom Sidney. Mind you, she didn't like Grace much either. But I wonder if we should check that Tom Sidney really is here on business? After all, we've only got his word for it.

So, Jim, the girl you met last week who can't walk very far can travel all over the world if the conditions are right. Ironic, isn't it? But no one ever sees me. I am not visible to most people in my astral form unless they are dream travellers too. Do something for me, Jim. If you can't bring yourself to believe me, then at least help me find out more about the Sidney's. I miss you, Jim, and hope to see you again soon.

With best wishes,

Connie

I hold my pen over the closing paragraph as I reread the letter, tempted to put a line through the salutation. *'With best wishes'* sounds awfully formal. In fact, the letter is more like a cross between a confession and a business proposition, spiced up with a smattering of science fiction. It does not read like a letter to a friend, let alone someone who could be dearer than that. But I am short of time, and I cannot rewrite it. So, I scribble a hasty postscript.

PS. – Please forward your reply to Peter Tremayne at Compass House, Newquay, to be on the safe side. If it comes here, Mrs Ponsonby may intercept it. CM.

Once again, I hover the pen over my initials, wondering whether I dare write a little X as a gesture of my affection, but I can't bring myself to do it. Jim has drawn a love heart, but whether he truly expected me to see it is another matter. And he kissed me before I left and must like me, so although logic tells me it's safe to send a kiss, fear of rejection stops me. I compromise by kissing the page, even though he will never know, fold the letter in two and address it. Then I place the envelope in my pocket, before hearing a knock at my bedroom door.

"Hello?" I say, and Elys walks in.

"Mrs Ponsonby wants you," she says brightly.

"You've cheered up."

"I know," she replies, flashing her ring finger.

"About time," I say. "What does Mrs Ponsonby want?"

"She's going into Newquay," says Elys as her smile falls away.

"Why?"

"You'd better go down."

I follow Elys and find Mrs Ponsonby dressed and ready to go out and waiting in the hallway. "Sorry, dear," she says. "You'll miss your breakfast, but I'm going to town, and you're coming with me."

"Why?"

"Quickly. We'll miss the bus."

I grab my bag and follow her out the door. "Slow down," I say, trying to keep up as she hurries down the lane.

"Sorry, Connie. I wasn't thinking."

I try again. "Where are we going?"

Mrs Ponsonby sighs. "To see the land agent," she says.

I stop and stare at her. "But I thought you were reconsidering?"

"I have, and I still think it's for the best."

The bus pulls up at the stop, and we are still a few yards away. Mrs Ponsonby raises her hand and waves at the driver. He tips his hat and waits while she strides ahead of me. I catch up, and the driver offers me his hand. We travel to Newquay in silence as I seethe, heart heaving with anger and feeling like she's ambushed me. Mrs Ponsonby looks no happier than I am and stares out to sea as if the answer lies in the deep Atlantic waters. The bus stops in the middle of Newquay, and we alight. Mrs Ponsonby waits and offers her hand as I negotiate my descent, but I wave it away and walk past her.

"Why have you brought me?" I ask coldly.

"I thought I should involve you from the outset. It will make things easier."

"I'm not a child."

"Quite. If you were a child, you'd be none the wiser until the day we left. This way, you will know exactly what will happen and when."

We stop outside the offices of May & Co in Bank Street, and I stand still like a petulant child. "I'm not going in," I say.

"You must, Connie. I won't leave you outside. I know you are disappointed, but I'm trying to treat you like an adult. Have the goodness to behave like one."

Her words hit home. I have begged her not to keep things from me, and for once, she is making an effort. I may not like the situation, but I recognise her efforts and reluctantly follow her inside. She must have made an appointment as the occupant of the only desk in the office stands and offers his hand.

"Ah, Mrs Ponsonby, I presume?"

She responds with a firm handshake of her own. I sit through a painful half-hour of sales talk and bargaining. Mrs Ponsonby is no pushover and negotiates a far better commission than the agent initially offered, but the result is the same. Pebble Cottage will be offered for sale at £750, and the agent will visit to take details early next week. I feel sick at the thought. We leave the building, and Mrs Ponsonby offers me a mint, but when she reaches into her pocket and withdraws the well-used packet, only one remains.

"You have it, Connie," she says as if a mint could make up for what she's just done.

"No, it's yours."

"I'll buy another packet," she says, heading towards the grocers.

"I'll wait outside," I reply, seizing today's first and only piece of luck. I've seen a postbox two doors down, and if nothing else, it gives me the means to post Jim's letter. Mrs Ponsonby trips off inside while I take a slow walk, use the postbox, then look up with the distinct feeling that I'm being watched. My intuition is correct. Two women of my age are standing on the other side of the road, openly pointing at me. One leans across and whispers in the other's ear, and they both laugh. I can't hear what they're saying save for one or two words, but 'thief' and 'ring' number among them leaving me in no doubt that they are spreading rumours. My first instinct is to blush and walk away. But walking makes me look feeble enough without dodging a confrontation too. I'd look even more guilty, and I've done nothing wrong. So, I stand there and face them head-on, hands on my hips, staring and daring them to say more. They are not expecting my response and exchange nervous looks as if waiting for the other to suggest what to do. And in the end, they scurry away without a second glance. It is a minor victory, but the feeling of power buoys my spirits. I'm still standing there when Mrs Ponsonby leaves the shop and walks briskly towards me. She admonishes me for wandering up the street, but when I tell her what happened and my response to it, she breaks into a satisfied smile.

"It's about time we did something about this situation," she says. "That silly rumour has gone on long enough, and though I disapprove of you hanging around the hotel, I don't like the way they've treated you. I'm going to see that manager and give him a piece of my mind."

"No, don't," I say, filled with newfound confidence. "It will sort itself out in the next few days."

She raises an eyebrow, but I don't elaborate. It's time I fought my own battles, and this thought plays over in my mind as we walk towards the bus stop. Mrs Ponsonby stands while I sit on a low wall while we wait for the bus to appear. I am lost in a daydream about Jim when I hear Mrs Ponsonby's voice.

"Good morning, Miss Napier," she says.

I look up to the nauseating sight of Charlotte Napier walking arm in arm with the girl who was gossiping so rudely only a few minutes before. Charlotte clearly intended to sail past us without speaking, but Mrs Ponsonby has left her in no position to ignore us.

Charlotte screws up her lovely face as she searches for something nice to say, and I shoot an admiring glance at Mrs P. I wish I'd had the nerve to speak, but I'm still haunted by the sight of Charlotte, Kit and Edgar watching my humiliating exit from the hotel on the night of the summer ball. Charlotte licks her lips. The silence is growing uncomfortable, and still, she can't find the right words to convey respect to Mrs Ponsonby while simultaneously directing her disgust at me. Finally, she speaks.

"Good afternoon," she says. "Isn't the weather fine today?"

"Have you found that ring yet?" Mrs Ponsonby swipes her small talk away with a pointed question.

"No," says Charlotte, shooting me a frosty glare.

"I'm sure it will turn up. I expect it's in the hotel somewhere."

"They've searched high and low, and I can assure you, it is not."

I try not to grind my teeth as I think of the ring lying in Mr Brookbank's drawer and wonder what Charlotte would think if she knew.

"You didn't see it, of course, did you, Connie, dear," asks Mrs Ponsonby, supportively.

"Not after I left the ladies' room," I reply.

"You were the last one out," snaps Charlotte carelessly.

"Meaning what?" asks Mrs Ponsonby. If Charlotte knew her as well as I do, she would stop talking now. Mrs Ponsonby is bristling with indignation. The more upset she is, the fewer words she uses. And she's down to two already.

"I meant nothing by it," says Charlotte with an insincere giggle. "But Connie was the last person to see the ring. That's all."

"So?"

Oh, dear. Things are hostile now. I could almost feel sorry for Charlotte, if only she weren't such a sanctimonious prig.

Charlotte smiles again but doesn't reply. I could let Mrs Ponsonby continue my defence, but I stand up and deal with Charlotte myself.

"Just so you're in no doubt," I say, "I did not take your ring. I have no interest in jewellery, as you can see." I show her my hands one at a time as I juggle my stick between them. "But I've heard some nasty gossip recently." I glare at her friend as I say this. "And I'm told that slanderous remarks can be quite hard on the purse." I sweetly smile while Charlotte stares nonplussed.

"Goodbye, Miss Napier," says Mrs Ponsonby as the bus draws up. We climb aboard, and I savour the moment as we travel, right up to the point where we see Pebble Cottage, and I remember that it's on borrowed time.

CHAPTER TWENTY-TWO

Netherwood

A harmonious mood settles over our cottage for the rest of the day, despite my upset at our imminent move. Mrs Ponsonby is resigned to it, Elys can't stop smiling since her re-engagement to Jory, and Jim's love heart has temporarily eased my disappointment at the prospect of leaving. Charlotte's Napier's discomfort following our hostile encounter is the icing on the cake, and I expect sleep to come quickly when I retire at ten thirty. I'm tired. It's a balmy evening, though not sweltering, and there's a light breeze coming through the chink in the window. But as I lie in bed, thumbing my way through one of Elys' awful magazines, I am unprepared for the wave of foreboding that rolls over me from nowhere.

At first, I think it's my imagination. The sky darkens even though it's dark already, and I can see the hairs on my arms standing on end. I place my hand firmly against my mattress in case I've plunged into unintentional astral travel without noticing, but my hand resolutely remains where it ought to be. The temperature in my room plummets, and my teeth begin to chatter. I draw my covers to my chin, and, while still sitting upright, I glance towards the window.

I don't notice it at first, but as my eyes grow accustomed to the increased darkness, I see a shape moving outside. My heart lurches as it hovers near my window, and I wonder, at first, whether it's another bat. But if it is, then it's bigger than any I've seen before. Scratching noises at the window, increasing in intensity, fill me with dread, and a long shape looms ahead. Or is it two? It's hard to tell, but the sound is getting closer and more persistent. The creature's wings are beating in time with my heart, but the rustling isn't. And the wings are clear of the window frame, so what's causing the noise? I stare at the black mass transfixed with fear. And as I watch the chink in the window with a growing sense of unease, a bristly protrusion forces itself through the gap and flails in the air. The spidery leg is slender and hairy, at least a foot long and attached to a bulbous malformed torso.

I freeze, then push back against the bedstead, logic battling fear. This creature isn't real. It's a figment of my terror. All I need do is think of something else, and it will vanish into the ether. But as I look again, I hear a repetitive thump. The creature is ramming itself against the window, trying to force its way through the tiny gap. A proboscis appears, the end dripping with drool. I try to look away, but my sight is sharper now, and I see its eyes, all eight of them, glowering at me in a travesty of order. My heart lurches as it forces another leg through, uplifting the latch. Then, in an unexpectedly agile movement, its wings stop beating, and the remaining limbs infiltrate the narrow gap as it enters my room.

Fox was wrong. This thing is real, and it's heading straight

209

towards me. A hundred thoughts flash through my head. I must leave. I must risk travelling on the astral plane. But I can't go to Wimbledon or Croydon, or anywhere I've ever been with Coralie. I search my mind in desperation, seeking a place, somewhere I've never been. Somewhere he'll never find me. And just as the creature reaches the bottom of my bed, I remember the trunk in Mrs Ponsonby's room and the name on the deeds. I scream the word inside my head, Netherwood, and hope that fear will grant me the gift of travel that so often eludes me. Nothing happens, and the creature draws closer, and I haven't got time to light a candle and watch a flame. It is coming straight for me, eyes like slits and a cavernous maw dripping with drool. I screw my eyes tight and imagine a naked light behind my eyes, dancing and flickering. I concentrate like never before. And just as I smell its rancid breath and feel the heat of its flesh, tingling streams down my spine, and I fall into the astral plane, hoping that I'll have a body to return to.

#

I briefly lose consciousness from the terror of the unexpected, ungodly visitor. It feels like several minutes have passed since the loathsome creature stood over me, and my astral body fled. But without a calendar or newspaper, I can't be sure. I don't remember travelling through the astral plane, and even though I have taken to closing my eyes recently, I have never blacked out before. Previously, I have arrived at my new destination instantly, always conscious of being first in one place and then the other with no gap in time, no matter how fleeting, and this loss of control does not bode well.

I am standing at the top of a long driveway leading to a large three-storey mansion a few yards from the main road in a town that I don't recognise. A crumbling red brick wall surrounds it and a smaller building, reminiscent of a stable block, sits to one side. Two pitted spheres top the entrance to the pockmarked drive, but even in scant moonlight, I can imagine the grandeur of the sweeping driveway in its heyday. The property feels familiar, and the carved stone sign tells me I have found Netherwood. Its pilastered doorway in the distance seems familiar, but I have never been here. So why does it feel like I'm coming home?

I'm still frightened. If I could feel my heart, it would lurch with nerves. I am alone in the dark in front of a decrepit, unloved house with boarded windows and a weed-strewn garden. I shouldn't go anywhere near the place. Anything could lurk inside. Crossley could be here, or the traitorous Cora or hordes of malformed creatures of the night. I should run somewhere safe, but I don't. Instead, I find myself drawn to the house, pulled in by an unstoppable force. And I go willingly.

I reach the door. A brass lion-head knocker hangs forlornly, and a gust of wind is all that it would take for it to fall to the floor and join the remains of the letterbox. I close my eyes and slide through the door into a spacious, dust-ridden hallway. Nothing remains of the floor covering, and several of the floorboards have collapsed. Doors lead off in all directions, but I walk left up a corridor and through a gap into what must have been the drawing room. Barely anything remains of it. Something has blown the windows out, which have been replaced with metal bars. The bowed ceiling hangs dejectedly, and the room reeks of damp. But the most notable damage is to the floor, which is quite literally missing. Floorboards remain at the edges of the room, splintered and damaged, but those in the middle have long disappeared.

I tiptoe to the edge and peer below, but the lighting is poor, and I can't see anything beyond. Then a shiver of fear sets my nerves jangling and I feel a sensation akin to nausea. I know what is happening. Oliver Fox would call it an existential crisis, and it's raging through my being at the thought of what would happen if I took a step into the void. Would I fall, or would I float? Could I easily get out again? I don't know why it matters, but for one moment, it takes on a terror almost as great as the creature from which I fled. I stand stock-still for a moment, paralysed with indecision, and then, in a moment of clarity, I let the fear take me. It's a strange sort of feeling without a racing heart or panting breath but terrifying all the same. A flood of pessimism engulfs me, leaving me devoid of hope. But I silently wait while it courses through my body and my patience eventually pays dividends. Bit by bit, the feeling disappears. I avert my eyes from the gigantic hole, and as soon as I feel up to it, I leave. I contemplate exploring the remaining downstairs rooms, but I'm too disturbed by the experience to stay close to the hole. So, I ascend the stairs, thankful to be in my astral form as they are in such a poor state of repair that it wouldn't be wise to climb them under normal circumstances.

I reach the top, turn right and pass through the door of the last room on the left. I know before I enter that it is a nursery, though I can't say why. The once jolly wallpaper still bears traces of a Victorian mother holding hands with her children beneath a rose surround, but it is peeling and covered in mildew. Despite that, this room is in better condition than the downstairs accommodation. Dusky pink curtains still hang from the windows, coated with years of undisturbed silken spiderwebs. A dark wooden chest of drawers is dusty but intact. It may still contain items, though I can't open it to check. But a framed photograph on the placemat sitting on top of the piece of furniture looks interesting. I can barely see it for dust, so I blow as if it would help, but of course, it doesn't work. Undefeated, I stand on the side furthest from the window and use the sliver of moonlight to its best effect. The picture shows a woman sitting in a chair with a plump baby on her lap. The child, no more than six months old, is wearing a lace christening gown. A tall man sporting a dog collar stands next to them, benevolently smiling as if he is gazing at his most precious possessions. My eyes prick as if with tears, but they don't moisten. I want to cry at this beautiful display of affection, but I can't. The disconnection between my body and spirit holds me back. But not enough that I can't recognise and envy the bond between parents and child; she's a lucky little girl to know such love.

I drift back up the corridor and examine the bedrooms – some with furniture, others empty. The largest room overlooks the rear garden; the rear field is closer to the truth. How long this house has lain empty is impossible to tell, but the neglected garden isn't just overgrown with grass and weeds. The head height brambles and shrubs have clearly run wild for a long time. I wonder why? Netherwood was a beautiful place once and could be again with a bit of care. This room, most obviously the master bedroom, is as dusty as the rest. A large four-poster bed with heavy drapes, threadbare and torn, dominates the room. And a dark wooden three-door wardrobe occupies one side, with two doors closed and the last open and dangling from its one remaining hinge. I peer inside to see an outfit hanging from an old wooden coat hanger. For a terrible moment, I fear it might be an occult robe. Then I recognise the compass and square of the freemasons. The way it is displayed would give me palpitations if my body was near. Every part of the masonic outfit hangs on a specially adapted rail showing all the regalia from the apron to an elaborate collar. The overall effect is one of a headless man. But the garment is harmless, and the moon casts a bright glow across the room. For now, I am unafraid and decide to continue exploring.

A small staircase leads to the upper level at the end of the left-hand corridor, and I can't help attempting to blow dust away again as I venture up the heavily coated stairway. I arrive in a partitioned attic room, standing in the servants' quarters and peer inside three small rooms, one of which belonged to a man, then stand in front of the abruptly ending upper corridor. It doesn't look right. There is no obvious door, yet the passage finishes well ahead of what ought to be usable space. I ponder the situation for a moment and decide it must be storage but how it's accessed is a mystery. I would walk through the wall if I cared more, but I don't and return downstairs. On my way down, I realise with a sudden jolt that I have felt no inclination to return to my body. Normally, I would have sensed a welcome tug by now, but nothing draws me back, and I worry that disaster has struck back at Pebble Cottage. I feel a swell of what might be panic if conditions allowed it and decide, after all, to occupy myself by trying to understand the strange configuration of the upper floor. I head down the left-hand corridor of the first floor again and enter the endmost room, which should, in theory, be directly beneath the closed-off area. Apart from dust and cobwebs, it seems perfectly normal and well proportioned, so I leave and enter the opposite room. The same applies. Frustrated and increasingly worried, I go back downstairs. If the answer lies in the drawing room, it can stay there as wild horses wouldn't drag me back, but just off the hallway is a partially furnished study, and as soon as I go inside, I can tell that the dimensions are off. Dented floorboards lie where a desk used to stand, and the sidewall contains a floor to ceiling bookcase devoid of literature and in a poor state of repair. But it isn't right. The room should be deeper, much deeper. It looks out of proportion but the only way to be sure is to go back into the drawing room, and I'm not doing that. So, taking advantage of my current form, I heave a deep breath and walk into the bookcase. I was right. Thankfully, it doesn't lead into the next room, and I find myself in a small enclosure in front of a set of narrow stairs rising steeply above. I can only just see them. It is pitch black behind the bookcase and even darker ahead. And the darkness is triggering a reaction – a tingling at the back of my head. The sensation brings a feeling of safety, and I risk spending a final few seconds ascending into the gloom. Halfway up, the stairs change direction, and I nearly walk into the wall. But I realise in time and continue upwards, finally emerging in a sloping ceilinged room running half the length of the upstairs. Moonlight streams inside from two long windows, and I look around with a horrible sense of déjà vu.

A painted circle with a crescent moon and other strange

symbols lie in the middle of the floor. Wall sconces run across the longest wall, and at the far end is an altar of sorts, covered in a dusty, ragged purple cloth with a pewter salver on top. Though not identical and much older, this place bears similarities to the attic room in the townhouse in Berlin. But there is nothing to suggest that it relates to Calicem Aureum. I peer at the symbol again, clearly visible despite the layer of dust and almost glowing in the moonlight, which falls in precisely the right place for best illumination. It reminds me of something, and I wrack my brain for inspiration. The memory returns slowly and only when I think of Oliver Fox and his potted history of astral travel.

Calicem Aureum was born of a dispute within a previous incarnation. And that group was the order of the crescent moon. Whoever lived here, whoever owned this house and created this room, was a member of that order. And far from Netherwood being a place of safety, I find myself in a room where someone has been dabbling in who knows what. Worse still, Mrs Ponsonby holds the deeds to the damned place. Just when my guard was down, when I felt I could trust her, this happens. Is she involved with these people? If Cora is corrupt, Mrs Ponsonby could be too. Are her friends in league? Is Isla Tremayne involved, or Peter for that matter? Crushed with despair, I have no fight left in me. The tingling fizzes like a surge of electricity. If I go back and find myself in the jaws of that fetid creature, it can't be any worse than knowing I have no friends. A flash of static streams through me, and I close my eyes and drift away.

CHAPTER TWENTY-THREE

Reaching for Jim

Friday, July 8, 1932

I wake in my room as if nothing has happened. It is dawn, and light streams inside from the open curtains. I gaze around, staring in disbelief at the orderly room. I can see no evidence that the creature was ever there, yet it wasn't a dream. I remember it vividly while desperately fearing for my life. I rise and walk towards the window. It is just as well that it is a balmy day, still and quiet despite the early hour. My window is unlatched and open to its widest extent, and if the sea breeze were up to its usual strength, the glass would have shattered. I approach the window and examine the frame. It is intact but coated with a gelatinous substance with an evil odour. I recoil at the smell and head straight for my water jug, unable to bear the thought of leaving it. Then I take my face flannel and start mopping up the mess. I wouldn't want to explain its presence to Elys. And it's a good thing that I deal with it quickly because five minutes later, Elys opens my door and enters, carrying a cup of tea.

"Are you alright?" she asks.

I bite my lip, not knowing what to say. "Why shouldn't I be?" I venture.

Elys places the mug on my bedside table and perches by the side of my bed.

"I'm glad you said that," she says, patting my hand. "You obviously don't remember."

"Remember what?"

"You were having a terrible nightmare, Connie. We heard you screaming blue murder. Even from the pantry, your cries were blood-curdling. Mrs Ponsonby and I raced upstairs as fast as we could. But by the time we got there, you were quiet. Deathly silent. For a moment, we couldn't be sure you were alive. Mrs Ponsonby took your wrist and found a faint pulse, so we covered you up again, and she sat with you until the small hours. You were breathing better by then, and she felt it safe to leave you."

"Where is she?" I ask, looking around in panic. Her description of Mrs P as a guardian angel does not match that of a woman who holds the deeds to a house used for occult purposes.

"In bed," says Elys. "As I said, she was up half the night in the freezing cold. Once I'd gone, she couldn't shut the window without leaving your side, so she stayed where she was. The cold kept her from falling asleep, she said. But I've assured her I will check on you, and she's not to get up before ten o'clock. So, what did you dream about?"

I shake my head. "I can't remember," I say, feeling guilty for the lie. But I can't tell Elys about the creature, or Mrs

Ponsonby for that matter. She'd think I was losing my mind. Perhaps I am.

"Well, you look a lot better," says Elys. "I was going to sit with you, but I don't think there's any need. But you mustn't go outside today."

I glare at her. "Why ever not?"

"Mrs Ponsonby says so. And don't argue," she continues as I open my mouth to reply. "She's worried sick, and you can give her at least one peaceful day."

I sigh but nod my head. I'm tired anyway and still torn about who I can trust.

"I've made some oats," says Elys. "Come and have breakfast with me when you've finished that."

She nods towards the tea, and I gulp it greedily, not caring that it's a little too hot. And when I've finished, I wring out my flannel and leave it on top of my wash basket. But the smell is vile, and Elys is sure to notice. Reluctantly, I hurl the cloth from the window into the shrubs opposite the front garden and tip the remaining water outside. Even then, the jug reeks of something otherworldly, but I can do no more, and I leave the room and go downstairs.

The dining room is empty, and Elys sits at the kitchen table with Mr Moggins on her lap. She jumps up and ladles a large bowl of porridge before spooning sugar over the top.

"Get that down, you," she commands. I try. Honestly, I try, but in the end, I am defeated by the quantity. Elys raises her eyes heavenwards when I place my spoon on the table.

"Mrs Ponsonby would hate the waste."

"Then don't tell her."

"Mr Moggins can have it."

The cat scrunches his face into the bowl, purring contentedly and emerges minutes later with white lumps smudged into his whiskers. He takes himself off to his favourite corner for half an hour's grooming while Elys probes me for more information about my nightmare, and I do my best to resist her. The conversation is getting uncomfortable when, to my immense relief, the doorbell chimes. Elys sighs and trots off to answer while I pour another cup of tea.

"It's for you, Connie," she says on her return.

"Who is it?"

"Best you go and see."

I open the kitchen door to find Peter waiting by the coat stand.

"Oh, hello. I wasn't expecting you."

"No. I'm supposed to be at the reading room, but it appears I have a new occupation."

I tilt my head. "I don't know what you mean?"

"A postman," says Peter. "I am now an unpaid deliverer of letters – a go-between, if you like. I say, Mrs Ponsonby isn't around, is she?" he asks anxiously.

"No. She's upstairs. Why?"

"Because she's not supposed to see this." He hands me a thick brown foolscap envelope with my name on the front above Peter's address.

"Oh, I should have told you," I say, blushing furiously.

"Yes. If I must play cupid, you should at least prepare me."

"It's not like that," I hiss.

"It's exactly like that," laughs Peter. "You like him a lot, don't you, Connie? I never thought I'd see the day."

I try to explain myself, but my tongue trips on the words.

"There's no need," says Peter laying a condescending hand on my arm. "I've got to go now anyway. Mother is waiting in the car."

"Tell me she doesn't know?"

"Of course not. She thinks I'm bringing you something to read." Peter nods towards a stack of books on the hall table that I hadn't noticed.

"Thank goodness," I say, impressed by his discretion and thoughtfulness.

"Must fly," says Peter.

"I need to tell you something."

"Is it urgent?"

"It can wait," I say uncertainly. Then I reassess the wisdom of telling anybody anything. Peter has been a good and dear friend, but I don't know who I can trust anymore. I desperately want to share my fears about the creature and Netherwood, but perhaps it is as well that he hasn't got time to listen. It gives me a chance to consider things further.

"Yes. It can wait," I say, more certainly. "Run along now, and we can speak another time."

Peter grins and mock salutes. Then he is gone, and I look at the envelope. Jim has replied quickly, and I don't know what is inside, but it is thicker than one page, which hopefully bodes well. I hug it to my chest, then make for the parlour before changing my mind. I can't risk anyone seeing me, and pausing only to put on my hat, I make my way to the beach and into the cave.

When I get there, I don't waste a moment. I lay my stick beneath the chair and slit open the envelope before extracting a sheet of paper. I peer inside. Something else is lying in the bottom half of the envelope, but it can wait, and I start to read.

My dear Connie

Thank you for your letter. It is a lot to take in, and I have walked Teddy twice already today while pondering my reply. I'm sure you understand how difficult it is to process your story, but it is also compelling. You write of things you couldn't possibly know – not just one or two coincidental matters, but everything, every part of my house. You write about the location of my clothes, even the first visit of Mrs Grady to feed my dog. And so, after considerable thought, I have no choice but to believe you. And this is born, as much of logic, as of my high regard. So, you can dream walk. We'll take that as fact. When are you coming to see me?"

I break from my reading and broadly smile as I clutch Jim's letter to my chest again. How typical of him to be so good-humoured about my confession. He must have harboured doubts about my sanity, at least initially. I read on.

I mean it. I long to see you again, whether in the flesh or, if necessary, in my dreams. And I promise I will keep our little investigation going for as long as I can. In fact, you will be glad to know that I sought out Inspector Morrish, Hedges erstwhile companion throughout the original investigation. He told me that everyone was a suspect at one time or other, even Mrs Noakes, though she was eventually ruled out. Apparently, they considered Grace's eldest son, John, for a while. He frequented both Tom Sidney's and Violet Sidney's houses and sheds and knew where they kept their weedkiller. Incredibly, he tested the substance on several small animals, killing them in the process. But Morrish and Hedges interviewed the masters at his school and his younger sister. And in the end, they decided he was too young and lacked an adequate motive. Morrish told me that they argued about suspects endlessly, and though both men had their suspicions, they could never prove it. Morrish meets Hedges from time to time, but they try not to talk about the case. It was one of Hedges few failures, and he has never come to terms with it. We were jolly lucky that he was so accommodating when we visited.

Anyway, to happier news. Mother has sent a postcard, and they are coming home soon. They are having a lovely time even though Mrs Callaway is under the weather. Too much of a good thing, I suppose. But I thought you'd like to read about their trip and see pictures of Seaford. It looks jolly nice, and I have enclosed the postcard for your perusal. Perhaps we could go there one day?

Write soon, dear Connie. I miss you.
Yours ever

Jim

#

My heart flutters as I read and reread Jim's letter. I gaze upon his words with an absurd smile plastered to my face. My revelation could have gone badly, but it hasn't. Jim not only believes me but misses me too, and he can't wait for us to be together again. I recline in my chair and look towards the calm sea, watching the tourists milling around the beach. They are out in force, and I would generally find them irritating, but the sun is shining high in the sky, and all is right with the world. I am happy and, dare I say it, falling in love. This moment is almost perfect, and only Jim's absence takes the shine away. Bubbling with hope and more peaceful than I can remember, I turn my attention to the brown envelope and spy the edges of the postcard at the bottom. Poor Jim. This larger than necessary envelope must have been the only one he could lay his hands on quickly as it is far too big for a postcard and a single letter. I idly wonder if he wrote to me while on duty and grabbed the only source of stationery he could find. But it doesn't matter either way. I am thrilled by his words, no matter how they arrived. Just as I reach inside again, I am momentarily distracted by peals of laughter coming towards the cave and watch two small children approach, dressed in bathing suits and carrying nets. I smile as they pass, and the little girl starts and clutches her brother's hand. She hadn't seen me, and I suppose it must be strange watching someone sitting in the mouth of a cave when you're not expecting it. She flashes a timid attempt at a smile, and they continue their journey up the beach. I am still grinning when I reach inside the envelope for the postcard, but the moment I touch it, fear lurches through my body, and I feel sick with dread. I examine the postcard, wondering why it has caused such an unexpected reaction. The innocuous front is a montage of photographs of Seaford. There is nothing strange about it, and I turn the card over and read the back, trying to ignore goosebumps racing down my arms.

Dear Jim

We have enjoyed our holiday, visiting both Brighton and Eastbourne though we prefer the tranquillity of Seaford with its walks and pretty coastline. We've spent many days sea bathing on the beach. I foolishly got sunburnt, and now my nose is peeling. Our guest house is basic but clean, and Mrs Lendy keeps us well fed. I could stay here forever if it weren't for you. But I fear we must cut our holiday short as Bertha is feeling unwell. She must have eaten something that disagreed with her, and although she improved for a while, she is poorly again. We'll catch the train as soon as she is up to it, so expect to see us in the next few days. Let Mr Callaway know we're coming, there's a good boy. Must go now, as Grace's daughter has just called us for dinner.

Much love

Mum

The news is trivial, the writing normal, and the postcard displays nothing of concern. Yet, I feel nauseous when I touch it. What is wrong with me? I hold it by the edges, peering at the photographs of the beach to see if I have missed something. It could easily happen in the shadowed light of the cave, so I rise and venture onto the beach, holding the card towards the sun, but see nothing to alarm me. I return to the cave but stumble as my stick clatters against a hidden rock, and I drop the card onto the beach. As I lean to pick it up, I realise that the feeling of despair has vanished. I stand, watching the postcard closely so I can immediately react if it looks like blowing away. But the sand is dry, and the day is still. It is safe, and I am content again, my mood as optimistic as it was before. I kneel on the sand and reach for the card, touching it with the tip of my finger. Once again, foreboding courses through my body and leaves the moment I remove my hand. There is no doubt about it; it is not just the postcard's content, but the item itself. Something evil lurks within, and the card is somehow tainted. I grasp it firmly and sit on the sand just outside the cave, not wanting the dark, oppressive nature of a confined space to influence my judgement. But from the moment I take the card, melancholy settles over me and clings like a grass burr on a woollen jumper. I reread it slowly, taking in every word. And by the time I have finished, I know what is wrong. The postcard emanates a strong, steady warning of danger. Danger to Mrs Douglass and Bertha, and the threat lies in Seaford. Mrs Douglass has inadvertently revealed a peril they don't know they are facing. She has mentioned her landlady, not once but twice. Grace Lendy. And I remember that surname as clear as day. Lendy was Violet Sidney's maiden name and a natural alias for someone running away from notoriety. Someone thought to be in Australia who clearly is not. A woman who is currently looking after two old ladies, one sick with food poisoning.

I didn't enjoy the experience of touching Annie Hearn's handkerchief, which told me things I didn't want to know. Back then, it revealed that she was alive. But the message within this postcard isn't quite so obvious. Though the women are in danger, the card doesn't say much about it. All I know is the distressing, all-consuming depression that descends on me when I touch it. But I can't knowingly leave Jim's mother and Oliver Fox's wife in peril, and I must contact Jim immediately, right this moment. He must go to Seaford and rescue them while it's still possible. I heave myself to my feet and make for the hotel.

CHAPTER TWENTY-FOUR

Emergency

I charge towards the hotel entrance, hauling myself up the steps as quickly as I can. I am unsteady on my feet and going too fast, but I can't waste any time. I need a telephone, and I need it now. I pass through the open door and up the hallway, not caring who is there. They can try to stop me if they like, but I will make this phone call, even if I must barricade myself in the office to do it. I walk alongside a couple of guests, trying to use them to block my visibility so I can get closer to my destination before someone sees me. But my old enemy, debilitating weakness, stops me, and I clutch one of the comfortable chairs in the reception area to steady myself as my head swims. After striding up the beach, my legs are like jelly. I wobble as I stand and curse my hasty reaction, knowing that this won't pass unless I sit down for a few moments. So, I take a seat with my back to the reception area, hoping nobody will identify me from the back of my head while I take a short breather. Several minutes pass, and I start to feel stronger, though sick with worry at the thought of Jim's mother being in harm's way. I try to rationalise my fears. Why would Grace Duff be a danger to two women she has never met? She has no vested interest, and they're not rich. But the postcard, which I'm still clutching, tells me otherwise. It speaks of pain and regret. I feel myself panting as a shadow looms behind me, and I hear a voice.

"Is that you, Connie?"

My shoulders sag as I hear Dolly's dulcet tones. She is the one person guaranteed to recognise me from a distance. I appeal to her better nature. "I need to use the telephone," I say. "Please don't tell anyone. It's urgent."

"Of course," she says. "I'll take you to the office now."

I sigh with relief, grateful for her willingness to risk her employment for my benefit. But as I turn and follow her towards the reception desk, Mr Brookbank appears and fixes me with a stare. Hope disappears in an instant, and I almost give up and go home. Only thoughts of Jim drive me on. I pretend not to see him and carry on towards the office, but Dolly stops and turns around as she reaches the door.

"Oh hello, I didn't see you there," she says, smiling at her employer. My heart sinks. Why is she so friendly?

"Miss Maxwell," says Brookbank, gesturing towards a nearby seat. "Why don't you sit down. I want to speak to you."

"I know I shouldn't be here," I say. "I need to borrow your telephone. It will only take a minute. Let me make a call, and I promise never to bother you again."

"Of course," says Brookbank. "Providing you let me apologise first."

I stop and hold the edge of the reception counter, reeling with surprise. Of all the things I expected him to say, this wasn't it.

"Sorry?" I repeat, almost lost for words.

"I must apologise to you. Please sit."

Time is not on my side, but I am so taken aback by his conciliatory tone that I do as he asks.

"I've written you a letter," he says, looking directly into my eyes.

I return his stare but don't reply.

"It's a letter of apology and an explanation. You see, we have found Miss Napier's missing ring."

About time, I think. "Where was it?" I ask.

"In the office. I can't imagine how it got there. I can only assume the silly girl picked it up and put it in the drawer for safekeeping. Not that I can get her or anyone else to own up to it, but that's another story. Anyway, I've only just returned from a short break," he continues, dropping his gaze to his lap. I keep a firm stare while thinking about his poor wife and his complicated home life. But I don't gloat. The terrible danger in Seaford prevents me from enjoying this moment of retribution.

"I found the ring yesterday afternoon, but I wasn't sure it was the right one until I telephoned Miss Napier. She came by this morning and identified it as her missing engagement ring. So that's that, and all is well."

"No, it isn't," I say. "Far from it. People are whispering everywhere I go. They think I'm a thief because of your very public questioning and my ejection from the hotel. I've lost my good name through no fault of my own."

"I know, and I'm sorry," says Mr Brookbank. "That's why I was writing to you. I hoped we could come to an understanding."

"Such as?"

"A nice meal here, perhaps several?"

I raise an eyebrow, which I hope conveys my disgust at his pathetic gesture.

"Or something else?" he asks, noting my disapproval.

It only takes a few seconds to think of a mutually attractive proposition, and I pounce while I can. "Full access to the library and use of the telephone whenever I want," I say.

"Is that all?" he asks, evidently relieved.

I nod. "But you'll need to let everyone know," I say.

"I'll do it at once."

"Thank you. Please, can I use the telephone now?"

"Certainly. I'll escort you."

I get to my feet and follow him, but not before Dolly indiscreetly winks at me in full view of her employer. We are approaching the office door when it opens and Roxy Templeton appears. She stares at me wide-eyed, and her lips disappear in a frown of disapproval.

"Ah, Miss Templeton. Kindly give this young lady a few moments of privacy. She needs to use the telephone."

"But, but," she stutters.

"Is there a problem?"

"No, Mr Brookbank. Not exactly. But the matter with Mr Sutton is still outstanding."

"I've settled the matter with Mr Sutton," says Brookbank.

"Not to his satisfaction."

"But it is to mine. And that's all he's getting. Was there anything else?"

Roxy Templeton shakes her head, glowering as she walks away.

"Help yourself," says Brookbank and ushers me inside. I wait for him to shut the door, then pick up the telephone and dial the operator. "Croydon police station," I say.

#

It takes several attempts to reach Jim. The operator puts me through, but the man who answers doesn't know where Jim is and leaves me waiting for so long that the call disconnects. I try again, this time getting a more efficient response, and within moments, Jim is on the line.

"Hello?" he says. "Who is it?"

Butterflies dance inside my stomach at the sound of his

voice, and an unexpected nervousness momentarily renders me dumb.

"Hello," he repeats.

"Jim," I say.

"Who is it?"

"It's Connie."

"Oh. Is everything alright?"

"Not really," I say, perching on the edge of the table. "This is going to sound silly, but I'm worried about your mother."

"Why?"

"You remember I told you about my dream walking."

"I could hardly forget."

"It's not my only unusual ability."

"Go on."

"Occasionally, when I touch an object, I feel something."

"Yes?"

"The postcard from your mother. It's not right. She's not safe."

"I don't understand."

"She's in danger. Don't ask how I know. Just accept that I do, and please believe me."

I hear Jim sigh down the crackly line. "This isn't easy to take in, Connie," he says. "How do you know your intuition isn't sending you off in the wrong direction?"

"It's a stronger feeling than that. But there's more. Her landlady's name is Grace."

"Yes, I know. I read the card." Jim sounds terse, irritated and far from convinced."

"Grace Lendy."

"Yes. Do you know her?"

"No, but you might. Lendy was Violet Sidney's married name."

Jim says nothing as he ponders my words.

"And we know she didn't go to Australia."

"You think my mother's landlady is Grace Duff?"

"Yes. Grace must have touched the postcard. I feel her

presence, and your mother isn't safe."

"Even if it is Grace, why would she harm two women who she doesn't know?"

"I can't tell you that," I say. "But Bertha is unwell. Perhaps she's met Grace before and upset her. I can't guess at any more than that. These feelings don't come with detailed explanations."

"What do you want me to do about it?"

"Drive down there."

"What? Turn up out of the blue, for no reason?"

Jim sounds incredulous, and I try to put myself in his position. I've telephoned him at the police station in a blind panic because of a wave of despair generated from touching a postcard. He must wonder at the wisdom of our friendship.

"It's up to you," I say, trying to be reasonable. "I realise how this must sound, and I've done my bit in making sure you know. I trust your judgement completely, and you should deal with things as you see fit, even if that means disregarding my warning."

There is another long silence. "It doesn't help that the car's in the garage," says Jim. "I couldn't drive down if I wanted to, and quite frankly, I don't know whether I should."

"I'm sorry," I say. I don't know what I expected from my revelation, but Jim's reaction is cold, and I can almost feel his regard for me slipping away.

"Are you sure my mother is in trouble?" he asks.

"As sure as I can be."

"Then I'll think about it. I finish here in half an hour. Is there a number I can call you back on?"

I give him the hotel number, and he rings off with a curt goodbye.

I sit quietly for a moment, torn between regret and relief at finally having passed on my concerns, then I leave the office and the hotel before returning to Pebble Cottage.

Mrs Ponsonby is back and approaches me as I arrive home, holding out a printed document.

"Do you want to see the sales particulars?" she asks.

"Not now," I say abruptly and head straight upstairs to my bedroom. I sit on my bed, knees to my chest, my stomach churning with nerves. Today started so promisingly, and now I have upset Jim and pushed his credulity too far. I should have ignored the nagging despair, should have waited. The whole thing could be a figment of my imagination, and with the postcard firmly in the envelope, logic prevails. I groan aloud as I remember Jim ending the call with none of his usual jocularity and no warm sentiment. I fear I have lost him, and tears prick my eyes. I try to blink them away, but it has the opposite effect, and before long, my cheeks are damp and my heart heavy with disappointment. Time drags by, minute by painful minute. Half an hour passes, then an hour, and by half past four, I accept that he will not call. And just as I am about to give up completely, Elys enters my bedroom carrying a note. "Dolly sent this," she says and waits while I tear it open.

I scan the page greedily. Dolly's writing is round and easy to read.

Connie, your friend called the hotel to say he has taken the train to Seaford, but his mother is out. He has gone to look for her and will send word as soon as he finds her.

Yours, Dolly

"Any reply?" asks Elys.

I shake my head. She lingers for a moment but leaves when she realises that I don't intend to reveal the note's contents. When the door shuts, I sigh with relief. Jim believes me. He wouldn't have taken the first train if he was entirely sceptical. But his mother isn't there, and he hasn't mentioned Bertha. I consider the possibilities. Perhaps Bertha is at the guest house, and Jim has gone to meet his mother, assuming she has gone out alone. Or perhaps Bertha isn't there, in which case Jim might be out looking for both of them. Are they safe or not?

He hasn't said, and now I am as worried as ever. I wish I were there. But the moment the thought crosses my mind, I can't help glancing at the window, looking for signs of the horror that plagued me the night before. I'm thinking about it because, despite the danger, I'm seriously considering dream walking to Seaford. It is a risky proposition, and even the thought of it spikes terror into my heart. I don't know why the creature appeared, but I'm sure it's connected to Crossley and, if to Crossley, then to dream walking by association. But for the interruption by Mrs Ponsonby and Elys the previous night, who knows what might have happened if the creature had reached me in the seconds before I arrived on the astral plane.

I would be mad to risk it again, and my teeth clench at the thought. I stand and pace the room, torn between concern for Jim and fear for my sanity. I glance out of the window. It is still early evening, but the sky has darkened, and a storm is brewing. It's nearly time for tea, and if I go down now, I won't be tempted to do something hasty. I open the door and make my way downstairs, but something stops me, and I stand halfway, paralysed with indecision. Elys crosses the foot of the stairs, carrying a tureen on a tray.

"Ready for supper?" she asks.

I shake my head. "I'm tired," I say. "Put a little aside for me, and I'll have it later if you don't mind."

Elys tuts loudly but agrees, and I make my way upstairs. Whether or not I risk a dream walk, I can't face food or polite conversation, even if it means worrying alone in my room for the next few hours.

I pour a glass of water and walk towards my window, unlatching it to its full extent. Then I peer outside when I'm satisfied it's safe to do so. I hang over the sill, staring towards the sea through the unnaturally dark skies, searching for inspiration. I am alone and adrift, and suddenly I'm struck by a terrifying revelation. Jim is in danger. He's in trouble. Not his mother. Not Bertha, but Jim. And I've put him there. The feeling turns into a certainty, and I slump on the bed, my stick falling to the floor. I reach for the envelope, take out the postcard, and a tidal wave of despair crashes over me.

I clutch the card to my chest and close my eyes, imprinting a naked flame on the back of my eyelids, and wait hopefully for signs of travel. They arrive almost immediately as my fingers burn from the touch of the postcard. They are painful, aflame, and spiked with electricity, violent and volatile. I am yanked from my bed, bumping through the darkness, not in the usual dreamlike manner, but with a sense of urgency and desperation. I close my eyes, fearful of what I might see and plunge downwards, hands flailing, hair trailing, in a terror-inducing drop without end. And though I can't feel the wind whipping or my heart racing, fear surges through me until I wish I were anywhere but here. Dead, in a coma, beyond suffering. And then, all motion stops. My eyes blink open in an automatic movement that requires no effort from me, and I find myself outside a small double fronted cottage on Steyne Road. It takes a few seconds to orientate myself, but as soon as I do, I see a slate sign on the wall bearing the words Merryweather's Guest House. I am here, in Seaford and striding towards me, with his hands in his pockets and wearing a worried frown, is Jim.

CHAPTER TWENTY-FIVE

The Guest House

I rush towards him, forgetting for a moment that I am in ethereal form, but when he looks right through me, my spirits fall. Jim moves purposefully and I turn and walk alongside, trying and failing to slip my hand into his. He doesn't know I'm there. I might as well be a gust of wind for all the attention he pays me. Jim strides straight to the cottage and raps the knocker loudly. He waits barely a moment before doing it again, displaying a sense of urgency at odds with our earlier conversation. Jim's hands are in his pockets, and he kicks a stone from the doorstep while waiting. It bounces off the iron boot scraper and straight through my ankle. I flinch unnecessarily, glad that it cannot hurt me. Jim tuts and hits the door again, this time with the palm of his hand. We wait and eventually hear footsteps in the hallway, and the door opens to reveal a teenage boy.

"Yes?" he asks.

"I called earlier and spoke to a young girl," says Jim.

"That will be my sister. She's out." The boy begins to shut the door, but Jim places his boot in the way.

"I don't want to speak to her. I'm looking for Mrs Douglass and Mrs Callaway."

"They're out too."

"So, your sister said, but they're not where she said they were."

The boy raises his eyes heavenward. "They've probably gone somewhere else."

"I thought Mrs Callaway was poorly."

The boy doesn't answer and shrugs as if he doesn't care.

Jim looks at his watch. "It's nearly six o'clock. My mother is usually at home by now. And talking of mothers, where is yours?"

"Out," says the boy.

"And when are you expecting her back? This is a guest house. Shouldn't she be preparing dinner?"

The boy sighs and answers monosyllabically. "Any minute, and yes." He attempts to shut the door again, but Jim is quicker.

"What's your mother's name?"

"Grace."

"Grace, what?"

The boy flushes and looks away, chewing his lip as he considers the question.

"What's your name. Your full name."

"John Duff," says the boy, then claps his hand over his mouth. "John Lendy, I mean."

"Can I wait inside?" asks Jim abruptly.

"No," says the boy. "Mother wouldn't like it. You need to go now."

"I'll wait outside then," says Jim.

"As you like."

The boy shuts the door, and Jim stalks up the short pathway, then stands facing towards the cottage with a frown on his face. I watch his handsome profile, wishing I could help, but his worry-lined brow and careful scrutinisation of the property indicate he's unhappy with the boy's explanation. I was right. Grace Duff and Grace Lendy are the same. Jim doesn't spend long on the pathway. He walks towards one side of the cottage, then the other, before discreetly hopping over a low fence. I follow him into a lawned garden utterly bereft of flowers. A wooden bench rests untidily among high grass, providing a joyless area to sit outside.

Nearby an iron drainpipe wends its way up the rear of the house and past an open window. A smile spreads across Jim's face as soon as he sees it, and I know straight away what he intends to do. Glancing left to right, Jim climbs onto a barrel near the pipework base, clasps the drainpipe and heaves himself up. Rangy and athletic, he's at the window in no time and reaches inside to loosen the latch. He peers into the bathroom and is lost from sight. I slide through the wall and find myself in a small kitchen with a tiled floor and flaking blue paint on the walls. I dart into a hallway and past an open door where John Duff is reading a magazine. Beside him, a much younger boy is drawing on paper with a piece of charcoal, his hands and face smeared black. Judging by the handprints on the fawn-coloured rug, the Duff boy will be in trouble when his mother gets home. But I'm not interested in the children and hastily climb the stairs looking for Jim. I find him in a bedroom off the main hallway, leaning over the second of a pair of twin beds, mouth pursed as he looks inside a handbag.

"Bertha Callaway's," he mutters, opening a leather card holder and retrieving a calling card. He stands and walks towards the wardrobe before throwing it open, then scrabbles on the floor. "Not here," he says. Jim systematically opens every drawer and cupboard, then looks below the bed while I watch. "Hmm," he whispers. "No sign of mother's bag, which is a good thing, but where is Mrs Callaway?" He is just reaching for a suitcase on top of the wardrobe when a door slams downstairs, and I hear John Duff greet his mother.

I can't hear her reply, but his subsequent shrill proclamation puts fear into my heart. "There was a man here looking for you," he says.

"Really. Who?" Grace replies.

"I don't know, but he asked my name."

"What did you tell him?" Grace demands.

"I'm sorry. I didn't mean to give it away, but I got your name right."

"Stupid boy," snaps Grace Duff. "Where did he go?"

"Away. The man said he would wait."

"I'll give him what for if he comes back here again," says Grace. "Watch Alistair while I'll make some tea."

"He asked about our guests," says John, disregarding thoughts of food. "Where are they?"

"One's in the cottage hospital with food poisoning," says Grace. "The other is with her."

"Will she die?"

"Don't be ridiculous."

"Aunt Vera died."

"That was different. Oh, John. Look at the state of your brother. Come here, child."

I am standing on top of the landing listening to Grace Duff while Jim hovers uncertainly by the window, in two minds whether to leave. I expect he is hoping that she will go to the kitchen and attend to the child, giving him time to exit in an orderly manner. But it is not to be. Grace walks Alistair upstairs, gently chastising him for the mess. I rush to Jim, trying to warn him, but he can't see me, and it doesn't matter. He has heard her tread on the stairs. The window is still unlatched, and Jim reaches for the drainpipe, tightly clinging as he descends. I watch from the window, trying to block him from her sight for all the good it will do. But as Jim moves tentatively down, the sky darkens, and a chill runs through me. Crossley is nearby. I can feel him. Somehow, he knows I'm here. A swirl of dark matter streams towards the window, and I instinctively lurch back, flattening myself against the wall. It stops and hovers by the window before entering the room where it materialises in the shape of Felix Crossley. I flee through the wall and into a cupboard on the landing, where I peer through an ancient keyhole. Crossley slinks from the bedroom, and I stand, paralysed with fear waiting for him to find me, waiting for the end. But I am wrong.

Crossley hasn't come for me. He isn't aware of my presence and streams, part human, yet wraithlike towards Grace Duff, who is walking towards the bathroom, still holding her child. Crossley approaches, but she doesn't see him, though she stops and stands stock-still for a moment while the child wriggles free and goes on ahead. Grace looks around as if she has forgotten why she came, then Crossley touches her in the centre of her forehead and she heaves an imperceptible shudder. Grace Duff is stationery as if frozen in time and Crossley walks in a circle, studying her from every angle. His touch has left a black mark where worry lines furrow her brow, yet she is oblivious to him. Part of me wants to warn her, but I am fearful of being seen. And I'm feeling an uncomfortable sense of déjà vu. Crossley touched Annie Hearn on the forehead too. I don't know what it means, but anything involving Crossley cannot be good. It feels like days before Grace Duff moves again, but it can only be seconds. Then the tableau breaks at the sound of a yell, followed by the crunch of damaged wood and fallen piping. I scream, a sound that neither Grace nor her children can hear, but Crossley's head whips around as he searches for the source. I close my eyes, imagine candle flames and try to return to my body. But with the commotion outside, I cannot concentrate. Grace Duff moves towards the window, and Crossley's nostrils twitch above his sneering lips. It is too risky to go to Jim. I can't help him and If I did, I would risk drawing danger towards him. Instead, I dart through the back of the cupboard, through walls, past a chimney and out the other side. I run, and I keep on running until Seaford is a distant pinprick.

#

I don't know how long I am running before my fear of Crossley gradually dissipates. I stop and take stock of my surroundings. I am on the edges of another seaside town, much bigger than the one I left. Crossley is nowhere near, and I don't know if he tried to follow me. I still don't understand his role in my life or where the danger lies.

On the one hand, he seeks me, yet he can't always feel me. And he has relentlessly pursued two women with whom I have crossed paths. Annie Hearn and Grace Duff, one a murderess and the other a possible murderess. What does he want with them? Why does he leave a black mark on their foreheads? Does Crossley exercise control over these women, and, if so, why? My mind is idling over these thoughts when I remember Jim. Oh, God. I heard him fall before I fled, and he may be lying there injured, in Grace Duff's clutches. I close my eyes and think of Jim, hoping to travel instantly to his side, but at that moment, I feel an urgent tug on the back of my head, and my scalp inflames with pain. I instinctively know that I'm being pulled back to my body and if I go, I may not find my way back to Seaford. So, I resist and push through the blinding headache that takes me. My eyes stream with hot tears as I try to pull away.

I must run. I can't risk the astral plane in case I am pulled back against my will. So, I set off back the way I came darting across the darkening cliffs, ploughing through pavements and people and buildings. Anything to get there quickly. Anything to stop thinking about the pain in my scalp. Eventually, I arrive outside Merryweather's boarding house. Darkness is falling, but I can't have been away for long. I haven't passed through the astral plane, and it must still be the same day, so it's just a matter of finding Jim. I enter the house through the front door, immediately hearing the chatter of children. There are three of them now, two boys and a girl. The boy listens to the radio while the girl reads, and the youngest child sits in her lap, docilely watching his brother through heavy-lidded eyes. But where is Grace?

I search the house upstairs and down, but there is no sign of her. I want to scream at the children to prompt them to talk about their mother, but they sit quietly, fully occupied in their various activities. Then it occurs to me that Jim might have just left. His mother hasn't returned, and he may have gone to the hospital. I am just about to follow when I realise, I haven't been to the scene of the fall, so I flit through the house and emerge outside to find a length of iron pipe splayed across the garden. The kitchen light illuminates the first few feet of the yard, and my hand flies to my mouth as I spy a small patch of blood, but there is still no sign of Jim. I wait for a moment contemplating the chances of him walking away from the terrible fall when I hear a woman's voice coming from an outhouse further down the garden. I can't get there quickly enough and force myself inside, only to see the awful sight of Jim kneeling on the floor with his hands tied behind his back and his mouth wet with an unctuous substance, still dripping down his chin. Grace Duff is sitting on an old wooden chair with a bottle in her hands.

"This will sort you out," she says.

Jim shakes his head. His ordinarily sharp eyes are bleary and unfocused.

"What is it?" he mutters. "It tastes disgusting."

"A slow-acting poison," says Grace. "We're going for a walk in a minute, you and me. A nice walk across the cliffs. You'll feel much better in the fresh air."

She flutters her eyelashes as she speaks, flirting siren-like with her captive.

"Where's my mother?" asks Jim, drooling as he speaks.

"At the cottage hospital with her friend," says Grace.

"She's had a touch of food poisoning, but that's all it is, Mr Douglass. They are going home tomorrow and have already purchased train tickets. I don't poison my short stay guests. It isn't good for business."

"Then why have you trussed me up like a turkey?" asks Jim.

Grace sighs and drops the brown bottle into a pocket in her apron. "Because I had a long-term guest last year who fared less well. Brian was a nice man and left me a small legacy when he departed this life, a little earlier than expected. Running a guest house isn't lucrative, and my financial position is precarious. I've always had money until recently. You can't imagine what a bore it is to need to take on domestic work. There will be other Brian's, lonely old men and women who are happy to pay for a little friendship at the risk of a reduced life span. It's a pity you asked John his name. Nobody knows our past, and that's the way it's going to stay."

"I'm a policeman," says Jim.

"So I gather," says Grace, removing his identification card from her pocket. "Which is another reason why it has to be this way."

Jim stares at her, rocking slightly. She frowns and removes the bottle, checking the label.

"We'll have to go soon," she says. "It's a fine line between drowsiness and death."

"So, you killed your husband?" asks Jim, sleepily. "We weren't sure."

"We?"

"I meant me."

I lean into Jim, trying to hug him and be close in his hour of need. Even though he is suffering with who knows what foul substance coursing around his body, he is still trying to protect me. I want to touch him, put my head on his chest and feel the beat of his heart, but my useless ethereal body passes straight through him, and a screeching pain sears through my head as my body orders me home. Jim is fighting for his life,

241

while I am fighting for my sanity. The pain is almost unbearable, and I know that I'm risking permanent damage stalling my return. Still, I resist the urge to go back.

"I didn't kill my husband," says Grace.

Jim's eyes widen. "Then who did?"

"My mother," says Grace.

"I don't believe you."

"She hated him," Grace continues. "She thought he wasn't good enough. They all did. They all knew what she was going to do. Tom, Vera, Margaret. Yet nobody stopped her."

"But you hated him too. Your affair with Dr Elwell..."

"A woman can have affairs and still love her husband. Men do it all the time."

"But he hurt you."

"I liked it. We had an understanding. And Edmund knew about Elwell. He turned a blind eye."

"Then you were innocent, after all?"

Grace Duff laughs, and her dainty voice trills with pleasure.

"Of course I wasn't. When I realised that my mother killed Edmund, I hated her for it. She took the poison from Tom's house, of course. Edmund was cashing in the life insurance policies, and it rankled mother in a way you cannot imagine. She thought we would live in penury, and it would reflect badly on her. But we'd always agreed to live for today and worry about tomorrow when it came. I didn't care what Edmund did with our money. We had always managed, and he made financial decisions with my full agreement. But I underestimated how much the rest of the family hated him. Mother poisoned his beer, but I believe that any of them would have done it if she hadn't."

"Tom knew?" Jim slurs the words, and Grace stands as she continues.

"Yes, Tom knew. I thought about killing him for his part in it, but I had to consider what would hurt Mother the most. So, I poisoned Vera's soup. It took a few weeks for Vera to die and another few for the truth to dawn on Mother. But it wasn't until Vera finally passed away that mother understood what I'd done. She asked me if I had killed my sister, and at first, I denied it. I didn't want Dr Binning or Dr Elwell to ask awkward questions. And they didn't. They took Vera's death at face value. But as the weeks went on, and Mother became more and more afraid, I decided to take advantage of the financial aspects of the matter. I started by putting arsenic in Mother's medicine the day before she died, and I finally told her what I had done and why I had done it. At first, she denied poisoning Edmund and said she was going to tell the police. But I knew she wouldn't risk it, and when I explained my plan, she listened. She owed me for Edmund's death which had left me in dire financial straits. So, I told her that she had nothing to live for with Vera gone, and if she didn't want the same to happen to Tom, then she had better take her medicine."

"How could you?"

"Easily. Mother said she could never kill herself. But I said she wasn't so much killing herself as saving Tom's life. So, she did."

"You're wicked." Jim's voice is trailing away, and he is fading fast.

Grace crouches beside him and snips the ropes away with a pair of shears. "We're going for a walk now," she says, pulling his hand. Jim staggers to his feet, swaying slightly. Grace puts Jim's arm around her shoulders. "Walk," she commands, and he follows, lacking the strength to resist. Grace manoeuvres Jim down the pathway to the bottom of the garden and through a small wooden gate into a scruffy grassed area. I follow behind, horrified at the sight of the cliff edge only a few hundred yards away.

As my heart lurches in fear, another piercing jolt of electricity passes through my skull. My head is on fire from the urgency of the tugs to the back of my head. I have been away from my body for hours – longer than ever before. I pull towards Jim, fighting every instinct to return, but I don't move. I can't. My spirit is paralysed, and all I can do is watch as Grace guides Jim away from me towards the sea. I try one last time, and then everything goes black.

CHAPTER TWENTY-SIX

Fate

Tuesday, July 12, 1932

Surrey Comet

A MISSING POLICEMAN

Although another search party spent all day yesterday seeking missing policeman PC James Frederick Douglass, not a trace of him was found. The search continues today. PC Douglass left Croydon police station on Friday, July 8, with the intention of collecting his car from the garage where it was undergoing repairs. Though his car is now on the driveway of

245

his house in Worple Road, Wimbledon, Cyril Fletcher, the mechanical engineer who fixed it, is by no means certain that PC Douglass collected it in person. The car was recovered from the forecourt of his garage by an unknown member of the public while Mr Fletcher attended to a breakdown in Purley.

PC Douglass' mother raised the alarm when she returned from holiday to find her son missing and his dog alone in the house. Several theories have been advanced, one of which is that PC Douglass may have gone to Cornwall to find a lady friend who has recently returned there. His mother, who was widowed some time ago, is distraught at the disappearance of her only son. Readers are encouraged to contact the police if they have any news on his whereabouts.

Newquay W I Magazine July 1932

A basket of fruit was delivered to Mrs Vera Ponsonby last week to mark the second week of Constance Maxwell's sudden illness. A loyal and long-standing member of the Institute, Mrs Ponsonby has acted as guardian to Constance for some twenty years. A fortnight ago, Miss Maxwell suffered a sudden cerebral haemorrhage in her sleep and now lies dangerously ill in hospital. We understand that Mrs Ponsonby has barely left her side during this time. It is hoped that Miss Maxwell will soon recover, and we will report back on her progress.

THE END

AFTERWORD

Afterword

The mysterious deaths of the Sidney family have formed the subject of several books and television programmes. Though theories differ, the consensus is that the murderer can only have been Grace Duff or Tom Sidney. I'm not so sure. Nevertheless, I made Grace a killer in this work of fiction due partly to the circumstantial evidence against her and because she makes a good villain. But I'm far from convinced of her guilt, and the behaviour of others around her is questionable, to say the least. Having accumulated information on the case, I discovered the witnesses to the murders frequently contradicted each other. But there was one fact about which they all agreed. Violet Sidney hated Edmund Duff and didn't think he was good enough to be part of the family. Violet had the means and motive to poison Edmund – more than Grace Duff, who, if not financially worse off by his death, was very little better off. The two doctors, Robert Elwell and John

247

Binning harboured suspicions of each other and did not seem to get along. During the course of the investigation into the Croydon poisonings, a fourth exhumation was also considered. It would have been on the body of Anna Maria Kelvey, who unexpectedly died while boarding with Grace Duff.

The elderly lady left Grace's children, John and Mary, bequests of £25 each in her will. She nominated Dr Robert Elwell as one of her trustees, and he received £50 for his trouble. At least one credible witness believed that Anna Kelvey died from unnatural means and was frightened of Grace Duff. But neither the Duff children's legacy nor Elwell's gift were enough to make murdering the frail Ms Kelvey worthwhile. However, some ten years after the Croydon poisonings, Elwell received a further substantial legacy from another elderly woman, Mrs Alice Esther Hall, in 1939. This time, he benefited to the tune of £4,000 'in gratitude for all his kindness in a time of great trouble.'. Miss Hall put the residue of the property in trust to her sister for life, then to Dr Robert Graham Elwell upon her sister's decease. Dr Elwell was well-known as a ladies' man who never married and conducted many affairs, including one with Grace Duff. Could he have had other motives for his friendships with ladies, both old and young?

I don't pretend to know who killed Vera and Violet Sidney, or indeed Edmund Duff. But it's not nearly as clear cut as some books suggest. If you have any theories or comments regarding this case, I would love to hear them.

You can contact me or find out more about my books on the website below.

Thank you for reading The Croydon Enigma. I hope you liked it. If you want to find out more about my books, here are some ways to stay updated:

Join my mailing list or visit my website
https://jacquelinebeardwriter.com/

Like my Facebook page
https://www.facebook.com/LawrenceHarpham/

If you have a moment, I would be grateful if you could leave a quick review of The Croydon Enigma online. Honest reviews are very much appreciated and are useful to other readers.

The Constance Maxwell Dreamwalker Mysteries

The Cornish Widow
The Croydon Enigma

***Book 3 in The Constance Maxwell Dreamwalker series
will follow soon***

Also, by this author:

Lawrence Harpham Murder Mysteries:

The Fressingfield Witch
The Ripper Deception
The Scole Confession
The Felsham Affair
The Moving Stone

***Book 6 in The Lawrence Harpham Mysteries will follow
soon***

Short Stories featuring Lawrence Harpham:

The Montpellier Mystery

Novels:

Vote for Murder

Printed in Great Britain
by Amazon

12888944R00145